Mothers, Daughters & Untamed Dragons

Mothers, Daughters & Untamed Dragons

a novel by

Aysan Sev'er

DEMETER PRESS, BRADFORD, ONTARIO

Published by:
Demeter Press
140 Holland Street West
P. O. Box 13022
Bradford, ON L3Z 2Y5
Tel: (905) 775-9089
Email: info@demeterpress.org
Website: www.demeterpress.org

Demeter Press logo based on Skulptur "Demeter"
by Maria-Luise Bodirsky <www.keramik-atelier.bodirsky.edu>

Front cover design: Dora Chan

Printed and Bound in Canada

Library and Archives Canada Cataloguing in Publication
Sev'er, Aysan, 1945–
        Mothers, daughters and untamed dragons / Aysan Sev'er

ISBN 978-1-927335-06-2

    I. Title.

PS8587.E836M68 2012   C813'.6   C2012-907265-6

*This novel is dedicated to my maternal grandmother
who taught me to appreciate epic tales and
to my paternal grandmother who taught me to love gardening.
Both hobbies became my loyal companions throughout
the parts of my life I spent on my own.*

Contents

Part V: The Fourth Generation

Part VI: Tangled Relationships

Part VII: Completed Cycles, Incomplete Dreams

"Challenge is a dragon with a gift in its mouth.... Tame the dragon and the gift is yours."
—Noela Evans (from Laura Moncur's Motivational Quotations)

"Motherhood is a dragon with a gift in its mouth.... Tame the dragon and the daughter will be yours."
—This is what Anna, the female protagonist of this novel, might say

Part I:
The Four Generations

1.

An Uneventful Death

AT LAST, IT HAPPENED. I died. I knew it was coming for a long time. I was waiting for my death, sometimes without emotion, but sometimes with trepidation. More than the death itself, the possibility of suffering frightened me the most. I was also afraid of being alone when it happened; struggling for my last breath while gazing at empty walls terrified me. My terror was a reasonable reaction to the isolated life I led in the latter part of my life. Loved ones had long gone or deserted me, and the few I called friends had found their maker ahead of me. Fortunately, when it came to my turn to join them, I did not have to stare at the empty walls. Although I do not exactly know how I died, I died peacefully. I was asleep.

It took them—the total strangers who lived in my apartment building—a couple of days to find me. Someone must have noticed the growing newspaper pile that was not picked up. So, after much deliberation, and in the company of the apartment superintendent, they let themselves in. Fortunately, my bed was clean, and I was in one of my more respectable pajamas, cotton, light blue paisley print. It would have been more embarrassing if they found me dead in one of my psychedelic pajamas covered in fire-spewing dragons and skulls. Indeed, I owned such vintage pajamas, and often wondered around the house wearing them, solely to delight myself. Now that I am dead, I can imagine more clearly what a bizarre sight I might have been, with my thinning white hair, shrivelled osteoporotic body, and skulls and dragons. The elderly are allowed a bit of eccentricity, but if I had been wearing my dragon pajamas, I would have pushed the boundaries of eccentricity into absurdity. However, on my very last night on earth, I was lucky; I died in my more appropriate paisleys, in muted colours and sensible cotton.

As far as my body, seen through my after-life eyes, I had not turned green and purple when they found me. And blessedly, there were not too many flies and bugs, since the room was very cool. I had the habit of sleeping with my windows ajar, regardless of the temperature. Since it was a cold January morning, the room was only a few degrees above the freezing point. The covers I was snuggled under were neat and clean, but profusely floral, despite the somberness of the occasion. I do not know about the smell though, since dead people cannot smell themselves. I reckon that it was not too bad, since no one ran out of the room gagging. The neighbouring apartment dwellers, who let themselves in to find my body, did not know me. To them, I was the "weird old woman" who lived on the same floor. So, when they found me, no one really cared too much, and the reaction was mostly a muted sigh—just another "oldie" bites the dust! That day, most of my neighbours had the fleeting luxury of being young.

It is a good thing that I had made all my funeral arrangements while I was still alive. Nothing fancy, but enough to pay tribute to the more "successful" parts of my life. I had asked for the placement of a Canadian as well as a Turkish flag behind my coffin. They were there, each spread out behind me in their red and white glory, which made me feel happy and patriotic. I had asked for Vivaldi's "Four Seasons"—more precisely, the autumn and winter sections—to be played. Indeed, the funeral home carried out my wishes in that regard. However, I had given clear instructions to place only yellow roses around my coffin, and had paid a handsome sum for them. Regrettably, the funeral home took it upon itself to send me off with a variety of flowers in mixed colours. They probably got a better price for the mixed flowers rather than the yellow roses I had ordered, and paid for. Misers! If I were still alive, I would have quarrelled with them and made them replace the cheap flowers with the roses of my choice. But they know as well as I that I am gone, so who is going to complain? If funeral homes feared ghosts, they wouldn't be in the funeral business.

The cheaper flowers in the cacophony of colours notwithstanding, my funeral was nice; honestly, much nicer than what I expected. Some of my neighbours showed up, especially those who found my body in my bed. Their faces were blank, their voices muted, to cover the absence of emotion. They said things like, "what a pity, she was a kind old woman," even though they had no clue whether I was kind or unkind. They were right about my being an "old" woman. I was eighty-four years old.

A few remaining friends, those still mobile, also came. I recognized the faces of some of my former colleagues, some I really liked, and some I really hated. The latter probably came to ensure I was really gone. Our dislike was mutual. There were faces I could not recognize. They may have been students from my career counselling years. They were kind enough to remember me, although I did not remember most. Greg's older daughter was there, and she placed a single yellow rose on my coffin. If I were still alive, I would have given her a hug for her sensitive and loving gesture. Greg's younger daughter did not show up, which did not surprise me. After my separation from Greg, his younger daughter had not kept much contact. Amongst my other "guests," no one was crying, but no one was laughing either. This was a good thing. I departed at just the socially acceptable time. People turned on you if you stayed around too long.

If you ask me how I know about these things, I will not be able to give you a straightforward answer. After all, being dead is new to me. All I can say is that I am kind of aimlessly floating around, looking down at earthly things through a translucent lens. I don't see faces very well, I only recognize the very familiar ones. I can make out shapes and I do see colours, possibly in somewhat duller shades than they would be in life. It is like having a gauze curtain between me and the rest of the people who are still breathing. In some cases the gauze curtain is dense, in other cases it is thin and almost transparent. My death, so far, is like being engulfed in a cloud of gauze. I can also hear voices, but they are low and muted. I am afraid I will no longer enjoy listening to Vivaldi or Beethoven or Mozart, or Karl Orff, since I will not be able to distinguish the glorious highs and lows in their music. This death thing seems to be a stretch of silence. I know no one can see me or hear me, and I am not even sure I have a voice of my own now. It is a good thing I talked so much during my working years; I got it all off my chest.

I have not met the Creator yet. Neither he/she nor his/her disciples greeted me. Maybe, there is no Creator, after all. Maybe, he/she is very busy. There are too many people dying these days and it is probably hard to keep up with millions of deaths a year, only from our world alone. Death is a booming industry. Not only the elderly like myself, but the youngest ones from the poorest of the poor are passing away. The war games men play are also costing thousands of lives each year, the lives of men, women and children alike. For all I know, there may be other worlds similar to ours, and that would definitely elevate life/death tallies the Creator has to keep. I wonder if there are super computers in the after life, and I smile to myself. Wow! I can still smile! Wouldn't that be something! Just having escaped the super computers of VISA, MasterCard, and Canada Revenue, I may now find myself caught up in the super computer of God.

Joking aside, if there is a Creator, I hope, he/she is a benevolent one. I am afraid of the ones who point fingers, and then send thunderbolts, fires, floods, and destroy nations. I have already endured a complicated life, so now that I am floating around in leisure, I do not want additional complications, judgments, blames, curses. I certainly do not want flames, since my skin is very tender. When I was alive, I stayed out of the sun, and religiously used sunscreens and gentle facial balms. The closest I got to any fire was an electrical fireplace. So, with all due respect, I am not a good candidate for Hell.

Once I passed over, I expected that my loved ones would meet and greet me. I expected them, so to speak, to show me around, give me a guided tour, share a few tips for surviving my own death. Above all, I really hoped to see my father and my maternal grandmother, Beatrice. I have so much to tell them, so much gratitude to express. I was also hoping to see Sophie and Agnes, and tell them what I had not been able to say in many of our growing-old-together years. In the case of Sophie, I had basically stopped talking to her when her mind slipped away, and all she could manage was to hang onto a few, small words. Sentences frightened Sophie; all she could understand were basic commands. In her final years, Sophie had become a pet rather than our mother: eager to please, but doing things which displeased everyone, like breaking and soiling things. Now that we are both dead, I thought, it would be the right time to really hear each other out. But Sophie is nowhere to be found. I wanted to see Mavis and tell her about my own garden, about the colours, the delicate perfume of my flowers, and the sweet taste of my fruits. I wanted to see Horus, Bambo, Boomerang, and my other small brigade of previous pets. I wanted to feel their luxurious coats, touch their velvet ears, stroke their damp muzzles and wiry whiskers. Yet, no one I know is here. Obviously, they have all moved on to another place. I am likely in a waiting area of sorts, a place that separates life from afterlife. As I said, I do not know the details yet, I am new at this thing we call death. I am a tourist without a suitcase, but with lots of emotional baggage.

Fortunately, there is a calmness about the new me, which is different from what was my mostly hectic life. I see things, I hear things, but from a distance. Nothing seems to upset me anymore. I no longer have heart palpitations. My memories seem intact. But my memories no longer cause me pain. I notice that I do not feel any joy, nor deep sorrow. The latter, I appreciate. I suffered more than enough, while I was alive. My heart did not just quit on me, it got broken, time and time again. Yet, I no longer blame anything, or anyone, for any of my life experiences, no matter how bad they may have been. That alone lifts a huge burden from my shoulders. So, death is like being emotionally anesthetized. If I had not been such a passionate lover of life, I might even say that I like being dead.

Death seems to clarify one's life. It provides a fresh perspective, like a view-finder. Or, like a movie, with bits and pieces of my past life parading in front of my eyes. The main characters of this afterlife movie are those who played a significant role while I was alive. The ones who stand out are the ones whom I loved the most, and whose actions and choices elated me or hurt me the most. My life was anchored around Negrisse, my daughter; Sophie, my mother; Agnes, my older sister; Beatrice and Mavis, my two grandmothers, and of course me: Anna. In sum, four generations of women inextricably tied to one another by bloodlines, loyalties, respect, and love on the one hand, and resentments, misunderstandings, and even hate, on the other. There were also a few men, in the form of grandfathers, husbands, in-laws, etc., but they were mostly in the background. Besides, in my family of women, men did not stay too long. They were either lost to death or divorce.

Just before I passed away, I finished writing a story about the women in my family, which I had started when I was young. My experiences, my joys and sorrows, my ups and downs are all reflected in this story. The completed story is tucked away in the bottom drawer on the right-hand side of my desk, a.k.a., my TV stand. I am hoping that someone will find it and read it, before my meagre possessions are sold or given away to Goodwill. I am hoping that someone will recognize the valuable lessons in my story for other women, and decides to seek its publication. I think the competing loves and the tensions amongst the four generations of women in my family can provide insights to other women who are caught up in their own familial generations. I want to forewarn the younger women about family dragons. Maybe, all I want is post-mortem fame through a published book. Who knows?

2.

The Dog Who Soiled the Carpet

THE DAY NEGRISSE MOVED OUT, she was seventeen years, five months, and four days old. Like most daughters, she had to free herself from the shackles of her mother's love, and she had to do it on her own terms. I thought I was going to die. I felt like someone had grasped my windpipe, and never let it go; as though someone had thrown my brain into the fireplace and someone else had tossed my heart into the washing machine and pressed the spin cycle. But, as I have found out since: women are resilient. They survive childbirth, they survive lack of gratitude, and they survive abandonment! Women are strong, like dragons.

I cried a lot at the time Negrisse left. I cried a lot after she left. I guess I cried for both of us since Negrisse did not shed a single tear. Since then, I have seen Negrisse only a few times. Our embraces have been either absent or cold and calculated, our eyes dulled with hurt, our speech laden with our unexpressed feelings and words. Each of us has developed an armour the other is unable to pierce. We are on the path of becoming total strangers.

I knew Negrisse's move was coming. As a matter of fact, I am mostly responsible for that outcome. But, that knowledge by itself did not lessen my outrage or pain when it finally happened.

One day, a few days after the New Year celebrations, Negrisse came home from school when I was still at work, and packed her books, clothes, and a few other belongings. She stuffed everything into two duffle bags and a paper bag, and left. The paper bag was made of shiny green paper, and had a very happy looking duck on one side. The bag had originally housed a Christmas gift, one that she seemed happy to receive: a collection of perfumed soaps, powders, and bath beads. Thus, seventeen years, five months, and four days of motherhood/daughterhood fit into two duffle bags and a scented shopping bag filled with things from the Body Shop. The enchanting aroma of sandalwood from the soaps, which she loved, still clung to her room. It was much too soon after Christmas for the perfume to wear off. Randall—my ex—probably was her conspirator and driver in this escapade, but I do not know that for sure. She may have taken the bus. She was travelling light. What I do know is that Negrisse ended up in her father's home, for the next year, waiting to become of legal age.

When I got home, I found the dark hole Negrisse had left in my life, a hole that has since never been filled. Like the black holes in space, the emptiness Negrisse's departure created in my life also sucked everything else in. The first casualties were my trust in others, my trust in myself, my ability to have a good time, and eventually, my health. Don't get me wrong; I am not blaming Negrisse for any of these things. After all, I am the author of my life, just like I am the author of this story. I have the ability to develop and change the characters and what happens to them, including myself. In the story, I can make Negrisse come back, I can make her cry and apologize. In real life, I do not have such ominous powers.

To make a long story short, when I arrived, Negrisse was gone. The heavy curtains in her bedroom were tightly closed, which was normal. Negrisse thrived in darkness, and avoided light of any kind. Her skin was always like parchment paper; her face had a luminescence, like the ethereal creatures that inhabit the depths of the ocean floor.

Her bed was made, which was totally unusual. In general, Negrisse successfully resisted all pressure to engage in house-related chores. Her bed was made only when the need to change her sheets became starkly obvious, even to her. Poor Horus, presented to her as a puppy on one of her previous birthdays, was whining in shame. He had soiled the expensive living-room carpet, maybe due to the absolute rejection he felt. Maybe, it was just because Negrisse, in her rush to escape, had forgotten to take him outside to do his business. Normally, I would have scolded Horus for messing up my beautiful home, for soiling my carpet with his discharged bodily fluids. Normally, I would have taken his deviation as a personal affront ... but not that day. That day, Horus's violation was minor in comparison to the other colossal violation in my life.

I sat on the floor, I don't know for how long, turning my back to the doorway of the now empty bedroom, staring at the opposite wall. As if I had eyes at the back of my head, I knew that the bedroom was not empty at all. The bed, the closet, the chair, the desk, the lamp were all still in there, the heavy curtains too. The room still smelled of sandalwood. Yet the emptiness was profound. I did not turn on the lights, not wanting to witness the void. I sat, my heart churning and jolting, and doing other things that hearts are not supposed to do, until Gregory came home.

Greg was my long-time partner, lover, colleague, all at the same time. But above all, Greg was my closest friend and confidant. He picked me up from the floor, like a rag-doll, and half-carried, half-ushered me into the living room where Horus had stained the carpet. We sat together for a long time, without words, in total communion with our mutual sadness. Later, he said, "you will now have to learn to live without Negrisse, like a paraplegic learns to live without her limbs."

I shook my head from side to side, as if in disbelief. That day, I did not have the confidence in myself to be able to survive without Negrisse. I did not say to Greg that Negrisse's departure was closer to a fatal heart attack than losing a limb. In a way though, Greg was right, people survive even massive heart attacks, but their lives are never, ever the same again. I eventually learned to live without Negrisse like a paraplegic learns to live without her legs, like someone who has had a massive heart attack learns to breathe again.

For days, I looked for a sign in Negrisse's room. I looked for a note. I yearned for a note that said, "I am sorry," or "I'll be back," or "I love you!" There were no notes or messages to be found; the missing duffle bags were a final and complete summary of her intentions. So, I closed the bedroom door, and did not open it again, for weeks, or was it for months?

After months, when I worked up the courage to open her door, her absence still hit me like a slap on the face.

3.

My Name is Anna

M Y NAME IS ANNA, or Anna is the name I would have liked to have, if I had not been given another one by my parents. Since my birth took place 7000 miles away from Toronto, in one of the subdivisions of the Asian side of the magnificent city called Istanbul, my real name does not sound like anyone else's. Moreover, the spelling is a mess. Anyway, it does not really matter if my real name is Anna or something else, what is in a name anyway? For this story, I will call myself Anna, for another story, I will pick another name, until I exhaust all the names I like. This is the prerogative of all storytellers.

I now work as a career counsellor in one of the community colleges in Toronto. I don't know how I ended up in this job, since I have a Master's Degree in Education. I would have liked to teach, but there was not much of a demand for teachers at the time of my graduation. So, here I am, sitting in a sparsely furnished office, with two iron and vinyl chairs facing my too bulky and too crowded iron desk. My walls are white and unadorned, with the exception of a large poster that promises fulfilling jobs and a bright future for the youth. I cannot say I like my job, since I find it stressful. Working with students who are caught between wanting to be an astronaut or a belly dancer is not much fun. The expectations of exceptionally happy marriages and success in business are also just as farfetched, especially for girls and young women. I do not say these things to the students who come to see me … why clip their youthful wings so early in life? I take my job very seriously, since I want to prevent the students from making catastrophic choices for themselves. I do not want them to hate me to the end of their lives. I do not want them to hunt me down and kill me, or come to my office and wail in public. Come to think of it, I fear the latter most. Besides, my job pays my bills, and covers my dental care. I need a lot of dental work, since I grind my teeth in my sleep.

Over the years, I even had a few success stories in my job. A young woman I counselled to pursue a degree in clinical psychology eventually became a well-known therapist. I keep seeing her on TV; her opinion is highly sought after to explain the unexplainable, like why men beat their wives to a pulp, or why men rape their neighbour's teenage daughters. She also seems to be good at treating men who fail to rise to the occasion. She has gotten herself a nice feminist reputation, assuming there are nice feminist reputations. In Coles bookstore, I looked through the self-help books she has written, and found many, but did not buy them. I also heard that she developed a severe alcohol dependency. I don't think my career counselling had anything to do with that. Of course, I could have counselled her to pick a career which was less demanding, like flipping burgers in a hamburger joint. Then again, she might have started to drink to cope with the grinding mundaneness of her existence.

Another one of my success stories is a young man who eventually became a funeral director of a local funeral parlour. I hate funerals. Too many flowers. Makes me remember my wedding. Also, I hate the term "parlour" in that context, since it sounds like a place you go to eat ice-cream, or a place you powder your nose after you use the bathroom. Well, there is a lot of powdering and make-up going on in funeral parlours these days. I have seen some laid-out guests look like Can-Can dancers, or one of the nightmarish clowns in Stephen King movies, through no fault of their own. The fault belongs to the overzealous make-up artists who work in the funeral parlours. The young student I once counselled did become a dedicated and hard-working director. He made sure that his customers were made up to resemble themselves while they were alive. He eventually moved to a chic suburb of Toronto, and opened up his own parlour. I received a gilded invitation card from him, for the joyous opening ceremony. I did not go. At the time, I thought I was a bit too young for his type of business. Later on, I will regret not having procured this particular parlour's services. Maybe, he would have honoured all of my wishes, including the yellow roses.

I ran into this young man, many years later, when neither he nor

I were young anymore. It was one of the chilling December days Toronto is famous for. I was dressed in multiple layers and colours to combat the cold. He was cloaked head-to-toe in black, minus the top hat. To be polite, I asked him how his business was, and he said: "Slow, they are not dying, they are hanging on for Christmas." What Christmas spirit! Although I was taken aback by his candidness, I couldn't help but admire his business savvy, his thirst for profitability. Yes, this seemed a perfect fit between a person and career choice. I was pleased with myself for having seen the connection so long ago, when both of us were much younger.

Another student of mine became a chiropractor. He loved it at first, and sent thank you cards to my office every holiday season. He said he loved every minute of his work, and enjoyed working with all of his patients. I was pleased and proud, like a hen with chicks. Then, he developed carpel-tunnel syndrome in both of his wrists, which made it impossible for him to continue his chiropractic practice. I heard that he found a job with an insurance company as an investigator of fraudulent workers' compensation claims. His thank you notes stopped abruptly. How could I have foreseen the biological weakness in his wrists?

Other than the grinding responsibilities of my job, I mostly lead a quiet life now. I do not smoke or drink, at least not for the last couple of decades. Before then, I did smoke, like a chimney, and I did drink, mostly in moderation. I had to give both up, not because of a newly found spiritual revelation, but because of my growing health problems. Originally, I was also a carnivore, often devouring chicken, beef and pork in one sitting. I became a vegetarian, due to the covert pleadings and overt urgings of Negrisse. She used to leave articles and pamphlets about the mistreatment of farm animals in strategic locations around the house, such as beside the toilet. Most of the pamphlets were from PETA, and featured stories about cows refusing to enter slaughterhouses, therefore being shot to death, or chickens flopping around for minutes after their heads were severed. Some of the articles were about the inexplicable violence used by slaughterhouse staff to do their work. The inhumanity ingrained in their work sometimes pushed these workers into committing cruel and unusual acts towards the animals already awaiting their agonizing deaths. The gory pictures and the gorier stories in these pamphlets were very bad for my digestion, so I stopped eating meat. Besides, at the time, I still had delusions that Negrisse and I could share goals and ideologies. I thought we could still be friends.

After Negrisse left without saying good-bye, I was tempted, more than once, to drive to Kentucky Fried Chicken, buy a bucket of chicken, and devour all fifteen pieces right in the parking lot. At that time, the chain was still called Kentucky Fried Chicken, since people did not have as many qualms about eating deep-fried, cholesterol saturated foods as they do now. Now, they call themselves KFC, hoping consumers will forget about the "fried fat" part of what they are buying. It also helps to forget that the average Canadian weighs at least ten pounds more than what their counterparts weighed a couple of decades ago.

Well, although I was tempted to eat chicken, and beef and pork just to spite Negrisse, I couldn't. I don't think she would have cared one way or another, but I couldn't bring myself to desecrating an ideal that was so important for her ... even in her total absence. I guess, people cannot swear or curse in a church, even if they are ex-communicated, or even after converting to Islam or Buddhism. So, even without Negrisse's critical supervision and judgmental eyes, I am still a sort of a vegetarian, although I occasionally consume small crustaceans. In my current eating habits, I draw the line just above cold-blood and pea-sized brains. In sum, you can say that my life is pretty ordinary, verging on boring. Of course, I have a long list of my own eccentricities, and some festering wounds, but who doesn't?

4.

Four Generations of Women

IN THIS STORY, I will call my mother Sophie. I chose the name Agnes for my older sister, since the pronunciation reminds me of angst. I have power over these names, at least within the context of the story. By the same token, I will call my maternal grandmother Beatrice, and my paternal grandmother Mavis, simply because those names feel appropriate for them. There will be other women tangled up in the story, and a few men, but this story is mostly about six women spanning over four generations.

Negrisse, who deserted me at seventeen years of age, is my daughter. I am sure she has a completely different story of her life to tell, which I know nothing about. Yet, whether she knows it or not, she is a very important part of my story, albeit in absentia. For the portion of her growing years that I was allowed to be a part of, she called herself Negrisse. I am going to call her with that name, since I do not have the power to change it. As it turns out, I have no power over her life either, not even in my own story. I do not know any of the people or events that surround her life. I have the suspicion that, sometimes, she is with my enemies, sometimes she is with my friends, but most of the time, she is with people I will never know. She is not with me.

So, my story is about Negrisse, Sophie, Agnes, Beatrice, Mavis and me. I am the so-called link between these generations, since the oldest ones died before meeting the youngest, and the youngest have never bothered to find out about the oldest ones. Come to think of it, I am also fast approaching my own demise, but it is too early for me to digest this mishap. I still feel alive on most days, and I still think in the present tense. The four generations of women in my story are tangled up through bonds of lineage. They are tied through umbilical cords and the blood and gore of childbearing, and the responsibilities for the born children. In a way, this story is not about a single family, but about all generations of women.

As the storyteller, I renamed five women out of six. Not bad at all! I also changed and invented many of their characteristics and events. However, Negrisse remains as Negrisse. I do not wish to reinvent her uniqueness, her beauty, her brilliance or her cruelty. I do not want to break the shackles of love and hate that bind us across space and time! I do not want to change things about her just because I am a disgruntled mother. Writing a story is one thing, but re-writing history requires a power that I do not possess.

The bind between mothers and daughters extends much beyond the one that links Negrisse and me. The literature is full of examples of mother daughter love, loyalty, conflict, and hate. The binds between Sophie and Beatrice, Sophie and Agnes or myself are also substantial, and at times, convoluted. Mavis's relationship with me through our paternal line does not qualify as a mother-daughter relationship in my story. Yet, she was the mother of my three aunts and, of course, my father. Of my three aunts, only two survived, so Mavis was also a mother who experienced a profound loss. In her case, the loss was to death, rather than to a one-sided choice.

The parallel rather than the vertical tie between Agnes and I is also important and noteworthy for its intensity, dynamic, and even dysfunctionality. We are sisters, we share the same mother, and each of us has mothered a daughter. So, the bunch of us are six players, six actors if you will, firmly separated in time and place, with blocks of overlapping existence. In this story, the life-long performance starts with Beatrice. Of course, there must have been equally rich stories about Beatrice's mother, her grandmother, her great-grandmother, etc. After all, women are not onions that grow from a single, isolated bulb. Women are like magnificent Banyan trees, with entangled and intertwined root systems. But, I know little about those earlier relationships, and feel too lazy to invent them from scratch. We were never one of those families who like to draw bushy family trees to keep up with our lineage. Therefore, I am going to stick to the six people at hand, the women tangled in love, devotion, and hate, within the four generations linked through blood, flesh, and distances.

In one way, and as mothers and daughters, we are so different from each other; yet not different at all. This is why I can easily change the names of the older generations, including my own name. This is also why I cannot change my own daughter's name; at the moment, she occupies the centre of the stage. She is equipped to play her part now, as she pleases, for a time, like each one of us did in our own heydays. Eventually, if she is blessed—or not so blessed—to have her own daughter, her own name may be replaced or discarded. She will then become another link in an eternal and all encompassing, sometimes enchanting sometimes macabre dance of generations of women. Will she call herself Negrisse then? Will it matter if her name was Anna or Sophie or Beatrice? Will she have the choices then that she now has? I doubt it.

The four layers, four generations to be exact, are not solid. They are not even totally opaque as of yet, since some of them are still going through transformations. Other than Beatrice and Mavis, who are already dead, and Sophie, Agnes and I who are getting old and fragile, the layers are not frozen. Our lives are still ebbing and flowing with change even when they appear to stand still. There is still hope for improvement. There are still major disappointments ahead. There are births, and deaths, yet to come.

The layers of the four generations are like transparencies, with their individual colours, their textures, and contours, their carefully slashed boundaries forming a topography of sorts. They are not like the two dimensional transparencies that our teachers used in classroom projectors, before the advent of Internet-linked smart-classrooms. The family transparencies I am thinking about have depth. They are like blocks of ice. You can more or less see through them, if the angle of vision and the lighting are correct. You can pick up each one of the four transparencies, like I am going to do, and subject it to variations of light and careful examination. Each layer is unique and will come alive with its own shapes, hills and valleys, light and dark spots. Each will form a beautiful, challenging and sometimes foreboding tapestry. There are sunrises, and sunsets, seas and mountains eternally locked in every one. There are people who dance, sing, cry, and mourn in each generation. There are a few who lurk around, vibrating with menace. There are black spots, hurricanes, and erupting volcanoes. Each transparency is etched with a wide range of emotion. Each transparency is etched with life and death. The dead continue to live within the transparencies of those still alive, although their stories lose their clarity and vibrancy across time. Through death, dragons lose their scales and fangs, and become butterflies.

My story is about the four transparencies placed on top of each other, anchored by the six women I already identified. These women are like a female Atlas, carrying the "world" of my family on their shoulders. I am one of the six. The story will have no existence without each of the four layers. The four generations I look through are from a thick book of many more transparencies, probably extending to Adam and Eve. The thick book also contains empty transparencies to be etched in the future, by new generations. My own mental capabilities, as the teller of these stories, do not allow me to comprehend the complexity of all generations in the past, or yet to come. Too many transparencies on top of each other make peering into them impossible. It will make my own four pages—layers—lose their depth, blur into a thick mess, like molasses. Seeing the dimensionality, the intricacies are possible if, and only if, a few pages are examined at a time. This is why I chose to look through the pages that contain Beatrice, Mavis, Sophie, Agnes, Negrisse, and myself. Four generations are plenty. Four is enough.

I am the third generation. I am an observer but not a bystander. I have my own biases that colour everything I look at. With my own jaundiced eyes, I look up through two, look down through one layer. When need be, I also look at myself. How objective are we as observers? How objective am I as a storyteller? The fact is, if there are any facts at all, I am embedded in my own transparency, in my own time and location. I am the bird that is locked up in the sealed glass wall-clock, coming out to chirp different tunes for each of the hours. My view might have been really different if I were not the trapped bird. My view might also be different when the clock I am captured in stops forever. The clock does not only keep the bird caged, but it also gives it life.

In the book of generations, I will put the bookmark between my own generation and that of my daughter's. The earlier layers of Beatrice, Mavis and Sophie, are there to shed light onto the last two. The love that binds all these pages together has its own glue.

The hate has its own gale force that blows people apart, like a fire-spewing dragon.

I see the transparencies of the generations as landscapes with their own rivers and valleys, lakes and rivers, sunrises and sunsets. In a way they are tangible, but they are also landscapes of emotions. The people imbedded in these emotional landscapes are like the mother-of-pearl mosaic pieces inlaid in luxurious Middle-eastern furniture. They shimmer; they have their own opalescence. They are like bubbles suspended in a cube of ice; they are like mosquitoes frozen in Baltic amber. Sometimes they appear in sunny areas; sometimes they are embedded within the eye of the storm. However, there are people, there are places, there are experiences that go right through all the transparencies, with much force, with much vigour. In a way, some events are like the butcher's knife, they slash through all four generations. Around these slashes, different lives from different generations coalesce, congeal, merge and become one. The slashes thicken, and form scabs. In a way, these slashes are the parts that keep this particular story together.

When I peer into the uniqueness and the sameness of the four generations of women in my family, the first thing that strikes me is the different colours. Each one has splashes of reds and blues and greens, here and there. Each also has more exotic colours like purples, aquas, and fuchsias and phosphorous yellows. However, each layer also has its own dominant colour. The predominant colour I see in Beatrice's and Mavis's generation is grey. Maybe, this has something to do with their whitish grey hair, at the time I knew them. Maybe, it is because of the lack of vibrancy in their lives, again at the time I knew them. Maybe, the grey represents the hardship in their lives. I see the dominance of a darker yellow, almost a mustard colour in Sophie's generation. It is earthy; it has a no-nonsense, stick to the facts and the rules nature. My own generation is definitely purple. Sometimes, it is lavender, fragrant and uplifting. Sometimes, it is a dark purple, like the sky before a storm, foreboding, pregnant with tears.

When I examine Negrisse's colour canvas, my heart fills with pain. It is covered with black. The darkness is like a curtain, heavy and non-penetrable. Maybe this is why I have been blind to Negrisse's wants and wishes. I have not been able to see through, so I did not see what they were. Maybe, this is why Negrisse has not been able to appreciate my own efforts; she has also been blinded by the same blackness of her canvas. I also see the dark purple reflections of my own moody canvas upon hers; I feel the frustration of not being able to look through. I despise the dark curtain over my eyes.

Part II:
Grandmothers

5.

Taş Kale (The Stone Fortress)

MY EARLIEST MEMORIES GO BACK to a small village called Aşkale, probably with a population of less than a thousand, and an additional few thousand stationed army personnel. The Aşkale of my childhood has a single road, and a few, barely passable side roads. Originally, it was called "Taş Kale," which means a stone fortress, but someone dropped the "T" along the way, and merged the two words into one. In a historic land such as Anatolia, name changes of cities and towns are common occurrences.

Aşkale was at the Russian border, when Russians were the enemy. So, the Turkish Army always dumped soldiers reaching many thousands into the barely equipped army barracks around that region. These idealist protectors of the fledgling Turkish Democracy of my childhood were carefully socialized to nurture a Soviet hatred, almost from birth. Most of that generation died with that hatred. I doubt that the more recent global love affair with the new Soviet republics has cured historic tensions in that part of the world. The socio-political angst that penetrated my early childhood was carefully manufactured. The Soviet Union was not perceived as just another political and ideological regime, but the cradle of everything that was evil. In a way, the mentality matched the "axis of evil" concept, which the second, and not-so-well-liked, President Bush invented many decades later. But, Bush's axis of evil were Iraq, Iran, and North Korea, not the Soviets. Later on, Al Qaida and its founder Bin Laden became the personification of evil, until the U.S. Navy Seals one day killed him in a remote compound in Pakistan. Then, Pakistan almost turned into another axis of evil, for hiding Bin Laden. The namers and the named change over time, but the construction of "evil" is a common, socio-political process. Countries that consider themselves on the "right" side of the moral spectrum seem to find it necessary to find another country, somewhat of an arch-rival, in order to further solidify their own stance. Of course, history is the only vehicle that can "judge" the morality of the sides, across time. In my childhood, evil was unanimous with the USSR, and we feared them as Russians.

In Aşkale, we, the members of the Turkish army and their families, and even their young children, were the protectors of the (only) good, and the (only) moral position in the world: ours. We protected our land as well as the borders of our "friends" in Europe and in America against a common enemy. Much later, I found out that our so-called European "friends" had repeatedly tried to degrade the pride of the Turkish people, and had occupied our motherland during our war of independence! Some of these so-called "friends" continue to treat the Turkish people as nothing but barbarians. However, at the time, I was too young to understand the two-facedness of friendships. In my little girl's eyes, the world had only two polar ends, and the Soviets occupied the "evil" pole. Prejudice has its own benefits; it oversimplifies things, which is why it is so rampant and so resilient to change.

In my childhood, we also made another major historical error by calling the peoples of all the USSR, Russians. As the 1990s clarified, the USSR was only a temporary unification of various republics, some of which could not wait to declare their independence. As we later found out, Russia may have been the largest and the most populous republic, but the USSR was not Russia, and Russia certainly was not the USSR. Yet, these distinctions slipped by me in my childhood, and the world continued to exist in clearly demarcated lines between the "good" and the "evil." So, in my childish nightmares, Russians came to my house and took me away. Russians took away all children from their parents, didn't they? The Russians who penetrated my nightmares did not have faces. Their faces were hidden behind the huge fur kalpaks they wore, and the raised collars of their itchy coats. Stereotypes do not need individuality anyway, so the "evil" in my dreams was personified as men in gigantic hats and coats. I would wake up in terror, terror of being captured, or just about to be captured. In my dreams, I froze; I couldn't run away. My only option to get away was to wake up. Sometimes I did, sometimes I didn't. If I failed to wake up, my Russian tormentors took me to Siberia. Ironically, Siberia was not much colder than Aşkale.

My dreams found their rich, raw, and interactive material from my maternal grandmother's stories. Since her husband's untimely death, Beatrice lived with us. Older women of her time had no place to go after the death of their husbands. Beatrice had only one child, my mother Sophie, so she was stuck with us, or we were stuck with her, however you choose to look at it. For me, this arrangement was a blessing. Beatrice loved me unconditionally, and I basked in her love. Besides, she told me stories.

The antithesis of Beatrice's love for me was the hatred she felt towards the Greeks. She was old-fashioned, and staunchly set in her ways. She was as stubborn as a mule. She never shifted her own axis of evil to the Russians, although the latter was the more fashionable enemy of the times. Beatrice's irrational feelings had a rational source. After all, my grandfather, whom I never met, had lost all his beautiful hair as a POW in a Greek prison. All the Ottoman sikke (gold coins) Beatrice was able to send as a bribe to the wardens had made very little difference for him. Well, maybe just a little difference. Even Beatrice admitted that my grandfather was not required to drink his own piss as a punishment, whereas all other war captives were forced to do so, at one time or another. The Turks have fought and won their independence wars before the United Nations wrote down their decrees about the humane treatment of the prisoners of war. According to Beatrice, Turkish POW's had lived and died under notorious conditions in Greek prisons.

Beatrice had many more war atrocities to recount, which she swore she had seen with her own two eyes. Her eyes were developing cataracts even then, so I sometimes questioned her vision, but I knew better than to bring this up. The village that enveloped her family's vast lands before the war of independence was on the European side of Turkey, and thus, happened to undergo the Greek siege. As an adolescent, Beatrice had witnessed killings of women and children. The occupying soldiers had the habit of placing a tomcat inside the loose pants (şalvar) of the local youth, and whip the cat from the outside. The soldiers would laugh and give each other pats on the back as the youth with the cat inside his pants screeched with animalistic sounds. The tortured young men Beatrice had witnessed had cried and begged, as they were being transformed to gnawed and mauled eunuchs.

Above all of the atrocities Beatrice recalled, and what bothered her most, was how her family attempted to save her own brother. Her brother was dressed in a woman's purdah to escape town during the early stages of the Greek siege. Beatrice claimed that she never saw her brother after that night. War was very dangerous for younger men, while the older men were already at the battlefields, or dead, or losing their hair in captivity. Beatrice recalled with horror her brother being diminished to wear a purdah. She fiercely rejected the degradation of turning a man, her own brother, into a woman, not even for the reason of saving his life. She had dichotomized views of the world, and believed in the bipolarity of good and evil. The good side was being a Turk, and respecting sharp divisions in gender. The bad side was represented by the Greeks, and effeminate men. Not once did Beatrice think that maybe the Turks, when they were the occupiers and the victors, might have done similar things on the lands they had seized. Never once, did she think that maybe war was an element of evil, it turned humans into monsters. Yet, for Beatrice, there was no blurring of the boundaries. Recognizing the possibility that the sides changed across time, and seeing evil in situational contexts were not possible in her surgically dichotomized world.

Some days, Beatrice told me colourful, intriguing stories which took weeks to tell, and which nourished my own imagination. On other days, she told me stories of shear human-induced horrors, torture, brutality and suffering. The first, made me a lover of storytelling, the latter gave me bone-chilling nightmares.

Rather than the black and white polarity of Beatrice's reality, the vision of a world that consists of shades of grey took many decades to emerge in my own mind. It also took endless soul searching on sleepless nights. I had to grow up. I had to move on. I had to shake off the hatreds that flourished in war-torn hearts. It was an arduous journey indeed. Eventually, I did cherish and keep Beatrice's endless love for me. I did keep her colourful stories as I slowly washed away the after-effects of the evil wars that had prayed on her life. I now have many students I counsel who are from Greek origins. They are just like other students; they want to be astronauts, they want to be doctors and engineers, they want to save the world. They help me to appreciate a world that contains hues of grey, rather than Beatrice's blinding black and white world. I also try to add to the multidimensionality of the students' worldviews. Who knows what horror stories their grandmothers told them about the Turks. Just like love, hate can only persist when it is reciprocal. I do not nourish hate. I certainly do not reciprocate in hateful ways as far as people are concerned. I do hate wars, regardless of their justifications. I expect civilized people to choose a pen over a sword.

I am glad I chose Canada as my new home. People from many different countries get to mingle here. Becoming a Canadian erases the many sharp edges of historical frictions. However, when I first moved to Canada, Sophie and Agnes saw me as a traitor. I saw the burning accusation in their eyes. I saw the deep hurt on their faces. Over decades, they too had come a long way; they too have dulled the sharp edges of their unilateral judgments. We can now reminisce about Beatrice without falling into the trap of her war-induced, ethnic hatreds. So, unlike my early childhood, my dreams are no longer filled with the fear of being kidnapped and tortured. No one, from any national or cultural background chases me anymore. Now I fear bioengineering of my food. I fear the chemicals in the water. I fear the pollutants in the air I breathe. I have allergies!

6.

An Early Lesson in Gender Relations

ASIDE FROM MY EARLY SOCIALIZATION in prejudicial views about the world, which took years to modify, Aşkale is mostly a blur. I know we lived in army barracks with small windows. Maybe, I remember this only because I heard it so many times. Maybe, it is just a pseudo memory I own from the few black and white photos that remain from that era. Another pseudo memory is when I stuffed *leblebi* (roasted chickpeas) deep inside my nostrils. *Leblebi* is a common snack in Turkey, and we used to consume plenty to combat our day-to-day boredom. I remember—or have I been told so many times that I think I remember—my father, sweating like a surgeon, trying to pull them out, one by one. His only surgical tool was my mother's tweezers. After the removal of the third chickpea (or was it the fourth?) from one side, I declared that my other nostril was also full! Once the emergency situation was successfully handled, and my father became my hero for once and for all, everyone laughed until they cried. To this day, I like roasted chickpeas, although I can never get over the stupidity of stuffing them into my nostrils. Yet, I take some hidden pride in having done something so utterly outrageous!

The *leblebi* incident, across time, transformed into family jokes about the size of my nose, and continued until I had a nose job. The jokes likened my nose to an elephant's trunk, with much room for hiding munchies. They were not meant to be cruel, but they were. They were not meant to have a lasting negative effect on me, but they did. I was partially responsible for the genesis of these jokes by doing what I did at the ripe old age of four. Eventually, I could not live with my nose. I could not live with that nose right on my face. At the time, I did not have a sense of myself as much better than the sum of my parts. My nose shadowed my whole self; it was large, long and purplish in colour (more jokes about eggplants). It was unacceptable, it had to go; it had to be reduced, it had to be re-shaped. I got my nose job after my father died. He would have never allowed such self-mutilation. Although my father would have been correct in his rejection of my blatant self-alteration, I have no regrets. At the time, the nose job served a purpose: it allowed me to grow my confidence without being the butt of cruel jokes.

Knowing first-hand how childhood jokes have long-lasting consequences, I never made jokes about Negrisse's physical features. I told her she was beautiful, which I honestly felt she was. When she was a baby, people would stop us in the park, or at the mall, just to tell me how beautiful she was. She had warm chestnut hair, and matching warm chestnut eyes with streaks of molten honey in them. She had a light Mediterranean skin, which was as smooth as a peeled egg. I could not stop looking at her and breathing in her beauty. As a young mother, I basked in her reflected light and glory. Negrisse was my sun, my moon, and my stars, all combined into one.

At puberty, Negrisse also developed a large nose. Her puberty nose was a combination of the length of my original nose and the width of Randall's bulbous nose. Amongst close friends, my ex's nickname was Karl Malden. Although I never uttered the word "nose" in her presence, and still saw her as beautiful as ever, Negrisse developed a poor self-image anyway. My unalterable belief in her beauty changed nothing. Like many other women I know, she had an internal clock that started to ring "negative, negative, negative." Fortunately, Negrisse was more resilient than I was, she never succumbed to pressure; she never got her nose chopped off. Instead, she dyed her hair midnight black, grew it into an unmanaged and unmanageable bulk, and let it hang all over her face. From certain angles, it looked like she had two heads, one made of hair, devouring the other one made of a pale-coloured flesh. To give herself some breathing room, she developed the habit of extending her lower jaw forward, and blowing upwards. Her attempts created a vertical tunnel of air in a densely populated shrubbery. The tunnel also gave her an opportunity to steal pictures of her surroundings, like snapshots frozen in a teased frame of hair. Why is it that as parents, we are so powerful when we do something wrong, but so powerless when we do something right? I should not have had my nose re-shaped. I should have kept my larger nose and been a better role model. Maybe, that was my falling from grace.

In sum, Aşkale was not the greatest place to raise children, although my parents did their best. It was high in altitude in far eastern Turkey, close to Mt. Ararat. At that time, no one was searching for Noah's Ark at Mt. Ararat. That interest first grew, and then died, long after we left. Aşkale was a cold, forsaken land. Our army barracks were buried under a deep blanket of snow for more than eight months a year, and housed no luxuries such as hot water or flush toilets. Did we have running water? Probably not. We had a wood stove for heat, and an oil stove for cooking. It was only when we were getting ready to move that the army finally brought electricity to the barracks, which was of no use to us.

The floors of the barracks were raw wood, which Sophie had to scrub with bleach to keep them looking clean. My parents shared a room. Beatrice, Agnes and I slept in the other. Some part of our bedroom doubled as a sitting room once we put away the roll-a-way beds, all army issue. One had to have a strong moral conviction to live under those harsh conditions. One needed even a stronger moral justification to drag one's young family into it. Fortunately, my father had both. The fear of Russians served the purpose. The difficult conditions never once made us wonder about why we were there in the first place. Also, there was an abundance of snow cones, made from real snow and a drizzle of honey.

To keep two little children, especially an inquisitive four-year-old like myself, under those Spartan conditions was extremely hard for Sophie. Besides, Sophie was not that good in things like mothering. Outside was dangerously cold; snowsuits in that part of the world were yet to be invented. We had no toys. I stuffed *leblebi* into my nostrils out of sheer boredom. One logical escape was my father's army jeep. When he was at "manoeuvres" in the mountains, whatever schemes they were manoeuvring for, his army jeep and his soldier-driver was at our service. This little bit of luxury was not exclusive to us, but was available for all army officers' families. There were no cars, cabs, or public transportation of any other kind. And the army did not want its officers' wives to ride on bull-wagons or mules, like the locals did. More accurately, though, when my father was up in the mountains, his jeep was at my service. The driver, different ones at different times, would give me short rides, and would let me sit on his lap and play with the steering wheel with the engine running while the jeep was parked. The engine had to run, or else both the driver and I would have become frozen. I loved these little escapes. These times were my best times, I felt important, powerful, grown up. Until one of the drivers exposed himself to me. When I went back home, I told my mother that our driver had something wrong with his zipper.

I not only possessed a big nose, but an equally big mouth. I still keep the latter in its original form. It is no wonder that I made a living from counselling students. I loved to talk. My mother had a bowl of beans in her hand, beans cooked in the style my father liked them, in lots and lots of olive oil. She let it go. In slow motion, I saw the beans tumbling out of the bowl like a waterfall, rolling on the floor, scurrying around, staining the bleached raw wood, looking like headless eyes. I watched in bewilderment, wondering if my mother was ever going to be able to get the stains out of the raw wood. She did eventually, but it took her many bottles of bleach. First, she had to ask me a million and one questions, which I did not find very relevant to the jeep driver's broken zipper. She kept asking, "Was it long? Was it long?"

At the ripe age of four, this was my initiation to gendered relations. Although the driver had only opened his zipper, and had not hurt me in any other way, my parents acted as if I had been murdered. They were right; men murder the trust women have in them. With their wars, with their guns, with their tempers and with their open zippers, men play havoc in women's lives. Other men, like fathers, have to clean up the mess, have to mop up the gore, with counter wars, counter arsenal, counter violence. They have to protect their land, and they have to protect their daughters. My father never allowed any one of us to ride his army jeep ever again. I certainly do not know what became of that driver who crossed the line. It was still shortly after the war, and the army was still the place for severe corporal punishments. I missed the jeep rides the most. I felt the whole thing was my fault. This is another aspect I learned about gender relations: even when men are the perpetrators, women internalize the blame. Like a genetic disease, self-blame passes from mothers to daughters.

Many years later, when I was a young adult, I watched the movie, *Marathon Man*, which won many awards for Dustin Hoffman and

Sir Lawrence Olivier (may the latter rest in peace). Sir Lawrence was a Nazi dentist who had accumulated gold from the teeth of Jews who were exterminated during WWII. He had managed to transport the gold to the U.S. and had hidden it in a bank safe, how and why are beside the point. He was ready to retrieve his stash. However, he thought that Dustin Hoffman knew something about some danger surrounding the safe (which, of course, he didn't; he just happened to be a jogger, inadvertently involved in the whole mess). The crazed and cruel character played by Sir Lawrence (was his name Adolph? Aren't all brutal people known by that name?) asked over and over, "Is it safe? Is it safe?" To extract information from Hoffman, he drilled on the live nerves of Hoffman's molars. The torture depicted in the film almost matched the torture Beatrice used to tell me about: the whipped cat in a young man's loose pants, scratching, tearing, shredding. Hoffman's character did not know the expected answer. He sometimes said, "it is safe, it is very safe." At other times, he said, "No! It is not safe." He was caught up in a world he did not understand, like worlds many women experience without being in films. They do not know when something is safe. They do not know when it is dangerous. They learn to expect the worst. This turns to be an effective education in gendered powerlessness and helplessness. I learned this lesson from our driver's "broken" zipper, and my parent's flurry of questioning that it engendered. Because I did not know the right answer, I sometimes said, "Yes, it was long" and at other times, I said: "No, it was not long." From my parents' reactions, I figured that all men carried hidden weapons beneath the zippers of their trousers.

Flashback: Anna at age five

My parents bought our first radio. It is a major purchase. This is my—and my whole family's— very first exposure to any kind of an electrical gadget in our home. So far, there are no electronics. Sophie still washes our dishes and clothes by hand, and sweeps the floors and the carpets with a straw broom. Once in a while, we hire a cleaning woman who does everything that Sophie does, but gets paid for it. Sophie's work is unpaid, and often unrecognized. Refrigerators and vacuum cleaners become available for middle-class families like mine when I reach my early teens. Dishwashers and televisions become available when I start university. My country folk never got into clothes dryers since the sun continuously blesses our climate, even throughout the winter months. Even when the cold stiffens the freshly washed clothes, so they look like two-dimensional ghosts, they eventually soften up and dry.

Our new radio is like a large breadbox with a polished wooden cabinet. I don't know the type of wood it is made of, but the colour is a warm, golden beige. With the exception of a tiny window in the front, the face of the radio is covered by a delicate bamboo-coloured mesh. The mesh is slightly textured. When the light hits the face from a particular angle, I can see the cavernous interior. There are two circular openings behind the mesh, like sideways turned soup bowls. They are the speakers. When the radio is on, the mesh covering the speakers slightly vibrates.

Near the bottom of the face, there are two large knobs. The knobs are dark brown, and go well with the warm golden colour of the exterior and the natural bamboo colour of the mesh. The knob on the left moves a perpendicular red line inside the window. The red line moves horizontally across faint, numbered lines, and helps to locate the few AM channels our radio is capable of receiving. There are no FM channels available at the time. The right knob controls the volume, but it is the left knob that is important; that is the one that needs patience and skill. As my father moves the left knob ever so gently, the red line moves from one spot to another, and we start to detect various hissing tones. Sometimes, the hissing becomes a loud metallic sound that is so disturbing that I have to cover my ears with my little hands. Then, the hissing slowly turns into a gargle, and human-like noises start to seep through. Eventually, a real human voice starts to speak, or a real person is intercepted while singing a song, accompanied by background music. At the end of his vertical red line journey, my father's face breaks out into a smile. He is the Atlas who has carried the weight of the world; he is the David who just slayed the dragon. Our radio is magical.

My parents placed the radio in their bedroom, possibly to keep its precious knobs from being manipulated by Agnes's and my own inquisitive fingers. During the day, no one plays with the radio, and the door to my parents' bedroom remains closed. It does not need a lock, since we know that we are never to enter my parents' room without permission. It is only after my father's arrival, and after Sophie washes the dishes, that we all get escorted into the room, and my father ceremoniously turns on the radio. He listens to the news. He also listens to the weather reports, which make predictions that rarely come true. Long before the advent of the satellites, reporting the weather was just a tad better than gambling. The predictor often lost.

On Thursday nights, the radio broadcasts one-hour-long plays. Some of the works are by Turkish playwrights, others are internationally known works. These are my favourite programs, even though I do not really understand the plots. Sometimes, the reception is not great, and it is difficult to accurately differentiate which of the characters is saying what. Still, our radio brings a bit of high-culture right into our home, since the location of our rented apartment is at quite a distance from the cultural core of Istanbul.

At the age of five, I listen to some Turkish plays. The main plots are always about wars, lost loves, saved honour. Turkish plays have a lot of deaths in them, especially deaths of women who sacrifice themselves for their country, or for their husbands or children. In Turkish plays, the drama imitates life. We also listen to a performance of Henrik Ibsen's, A Doll's House. Needless to say, I don't get it. Maybe, my parents did not get it either. We all blame Nora Helmer for breaking up her marriage. Unlike their Western sisters, Turkish women did not learn to fight for their rights; their political rights were given to them from the top down. For all I know, they are still struggling with their personal, social, and cultural freedoms. At a time when I am only five, there are no divorces in our immediate or extended families. The older generation of women who now live with their daughters are widowed, not divorced. So, it seems natural that we all blame Nora for being so unreasonable and selfish. We expect her to do what Turkish women do: sacrifice.

It is only when my own generation moves into adulthood that divorce becomes common, but still frowned upon. First, my oldest aunt's daughter gets a divorce, but only when her husband's infidelities become too frequent and too public to ignore. Then, Agnes and I get a divorce, even though our husbands did not cheat on us behind our backs. Since then, each of our daughters has already tried it once. Since Sophie's generation, all women in my family have become Ibsen's Nora, and I think, it is a good thing.

7.

Beatrice

BEATRICE LIVED WITH US, like most maternal grandmothers did in my country of origin. Paternal grandmothers lived with their own daughters, if they had them. If not, they moved into the home of their daughters-in-law, and often, there was trouble. The worst trouble was when the wife's, as well as the husband's, mothers had to live with them in the same house. Then, it was a right-out war, which the paternal grandmothers often won. Patriarchal beliefs have a way of rubbing out on women who are close to the patriarchal heads. In my family, this was not the case, only Beatrice lived with us. Mavis lived in her own house, and died of a heart attack while visiting one of her daughters. Mavis was resourceful like that, and I will have numerous occasions to return to her life.

As long as I knew her, Beatrice looked a million years old. I was shocked to find out that she was only in her early seventies when she actually died, and by then, I was about ten. Chain-smoking was Beatrice's full-time occupation and the primary cause of her eventual demise. Even decades after her death, I still think of her as the hub of a dense cloud of smoke. She was a volcano, spewing ashes and smoke wherever she went. Well, to be exact, she did not go anywhere special, she just went to the bathroom when the nature called. Sophie did not want to take Beatrice out very often; she claimed that Beatrice slowed her down. Moreover, when Beatrice had to walk even for a short distance, she complained about aches and pains. At that time, we had to walk for a bit in order to take public transit. Cars were available only for the rich, not middle-class families like mine. So, Beatrice sat down on her favourite couch, and chain-smoked all day long, and part of the night. At night, she went to bed early, and that gave her tormented lungs a rest.

I called Beatrice "Nane" which was a play on the word, *anneanne*, which means maternal grandmother in my mother tongue. *Nane* also means "mint," which was the last thing Beatrice smelled like. She always reeked of tobacco smoke, although she was meticulously clean. Smoking was considered a birth right in the remote part of the world we lived in at the time, so I did not complain. However, Sophie complained relentlessly. She did everything in her power to make Beatrice feel bad about her habit and often accused her of poisoning the tender lungs of my sister and myself. The tension in the air between Beatrice and Sophie was as thick as the billowing clouds of smoke. So, Agnes and I opened the windows. The smoke funnelled out, the tension remained.

This was not something I thought about at the time, but which occurred to me later: Sophie never complained about my father's smoking habits, although they were just as bad as Beatrice's. Was this because my father paid the bills? Was it because men's deviance was tolerated and women's was not? It was surely due to the greater power of men, especially in the patriarchal corners of the world we lived in. So, my mother was silent about my father's smoking, but doubly resentful of Beatrice's: once for her own, and once for my father's deviance.

From the earliest days I can remember, Beatrice was an extremely slender woman with a severely curved spine. She was a bag of bones in Mardi Gras. To my child eyes, she looked emaciated, yet ominous. Since osteoporosis was not a word that was part of our daily language, all I could see was Beatrice's mighty hump. She looked aged, convoluted, imploding, as she sat in the eye of her billowing clouds. I loved her just the same, and never once wondered if she may have looked different when she was younger. In another appearance, in another time, in another place, she wouldn't have been my beloved Nane. In my whole life, the only unconditional love I experienced was the love Beatrice showed me. Other loves were always conditional, on a lot of things.

Throughout my childhood, I overheard stories about Beatrice, although none were intended for my ears. Some led me to believe that Beatrice was originally from an exceptionally respected farming dynasty. Her father, her father's father, etc., not only owned farms, houses, herds, but also total villages, in an especially desirable part of Turkey that falls on the European side. There were also rumours that Beatrice's mother had her roots in the palaces of the Ottoman Sultans. I never found out if this meant a harem existence for the maternal foremothers of Beatrice. Even in her deteriorating physical shape, Beatrice had an uncanny presence and dignity about her.

Other stories I overheard concerned how her husband was captured and tortured in one of our endless wars of independence. It was at that time that she had sold most of the things she owned, converted her riches into *sikke* (Ottoman gold coins), and bought her husband some dignity in the undignified world of his POW life. The rumour was that she had eventually managed to get her husband released from the POW camps. By that time, it seems, she had not only prematurely aged, but also had lost her wealth. The husband who had returned from the POW camps was not the same either. He had become mean and selfish. He cheated on her repeatedly, and suffered from ill health including some complications with sexually transmitted diseases. Shortly after the end of his POW life, he suffered a fatal heart. He was only forty-eight, and Sophie was only seventeen, and newly married when all these things had to come to an end. Due to the war-torn nature of Turkey at the time, Sophie never had a chance to say good-bye to her beloved father, but only had made it to his funeral. Sophie loved her father, and missed him all her life. In her advanced age, when her mind was mostly wiped clean by dementia, Sophie could still recall the minute details of her interactions with her father when he was still alive. Sophie was more eager to forget about Beatrice.

The couple of years of my grandfather's POW existence were recalled in detail, as an epic tale in my family. So were the details of Beatrice's self-sacrifice for her husband. Even the bad behaviour and questionable judgment he had shown after his release had not dampened Beatrice's love for, and devotion to, her husband. It was also rumoured that Beatrice had stopped eating for weeks following her husband's death, that her hair had turned white overnight and that she had suddenly and inexplicably lost most of her teeth. These whispered stories I heard in my childhood made Beatrice a legend among my mother's chatty friends, and a silent heroine of sacrifice in my childish eyes. Beatrice personified the suffering of women, which in Turkey, is deemed as a good thing.

After the funeral, Beatrice had moved in with Sophie and her husband. It seems Agnes was merely a baby at the time, and it was another five plus years until my own arrival. However, Beatrice's position in our home was always tangential, since Sophie always saw her own mother as an outsider; partly because Beatrice did not help with cooking or cleaning the house. When asked, she always said she did not know how to do housework since she had always had servants at her service. Sophie never failed to remind her that if she hadn't blown away all her wealth, maybe we could also afford a servant. This accusation deeply troubled me since Sophie professed to love her father so much, but yet, complained about the fact that Beatrice had spent her wealth on procuring his release from Greek prisons. What was clear was that Sophie and Beatrice personified mother/daughter tensions, which seem to be particularly vicious in my maternal family line.

Beatrice never said a bad word about my mother, at least, not in my presence. Maybe, her silence was the price for her dependency. In Turkey, like in many other parts of the traditional world, widowhood plunges women into a life of dependence on others. So, Beatrice ground her false teeth, since she no longer had teeth of her own, and smoked her cigarettes, one after another. She sat stoically on her couch, and only showed pleasure when Agnes and I were around. In our absence, she stared out the window, at nothing in particular.

Beatrice never talked about her past. There were times, nonetheless, when I would sneak up on her while she was staring at a picture of my grandfather. A completely bald, but an enchanting man stared back through the crackled surface of the yellow paper. He had jet-black eyes, which Sophie inherited. His stare did not mean much to me, but it never failed to moisten Beatrice's eyes. Beatrice's eyes did not have colour; they had no sparkle. They were two little indentations in her sallow, shrunken face. I never saw her actually cry though. Sophie told me Beatrice had cried so much for so long that she had dried-up her tear ducts. I had seen dried-up wells in our neighbourhood. I clearly understood the reason for Beatrice's missing tears.

Other stories surrounding Beatrice's earlier years were that she was a "spinster" until the ripe old age of twenty-six. Obviously, she was rich, but may not have been beautiful. When my grandfather eventually asked for her hand, she had accumulated nine hope chests filled with objects made of solid silver and gold, and an incredible variety of silk embroideries. Even her bath towels were jewelled and embroidered. Moreover, her dowry included a whole street of houses in a farming community, the best watermelon, onion, and wheat fields in the region, a farmhouse and a barn complete with good quality work horses. It seems my grandfather had brought little to the marriage except his handsome looks and a degree in rural engineering. However, Beatrice always thought that she had gotten the better side of the bargain. Even now, women's love trumps their entitlement for equity in marital relations.

By the time I was around, and had a sense of my surroundings, Beatrice had little left of her former glory. The war, which had indirectly snuffed out my grandfather's young life, had also devoured Beatrice's worldly possessions. She had bequeathed the remaining patches of land she owned to my mother, and moved into our house to await her end. The only thing she still owned was a large suitcase, tucked away at the bottom of one of the most inconvenient closets in our home. The suitcase was filled with her most intimate possessions and a few sets of clean clothes. Since her cigarette supply was also stashed in the same suitcase, everything uniformly smelled of tobacco. However, Beatrice's persona was not confined to her meagre possessions. Her glorious past and her unquestioning love for us enveloped her with a luminous aura, visible even through the billowing clouds. Despite the huge hump crouched on her fragile back, despite the clothes she wore which had long outlived their fashions, Beatrice imbued her own elegance.

8.

Beatrice's Stories

BEATRICE WAS AN INCREDIBLE NARRATOR. Most of her stories lasted many nights. In a way, she was like Blue Beard's only surviving wife, or TV series like *All My Children* or *The Young and The Restless* of decades yet to come. In her stories, there were young maidens, and exceptionally handsome and courageous heroes, often riding either milk-white or jet-black horses. There were castles and palaces as well as gold, rubies and emeralds as "large as the eyes of camels" (her expression). There were also villains, sometimes more than one, who sizzled with the evil they possessed. There were famines, floods, and of course, wars. There were painful separations, sometimes due to simple misunderstandings, but often as a result of violent combat. All of Beatrice's stories were about men and women, of love and hate, of separations and reunions. They all had happy endings, but I had to be patient and wait for them. Beatrice could not be rushed. Her stories were long. Some of her tales did not come to a conclusion for a month. The suffering of the beautiful maidens was immense. Many different people, mostly but not exclusively men, did horrible things to them. Eventually, all the bad women died torturous deaths, but the evil men sometimes died, and other times survived to appear in other tales. Men also had other troubles; as a rule, they had to maim or kill one another. They had to declare wars, lose their memory, or limbs or body weight. They had to kill and plunder and take hostages. Most of all, they had the singular responsibility of saving maidens who were chastely waiting for them. All chaste maidens eventually got married.

Beatrice never repeated a story, not even twice. Once the story was finished, which might have taken a few weeks or a month to tell, she introduced fresh new characters, in a fresh new story line.

They had different names, different placements in life, different love attachments and they experienced different torments. Some got sick with non-diagnosable diseases. The blood and gore that took place before the lovers eventually united was a staple in all stories, although the faces of the villains changed. Many villains had beards and body odour. Some had humps like the one Beatrice had, but Beatrice was no villain. All the heroes were clean-shaven, unless they were captured by the enemy. Beatrice's heroes never suffered post-traumatic-stress disorder. All the maidens had perfect teeth, "like pearls," although all Beatrice's generation of women smiled with false teeth.

Sometimes, I begged Beatrice—my dear Nane—to re-tell a story I particularly liked. I would try my best to remind her of the characters, or the plot, or the names of the maiden and the hero, to no avail. She could never re-construct any of her previous stories; most of the time, she would not even try. So, there was no rewind button in Beatrice I could press; once she finished a story, it was done, forever. Most likely, she made them up as she went along, without the need to look back, without the need to "save" it for a future occasion. Beatrice's stories were like taking a bath, once finished, you threw out the water. At the time, we did not have bathtubs though we had a wall-to-wall tiled room with a drain on the floor. We had bath stools that we placed near the drain, and we soaped and rinsed ourselves by scooping water from a huge bucket. These tiled-rooms were home-size variations of Turkish baths, low tech, but perfectly functional.

I deeply regret that none of the stories Beatrice told me survived the decades that have passed since her death. They are like pressed flowers from a long past, where the depth, the colours, the edges of their original glory are long gone. When I want to hold onto them, they shatter into a million pieces. What did endure is my passion for stories. In a way, Beatrice gave me the greatest gift in my life: the ability to tell stories, my own and others'. I learned to invent stories, with little effort, as she had done. It is too bad that I do not have a grandchild to whom I can transfer this amazing gift. Still, I look at stories as arteries in a body; they carry the oxygen that makes life possible. Rather than telling stories, I just write.

We also played card games together, just Beatrice and I. When I got slightly older, and when she became much more fragile, I sometimes cheated in the game to tease her. She never cheated back. Beatrice had zero tolerance for lack of fairness, even in my childish games. She had already endured so much unfairness in life. Beatrice was one of a kind. My Nane anchored my days, and she was the one who also anchored my childhood, or else I might have become unhinged, I might have floated away. I could not have imagined a childhood without her bony hug, without her stories that eventually transcended all evil. Although she herself was drawn into her own solitude, her stories exuded hope. I am so sorry Negrisse never met Beatrice, never knew Sophie, never basked in the self-giving love of a grandmother. Before she celebrated her first birthday, Randall and I immigrated to Canada. Negrisse had to grow up like a potted flower, only getting nutrients from her own shaky roots in the pot. She never learned to be part of a much larger garden, where the colours, fragrances and roots are all tangled together, where the total is more enchanting than the sum of its parts, where there is beauty as well as chaos.

Flashback: Anna at age five

Sophie is at one of her migraine retreats again. Her bedroom drapes are drawn; her door is closed. Beatrice tiptoes around, preparing simple meals for me and for Agnes. Beatrice also tiptoes in and out of my parents' bedroom, delivering water, soup, and pills. The soup comes back barely touched; the pills disappear. Obviously, Sophie is trying to get better before my father returns from wherever he is.

Beatrice combs Agnes's long hair, and braids it into two thick braids. Agnes does not complain as much as she does when Sophie performs this morning, pre-school ritual. One reason is that Beatrice is exceptionally gentle with us. The second reason could be that Beatrice is not a perfectionist like Sophie. On the days my mother retreats, the hair split on top of Agnes's head is not razor-sharp. Her long braids look presentable, but not perfectly even, or meticulously matched. The taffeta bows attached to the end of her braids are clean and ironed, but not necessarily starched. These infrequent escapes from perfectionism make better-behaved and happier children out of Agnes and I. It is Sophie's grinding perfectionism that drives us crazy. Sadly, it is also Sophie's perfectionism rather than Beatrice's flexibility that we emulate in our own adult lives.

Once Agnes leaves for school, I have Beatrice all to myself. She combs my hair too, but it takes a few seconds. My hair is thinner than Agnes's, and only a couple of inches long. Then, Beatrice stokes the fire in the stove. She always starts the fire about two hours before we wake up, so the room will be warm when we get out of our beds. We burn coal, which gives a lot of heat, but which also turns our white walls a grimy colour. Every couple of years, a painter arrives and places a fresh coat of white lime over the blackened layer. No designer paints are available in my childhood. Walls come in white or blue, the latter with the help of some laundry brightener.

Beatrice and I have breakfast. The top of the stove doubles as a cooking surface where Beatrice toasts our bread. She dips her pieces in her tea before eating them. Probably, her dentures bother her, but Beatrice never complains. Beatrice takes some tea into my mother's room, and the glass comes back empty. Things must be improving in there. Soon, my mother will start walking around, with a scarf tightly wound around her throbbing forehead, and her hair sticking out on top of her head, in total disarray. In a few more days, she will be braiding Agnes's hair into perfect braids. In a few days, Agnes will be bitterly complaining, because the roots of her pulled hair will hurt.

But today, there is still time for uninterrupted leisure. Beatrice sits down and takes a few minutes to arrange her aching bones, her already severely curved hump. She arranges her bony arms and hands, covered with crisscrossing veins and age spots. I snuggle as close to her body as I can. I want to absorb the love she exudes for me. Then, she starts one of her epic tales from where she left off the day before.

In today's segment, the story of a heroic prince who was captured by his enemies continues. They throw him into the dungeon, with little water and occasional scraps of food. The dungeon is rancid with human excrement. The prince loses more than half of his body weight, but he never loses his dignity or his hope. In the worst of times, when his skin cracks, his shirt rips, and his sores become infected, he can still visualize the clean, natural perfume of his princess. The princess is dressed in an all-white gown, and her liquid brown eyes and flame-red hair are urging him to live on. The emaciated prince finds in this mirage just enough courage to live through yet another day of torture. I see myself as the princess, and I also urge him on!

In Beatrice's tale, the princess does more than just appear as a vision in her prince's dungeon. She cajoles her influential father, brothers, and cousins to gather a small militia of armed men. She also uses her wit by making elaborate plans about when to attack the guards of the dungeon, and how to retrieve the tortured prince. She gives orders about his aftercare as well. She instructs the to-be rescuers not to feed the prince large amounts of food at first, in case his shrivelled-up body cannot cope with the sudden change. She instructs the rescuers not to scrub the filth and grime from his body, in case they hurt and aggravate his wounds. She would rather take care of his prince herself, slowly, with care and with love and devotion. After all, even witty princesses are there to provide care and comfort for their men. In Beatrice's stories, they provide all this care without dirtying their hands or their exquisite clothes.

I listen to Beatrice's story, visualizing every detail of the suffering in the dungeon. I also visualize the beauty and applaud the absolute dedication of the princess. I promise myself that when I grow up, I will serve my own charming prince. At the time, I fail to make the connection between the prince in the dungeon and my maternal grandfather's similar ordeals in the POW camps in Greece. I also fail to see the connection between the dogged determination of the princess and my own grandmother's super-human efforts to broker freedom for my grandfather. My five-year-old mind fails to see the similarities because my grandmother looks old, and bony, and is dressed in her everyday clothes of tans and browns. She does not look like the princess in her own story, although her sacrifices for my grandfather must have been just as heroic in her time. My five-year-old mind has already learned to ignore women's heroism, if they do not resemble fairy-tale beauties.

9.

Mavis

I WAS JUST A LITTLE GIRL when Mavis died. Sophie called it a "clean death," which meant a heart attack. This type of death is common on my father's side. The women of my maternal side hang around, their deaths complex: too much emaciation, too few pleasant memories, too many fragile bones, and too many bedsores.

Unlike Beatrice, Mavis did not live with us, and it is my suspicion that Sophie liked it better that way. Mavis was old, possibly much older than Beatrice, but had an inextinguishable spunk about her, which comes from being able to live alone. For her time, and for the socio-cultural restrictions in which she lived under, Mavis was an uplifting deviation from the norm. The norm was for women like Beatrice, aging and fragile, to be warehoused in their daughters' homes. Mavis lived free and independently in her own home; she was free in her own garden, free to do as she pleased. She grew flowers. When she was alive, her life meant very little to me because I knew very little of her. So, her death was also easy; it was like changing the colour of the bedroom curtains. Beatrice was the pillar of love in my childhood. Mavis's importance, on the other hand, was indirect and long-term. Her contribution to my life only bloomed over time. Her unvoiced modelling was like fine wine—it had to age, and it had to wait for me to age.

Mavis was not the white-haired, really old woman all her life, as I knew her. She had her own childhood, of sorts. As I found out from stories and card-game-day chatty gossip of Sophie's friends, Mavis's childhood was somehow linked with the history of the Ottoman Empire's collapse. Since I was too young to understand the implications of the ominous Ottoman history, I did not understand how the Mavis I knew was part of something I did not know about.

As it turns out, the end of the nineteenth century was not kind to the once all-mighty Ottoman Empire. Rather than more lands, more riches it was accustomed to capture and accumulate, the Empire had lost wars, lost lands, and had to deal with the internal uprising of its own peoples. The Empire also had to deal with the greed of its disgruntled neighbours. This was also the time when once peaceful and generally loyal peoples of the Balkans started to rise up against the Empire, and harass the Ottoman-originated Turks living amongst them. In a way, the Balkans in the late nineteenth century were a precursor to the ethnic cleansing scenario that repeated itself in the late twentieth century, when the former Yugoslavia collapsed and Bosnians got slaughtered by their very own Serb neighbours. The difference was that when the Ottoman Empire collapsed, ethnic cleansing happened in parts of Hungary, Bulgaria, Greece, as well as Yugoslavia. In each case, there was a lot of bloodshed between armies, but also amongst common peoples. In each case, there were many mass graves dug, many bodies of the old, the crippled, women and their children dumped into graves. In each case, most of the initiators of these atrocities went free. Some even became heroes and received medals to display on their chests. War blunts morals, and turns them upside down.

My young mind did not understand these complexities. What I did understand—at the more primitive level of my spinal cord of emotions rather than the cortex of my brain—was that many people were killed. I understood that some escaped, some killed, and some initially escaped and then killed or died of exhaustion. Due to the political developments of the time, our settled ancestors in Europe for generations were reduced to reluctant immigrants and refugees, leaving their homes, mosques, and businesses behind in their flight. They had to abandon their goats, cows, their cats and dogs, their cooking utensils. Some left behind their aged parents who were considered too slow for an impending fugue. These threatened groups running away from death and torture tried to find security and solace in the Ottoman hinterlands. They had moved their horse carts, their children, and wives—assuming the latter were still alive—through demonstrations of hate, thrown rocks, and the occasional spray of bullets. They had pushed backward, gone east, in small and larger groups to their ancestral homelands in Anatolia. When I was very little, there were a lot of people we knew who were displaced Turks. The term used for them was *göçmen* (refugee). The older ones spoke a barely understandable Turkish, the younger ones were already fully integrated, fluent in their new language. In the faces of the older ones, the troubles of their flight were etched. The younger ones were ready to forget or even deny the suffering of their parents.

For the refugees who had to leave all their worldly belongings behind, the move was an arduous voyage indeed. They had inched along, horse cart after horse cart, woman after woman, a child after a child, through the cold, mountainous Balkans and temperamental rivers, and fell exhausted in barren lands. They had endured the hostile rejection of people they once considered friends and neighbours, and saw crimes against humanity committed by once law-abiding citizens. Some of these refugees had succumbed to disease, bullet wounds, and a blow to the head with a rusty shovel or a garden rake. Younger women had been raped; children had been lost, stolen or murdered. Babies had died when their mothers' milk turned sour or totally dried up. The fleeing families had to dig for roots, steal chickens, or eat grass soup. This is what ethnic wars do to people; they reduce both the dejected and the rejecter into animals.

Sophie's chatty friends used to say that Mavis, as a newborn baby, was part of this tragic exodus. It seems, amongst the retreating crowds of Ottoman Turks, there was a young couple who had exchanged their wedding vows not more than a couple of years earlier. Later on, no one remembered their names, or where exactly they were from, but a few recalled that the couple was hanging on to a newborn named "Mavis." The young couple was desperately trying to reach a safe place, mostly for the sake of their infant daughter. In the frightening world of exile from their homes and communities, what seems to have bound them together was the hope of re-establishing a life of abundance and dignity, in the welcoming arms of Anatolia—once they reached it ... if they reached it.

Alas, the journey was long, the terrain treacherous, the couple too young and naïve, and the hostility of the locals impossible to overcome. The harsh conditions had eaten into the hopes of the new couple, like moths eating into fresh wool, leaving them hollow and tattered. No one remembers who got sick first: Was it the young mother who had given birth a short time ago, or was it the young man who was under a Herculean pressure to protect his wife and baby daughter? Maybe their broken hearts and shattered dreams made them get sick at the same time. These are long-term casualties of war. Even though the winners and the losers are quite clear in the beginning, accumulated despair taints everyone at the end.

From the hush-hush stories I heard from Sophie's chatty friends, my young mind arrived at a "truth" of some sort. It was obvious that the young parents of baby Mavis crumbled under the pressure of sleeplessness, scarcity of food, the sheer exhaustion of the walk, and the lack of clarity of their future. How much longer could they walk? How much longer could they carry? Even their precious Mavis, with her skinny arms and legs, might have turned into a load of stone, difficult to bear, for her ailing parents. Many years later, I saw the same theme played out in an award-winning film, *The Silence of the Lambs*. In the movie, FBI agent Clarisse is forced to remember a childhood torment that tainted her life. After her parents' untimely death, Clarisse finds herself in the care of distant relatives who are sheep farmers. One night, she awakens to heart wrenching cries in the night, and finds out that the little lambs she loved so much are being slaughtered for the spring lamb market. She desperately tries to save one, at least a single one, from being slaughtered. She tries to run away in her sleepwear, carrying the little lamb in her arms. But the weather is so brutal, her childish arms so fragile and the lamb so heavy, that she can only go a few hundred yards. Despite her efforts, she fails to save the lamb, but she still hears its shrill cries. I saw the *Silence of the Lambs* when I was a young woman, living a peaceful and predictable life in Canada. Yet, in Clarisse's dilemma with the little lamb, I understood Mavis's parents' dilemma of carrying Mavis to safety. Under the harsh conditions of the exodus, she must have felt so heavy in her exhausted parents' arms.

In Mavis's case, her parents had sacrificed themselves, rather than giving up on their little lamb. No one knows if one parent survived the other, or if they mutually let go of their shattered world at the same time, clasping each other's hand. What we know is that the young couple entrusted their baby girl to another couple in the refugee caravan, as their final selfless act. No one remembers how they said goodbye; no one knows how they pinned their hopes, their prayers, and their love onto their infant child who had to grow up without them. The caravan was moving and they were no longer able to move with it, they had no time. Thus, whether Mavis realized it or not, she continued her long journey, with only the swaddling clothes she had on, and away from the protective arms of her parents. Basically, Mavis started her life with two strikes against her: she was an orphan and a refugee. She must have been very resilient to survive her infant years at the care of total strangers who themselves were walking towards an unknown. After many generations of absence, the sons and daughters of the once victorious Ottoman Turks were returning to Anatolia, no longer victorious. They were returning with physical wounds to their bodies, and emotional wounds to their hearts.

Being forced to become a refugee involves little voluntary choice. It is usually the result of a life versus death struggle. Uprooting oneself from one place and trying to establish roots in another is a taxing process, even under the best of circumstances. Refugees often look death in the eye. People are not tumbleweeds; they yearn for their roots. They yearn to belong. They face prejudice. The process is the hardest for the first generation that has made the move. Sophie's chatty friends did not have too much to say about Mavis's early childhood. Somehow, she had grown up; somehow, she had gotten married. It seems my paternal grandfather was much older than Mavis, which was not uncommon in those years. My paternal grandfather, whom I never met, was a well-established businessman. He owned a whole street of shops that manually produced cotton-filled comforters. It was a good business; people needed comforters to warm themselves in the winter months. Moreover, there was never a shortage of people since more and more migrants and refugees flocked to post-war Istanbul.

While still young herself, Mavis gave birth to three daughters, who were all considered blessings. Then, my father was born, the single male heir, an absolute must in a patriarchal society. Having thus created his legacy, my grandfather passed away before my father turned ten years old.

Whether Mavis loved her husband or not, no one knows. In those days, love was never a requirement for marriage. In her old age, when I knew her, her husband was never a part of her conversations, her garden and flowers were. Her husband was significantly older than she was; some estimates are that he was twenty to twenty-five years her senior, but obviously the couple had experienced some marital bliss. They had produced four healthy and attractive children. Besides, especially in those years and in that land, women wanted security; they needed security. If there was any love, it was an added bonus. The real challenge for Mavis must have come when her husband died, when she was still a young woman. She was a single parent at a time when that concept did not even exist.

Mavis never remarried. Moreover, any form of cohabitation or another kind of a meaningful relationship was never an option for "decent" women of her time. It is still mostly frowned upon in Turkey. I think she could have remarried. As a matter of fact, women in her situation were expected to remarry, since the severity of the public/ private divide made women totally dependent on men. Yet, Mavis chose solitude. She chose to raise her four children alone. She chose her garden over a second husband.

From what I can gather, my grandfather's property and business income was more than sufficient to take care of his family during his life. The family owned a three-level, mansion-like-house, in a respectable part of Istanbul. The house sat on a hilltop and had a breath-taking view. It also took one's breath away to climb the hill to get to it. I know, because my own family lived in that house after Mavis's death. What I don't know is how Mavis lived there, first with all her children, then all alone, in her elderly years. There was no public transit to the hilltop. The road was cobblestone, the incline not very good for the hooves of the horse buggies. When they had to climb, the buggy-drivers tripled the price. So, except for emergencies, Mavis must have carried up her own groceries, and even garden supplies.

So, the predicaments of life that started when Mavis was only an infant followed her into her young adulthood. Mavis had to find some men to keep an eye on the shops, since women of her era did not do those types of work on their own. We do not even know if Mavis was literate. The male shopkeepers would not have talked business with a woman, anyway. Whoever those men who helped her were, they must have lined their own pockets, and feathered their own nests, over time. Eventually, Mavis lost ownership of most of the shops her late husband once owned. At her death, there was only one shop left, from a whole street full of shops. From Sophie's huffs and puffs, I have the sense that my father was contributing to Mavis's up-keep at the end, but it couldn't have been too much. If my father were to give his mother a lot of money, Sophie would have blown her top like a volcano. Besides, Mavis had some money trickling in: she rented the first floor of her mansion, and also collected some rent from the remaining shop. Although my father was a very generous man, Sophie was not a generous person to begin with. In addition, she was squirreling away money for Agnes's and my higher educational years. Mavis was very low on Sophie's priorities.

Mavis's chain of troubles had not ended with the death of her husband either. She had to go through the pain of losing Angel, her youngest daughter. For as long as I can remember, the youngest one of my aunts appeared only as a life-size portrait on the wall of Mavis's home. The portrait had an antique, gilded frame, and was always covered with a black silk cloth when Mavis was alive. The black cloth was so old that it had grown a greyish patina of its own. I know this because when my family moved into Mavis's house after her death, the first thing Sophie did was to pull down the black curtain and dispose of it. She gave it to one of my two living aunts. Sophie had little regard for sentimentalisms. We never had portraits of dead people on our walls. Come to think of it, we never had portraits of living people either. The only thing Sophie chose to hang on our living-room wall was a hand-knotted, silk rug. Even when I was a child, the silk rug must have seen much better days. We also had a hanging calendar, often showing snow for winter months, and brilliantly coloured flowers for spring and summer. I do not recall the calendar depicting the fall season, since trees in Istanbul do not turn into brilliant colours in the fall like they do in most parts of Canada and the States. They are either evergreens, or they are still variations of green when they shed their leaves. So the autumn months of the calendars on our walls have not registered into my memory at all.

Part III:
Mother as Daughter and Wife

10.

Sophie

SOPHIE IS MY MOTHER. As she told us many times, somewhat accusingly, she had married my father at age sixteen, and had given birth to Agnes within a year. My father was twenty-seven. In the war years, these early marriages were common, but my mother was not able to forgive her parents for marrying her off at such an early age. Sophie was under the impression that if her parents had held up longer, they may have received a better offer for their daughter's hand. If anyone asked me, and of course no one did, I would have said that my father was an exceptionally good catch. He was young, handsome, a decorated officer in the Turkish army, and was absolutely dedicated to his family. So, who could have topped him? However, I have to admit that I have always been partial to my father. Her muted complaints aside, I think Sophie also loved and respected my father in her own, hard-to-show way. For one thing, she was unusually jealous of my handsome father. Her complaints about having to marry him at such an early age rang hollow after a while. I think, these complaints had less to do with my father than the ongoing tension between Sophie and Beatrice. Mother/daughter tensions are deeply rooted in the DNA of my family of women. I call my family a family of women since we either scare off the men in our lives, or we lose them to an early death.

In Sophie's marriage, the second and the last child who was allowed to make an entrance to this world was me. I was told that I was born with my umbilical cord wrapped around my throat, and that I looked like a hung convict in the gallows. A savvy midwife I never had the pleasure of meeting had saved my life by untangling me from the suffocating grip of the cord. The cord was thick and pulsating. I was all purple and blue, and there was some question about my survival. Well, I survived this unnerving early mishap, and numerous others in my life. Maybe, my life-threatening birth was the reason my father loved me so much; he must have agonized over the possibility of losing me. So, my father always sheltered me from all harm, throughout his life. When he died, I felt like a fish out of water, gasping for air. I did not know how to survive outside of my father's protective presence. I felt skinned like a baby seal in the Canadian arctic, cruelly exposed to the murderous elements.

Between Agnes's birth and mine, Sophie had numerous miscarriages. After my birth, she continued to have miscarriages. Although some of these occurrences may have been natural, others were certainly self-induced. What I know now, which I did not know as a little girl, was that women of her time had little control over their own reproductive powers. As loving and caring as they may have been, men like my father may not have been too sensitive about the consequences of their sexual desires. So, my mother being exceptionally sick at times, and being exceptionally healthy at other times, was like a revolving door in my childhood. She spent her very sick periods behind closed doors, and doctors, almost all of who were male at the time, went into the room with large doses of penicillin. This was a time before disposable needles. The doctors making the house calls boiled the needles they used in a chrome-plated, rectangular container they carried with them for this purpose. Although the chrome exterior of the boxes glittered with confidence, the interior surface of the box was covered with yellowish-mustard coloured calcium deposits. At the time, no one considered these signs of hygienic slips as something dangerous. What was really dangerous was what women like Sophie did to themselves.

When the needles—and the syringes—were sufficiently boiled in their chrome coffin, the doctors took them out with metal forceps. They assembled the different parts of the syringe, again using metal forceps. At last, they sucked the different concoctions they were to inject into my mother from miniature bottles with rubber caps. The needle went through the rubber just like going through flesh. I was allowed to keep the empty bottles. They were a kind of compensation for the fear of losing my mother. I still collect miniature bottles, but my collection now consists of mini perfume flasks. Times have changed. I changed my country. I grew up. I have control over my reproduction. Doctors do not make house calls to shoot me up with penicillin to combat blood poisoning. In Toronto, no doctor makes a home visit anyway.

As I said, self-induced miscarriages brought my mother exceptionally close to death, more than once. In each new episode, Beatrice's facial wrinkles reached new depths, her sallow skin turned more ashen, and her stories took on more gothic nuances. But she always stood erect, as much as her advancing osteoporosis would permit. She cooked our meals, made our beds, combed our hair for school, and attached starched ribbons to our braids that were almost as large as our heads. Beatrice also kept on telling us her stories about heroes, about villains, about maidens in danger, until Sophie got well. Then, the cycle repeated in a couple of years. Each time, there were new additions to my miniature bottle collection, new shapes, new colours, new labels. Although women's sexual rights stood still, pharmaceuticals advanced at an alarming speed.

Sophie was an only child, spoiled to the core; she clearly had a negative view of large families. Her fear of large families trickled down to Agnes and me; we each ended up having one daughter. Our daughters, in turn, chose to remain childless. Soon, our matrilineal family line will become extinct. Our patrilineal line is already extinct, since my father was the only male heir, and he produced no sons. Some days this possibility of extinction makes me sad, on other days, I feel a relief. Maybe we should leave raising daughters to other women who have experienced more positive transgenerational relations. Maybe, the intergenerational conflict amongst women is ingrained in the extra X chromosome we carry.

Like every other woman of her time, Sophie lacked control over her sexual life, so she did what she had to do, after the fact. She induced her own miscarriages. One winter, we almost lost her to yet another unwanted pregnancy. Since we did not have running water at that particular house, it was a challenge for Beatrice to wash and bleach the blood-soaked sheets. The male doctor who eventually saved Sophie's life almost threw up in his boots when he found out how she had poisoned herself. That time she had used shoe-glue piled on the blunt tip of a knitting needle. Women of my mother's era were like alchemists; they had a working knowledge of the use of poisons. I was still much too young to grasp the nature of the situation, but even

I understood that Sophie's situation was grave. Regular illnesses do not make people throw up day and night, non-stop. Regular illnesses do not paint the sheets and the covers crimson with blood. Regular illnesses did not make Beatrice shed tears; she was a war widow, she had seen atrocities, but seeing her only daughter in a pool of blood time and again broke her heart. I sensed that what my mother had was one of the "unmentionable" women's ailments. Women like Sophie and Beatrice were very secretive about the dangers that lurked inside their bodies. It took me many years to learn to trust my own female body, rather than fearing it.

Sophie's fever busted the glass thermometer placed under her arm, the mercury in the little tube boiled over. Adult women of that age were used to on-again, off-again health problems, which they discussed in hushed voices, but the ferocity of that particular incident scared everyone, everyone other than Sophie, that is. Maybe, she was scared too, who knows. Obviously, having yet another child scared her even more, so she tried the same procedure at least one other time. This was a time before the birth control pill, before a man would ever consider using a condom. This was a time when women's bodies were women's enemies. Although my childhood was threatened many times with the possibility of being orphaned, as an adult, I respect Sophie for not bringing unwanted children to this world. Her ability to cope with children was limited, and even my own birth may have pushed her beyond her comfort zone.

With the exception of her recurring health crises, mostly following my father's yearly arrivals from whatever dangerous part of the land his command post was stationed in, Sophie is mostly a blur during my tender years. Rather than being the central figure as my mother, she somehow chose the periphery; she stayed in the distant fringes of my life. I don't know whether I was responsible for the distance, but I had the distinct feeling that I might not have been what she really desired from life. Could it be that she wanted a boy? Could it be that she thought my father wanted a boy? I don't know. What I do know is that almost all the affection I received as a child came from either Beatrice or my father. It was a lot of love, mind you, but the source of that love was rarely my mother. Instead, Sophie loved Agnes the best. She was a person who could love only one thing at a time. Showing her love somewhat exhausted her, and she could only engage in spurts of affection, a little at a time, like the blue flashes of light in a plugged-in electrical toothbrush. Sophie's love was like the flashing lights of an ambulance that only appeared in an emergency.

Sophie loved going to movies that featured love stories, and she dragged Agnes and me with her. There were never any suggestive scenes in those movies, never uncovered flesh, let alone open coupling. The movies were not rated; anyone who paid the fee could watch them. Women characters wore elaborate hats and gloves in those movies, and kept them on even during scenes of passion. Love was expressed through small gestures, like the mist in an eye, a barely audible sigh, or a crushed flower under the pillow. The greatest expressions of carnal desire were depicted as a waterfall, or an airplane taking off during the war. Jean Simmons, Joan Crawford, Betty Davis did not jump into bed with men. The movies ended with a marriage when the heroine was good, or with a death when the heroine was bad. The moral code of the time demanded that bad women should die. Slightly bad women died in their beds, still wearing make-up, albeit lighter shades, hair still coiffured. Really bad women—the ones who had slept with their best friend's husband—died more violent deaths, like being shot, or burning in a house-fire, or driving over a bridge. Only the pure and virginal women were allowed to live and get married.

On bad days, when it was raining or windy, even when there was the occasional snow on the ground, we walked more than half an hour, each way, to catch one of the discounted matinees. Each show consisted of two movies, at first without sound, later with sound but still only in black and white, and later still in washed-out and unnatural colour. Sophie bought roasted peanuts and sunflower seeds, and we ate and watched, watched and ate. Sophie also kept track of visiting circuses, theatres and whatever other cultural event that came close to our home. Many years later, after my father retired, and before his heart attack, he also joined us on the movie excursions and overdosed on roasted peanuts with us.

During those movies, we did not get to see what happened after the marriage ceremonies of the good heroines, nor how many children they produced. We did not get to see whether any of them had to use shoe glue and knitting needles. Sophie must have loved this platonic love, where women kept their hats and gloves on, even in love scenes. Sophie was not fond of physicality; she was not fond of receiving or giving hugs. Even after she reached her golden years, and mellowed substantially, she could best love from a distance: only one friend, only one cat, only one daughter, only one granddaughter at a time. I did not make her list of "ones," and neither did Negrisse. My father, who obviously had a different conception of love, and an endless reservoir to provide it, suffered a heart attack, and was gone.

I first developed the courage to accept this shortcoming of my mother when I reached my own adulthood, but it always hurt me, like joint pain. It is really a mystery how children pick up emotions, or their absence. In tangible ways, Sophie never denied me anything. I had decent clothes. I received a private school education, due to many sacrifices of my parents, just like Agnes did. In a way, I had whatever my family's middle-class budget could offer, although some of the offerings were my sister's hand-me-downs. Agnes never had to have my hand-me-downs, due to the chronological order of our births. Yet, Sophie always found ways of altering the hand-me-downs, so no one would see me in exactly the same version of clothes Agnes once wore. She would make tops out of skirts; she would add ruffles, bibs, and embroideries. She would knit vests to go with the old skirts, which gave them a new life. These little creativities gave Sophie pride in her parenthood. Maybe, her creativity in dressing me up in altered, but nice-looking clothes was a form of love. Maybe, it was compensation for its absence. So, in terms of the actual behavioural output, Agnes and I received more or less equal treatment. Why I felt my mother liked my sister the best was for reasons that were not tangible, just felt. Still, I felt like an intruder in my mother's life, a complication, a botched miscarriage. I had to work hard to be acknowledged. I had to settle for the crumbs of her affection.

Food was occasionally abundant, but more generally, just sufficient in my childhood. According to the season, horse carts full of onions, potatoes, cucumbers, squash, watermelons, and other goodies arrived from what little remained of Beatrice's once legendary farming lands. When Sophie sold the last bit of Beatrice's farm, this abundance came to an abrupt end.

Whether a lot or just sufficient, food was served according to the status hierarchy of our family. When my father was at home, which was rare, he was served the best of everything. Also, special foods that were not part of our regular diet suddenly appeared on his plate. The twin justifications for feeding my father better than the rest of us were fed was that he had to work and support us, and that he was a picky eater. Both were true! My father did support us and he was indeed a picky eater. He struggled with the food on his plate, like a painter mixing paints on his pallet. He had to rearrange the colours, the textures. He had to add salt, pepper; he had to douse the plate with more olive oil. He added fresh dill or fresh parsley; he added lemon juice. He added a pinch of cumin. At the end, his food was not only different, but also much tastier than what was on our plates. Yet, he never failed to offer me a choice piece of his special food, so I got to taste the best part of his special fish, or had a few of his sweetest cherries, or some morsels of his aged cheese. For me, those bits of my father's special food personified his love for me.

Given the first rank of my father's access to food, the hierarchy in my childhood home demanded that my sister and I get the next best pieces, in equal amounts. Beatrice and Sophie got the last, which meant the less desirable parts of meat, the burnt corners of pastries or the dried-out vegetables and fruits. Sophie did not mind these rules, since they were of her own making, but I think Beatrice did mind. Beatrice was brought up in an exceptionally affluent home. She was used to servants, gardeners, cleaners, horse-cart drivers, and even young girls who were hired to be her companions. Her mother's estate included herds of sheep, so butter, milk, and meat were plentiful. Although Beatrice never complained, having to eat the burnt corners of pastries, blemished fruit and leftovers from the day before was hard for her. Without words of criticism or expressions of ingratitude, Beatrice held her head high, ate little, and looked increasingly emaciated. She resembled a skeleton stuffed into a nylon stocking when she died. We could actually see all the contours of her bones.

In our home, nothing went to waste. The difficulties experienced during the war times were so great that they loomed over our heads even in years of relative abundance. Leftovers became soup. Hand-me-downs from my sister were re-fashioned for me, and worn out sheets were first transformed into pillowcase, and later cut into neat squares and rectangles for dishcloths. The only things my mother threw away were the priceless antiques we inherited from Mavis. I always wondered why my absolutely frugal mother had so little reverence for irreplaceable antiques. I think it was their association with Mavis that fuelled the mass discarding of those irreplaceable items.

The next thing I remember about my childhood was my mother's migraines. When Sophie was having one of her migraines, she would tie a scarf around her forehead so tight that her hair would stick out on top, like a mop. Underneath the grip of the scarf, her eyes would bulge out. When she had her headaches, she locked herself into her bedroom, sometimes for hours, mostly for days. In such times, the air in our home became heavy, soupy, almost like the air before a thunderstorm. Agnes and I were instructed to be extremely quiet and tiptoed around. Sophie could not bear to see lights, so Beatrice kept all the curtains closed. Sophie could not bear the odour of food cooking so we ate cold sandwiches. During my mother's migraines, time stood still. Although this was a time way before the lunar conquest, we resembled astronauts hopping on the moon, in slow motion, in total silence. Despite all these restrictions, I did not feel deprived as a child. Beatrice's stories made everything better, and brought light into my days even when the curtains were tightly closed and the ceiling lights were turned off. Besides, I knew from experience that my mother would eventually come out of her bedroom, without the scarf, her eyes back in their sockets. When she did, she resumed her regular self: busy, creative, critical, and aloof.

In times that were not tainted with migraines or near-fatal miscarriages, Sophie displayed many talents. She was proud of her talents, and she made sure to let all her friends know how good she was at doing certain things. Our home was always scrubbed, so were our faces. She embroidered the most beautiful pillowcases. My favourites were two black velvet pillows with a bunch of roses on them. It took her two full years to finish them, because she wanted just the right colour for the buds. She made endless trips to every craft store that she could think of to find the exact tone of peachy red she had in mind. The roses already in bloom on the black velvet pillow had to wait until the correct colour of the thread was found. Sophie's crafts did not come in pre-measured, pre-selected, pre-cut, pre-thought-out packages. She created them from scratch, designing the shape, colour, and texture of each individual stitch. They were museum-quality art.

Sophie also painted, but she would have starved as a painter. Once she painted birds: a set of two panels. In one of the panels, a fluffy, yellow and a grey bird was perched on a cherry-tree branch, full of pinkish-white blossoms. Sophie captured the tension in the little feet so well that the yellow and grey bird appeared to be getting ready to take off. It was life-like.

The bird in the matching set was a cardinal, on a willow branch, brilliant with its crimson feathers and tar-black eyes and the base of its beak. Yet, the cardinal took about four years to get complete. Sophie had to find the exact yellowish, pinkish orange she had in mind, before the cardinal could grow its beak. We had trial beaks of every orange in the world except the one she found acceptable, until the perfect colour became available in the market. The bottom line is that my mother was a perfectionist. Everything she did had to be perfect or it existed in a state of incompleteness. Maybe that is why she had those killer headaches. Maybe that is why I have them too. Maybe that is why Negrisse had to leave. It is not easy to be the daughter of a perfectionist. I know. I was a daughter before I became a mother. But the black pillows were astonishingly beautiful. I often wondered if the roses Sophie created would begin to smell like real roses. Once it grew its beak, the cardinal was also beautiful. I would not have been surprised if one day, it took flight. Sophie's friends were astounded with her creations, and she glowed in their praises. Of course, her friends only saw the finished product. They were not around when we had to close all curtains and eat cold sandwiches, while she locked herself up and suffered through her migraines.

Sophie made the majority of our clothes. They were not put-together rags. Each was a work of art. When she saw a new design displayed in a pricy store window, or in the newspaper, she would re-create it or design something even more beautiful. We had designer sweaters, skirts, coats that we could not have been able to afford to buy. She made them from remnants: the leftovers of discarded older clothing, yard ends, and threads that other people would have thrown away. As children and as teenagers, we never missed a single fashion. Probably, I was the first one to have a poodle skirt in all of Turkey. The skirt was full, a juicy watermelon red, with a large black poodle embroidered on the lower left side. The poodle had dimension: it had a curly coat, each curl cut and sewn into place from pieces of silky yarn. The poodle also had a shiny collar, studded with rhinestones, and a long leash. The leash went all the way across the front of the skirt, and gracefully ended in the outside pocket, on the right hip. This skirt was my most favourite outfit of all time; moreover, it was not a hand-me-down creation. It was made just for me, from scratch. I also had a dress that was one of my mother's one-of-a-kind masterpieces. She had knitted by hand, from recycled wool. Some earlier sweater of my mother's or my father's had been taken apart, unravelled, washed, dyed into an azure blue colour, and knitted back into a little dress. The top of the dress had a bib, and large, ruffled straps. The bib was adorned with a horse cart, a galloping horse, and a driver with his whirling whip snaking in the air. This intricate and quite captivating scenery was not embroidered on top, which would have been hard enough to do, but actually knitted in, with different colours of yarn. The dress also had a rounded bolero, in the same azure blue, and tastefully trimmed in the three colours used in the horse-cart. The colours were red, a dark gold and white. I felt like a princess when I wore this dress. The only drawback was that the dress was not washable, because of all the home-dyed wool that had gone into making it. So I could only wear it sparingly, and always with strict instructions about not getting dirty while I had it on. So, I stood like a robot, moving languorously from one place to another only when absolutely necessary to do so. It was made of wartime wool, so it was itchy. The dress was never comfortable, but so pretty. Expectations of not getting the dress dirty extended into the rest of our childhood. Cleanliness was yet another aspect of my mother's obsessions. I still cannot put my knees on the ground when I do my gardening, so I end up with a debilitating backache. Parental expectations stick to you like a stamp on an envelope. They do not peel off, even when they have served their purpose and you want to be rid of them.

I kept the dress with the horse-cart, and actually dressed Negrisse in it when she turned four. Somehow, in the various closets it was stored in as I moved from place to place, it had turned shabby, all on its own. The home-dyed blue had faded, the horse cart had sagged and unravelled, the once galloping horse had gotten old and mangy. Even the once mighty whip of the driver had deteriorated, and became a bare thread. Negrisse promptly objected to wearing that shabby-looking dress, and I could not help but agree with her. I took a single picture, and placed it beside my own picture wearing the same outfit, a quarter of a century before. Both the pictures are getting old now, yellowing and cracking. My own picture was already in black and white, and Negrisse's picture is quickly losing its colour. Like the dress, I too am getting old, I am losing the stitches that once held me together, and I do not have the power or the desire or the energy to crack the whip. Yet, I am not able to discard the dress. It is still at the bottom of one of my drawers. I am quite sentimental about the small gifts from my childhood, especially when they were from my mother. There were so few. After I am gone, anyone who opens my drawer may be confronted with an army of moths, and wonder what on earth I was keeping in there. The driver of the horse cart will be too mangled to tell the story of the dress on his own.

In addition to going to the movies, one of my mother's favourite pastimes was gambling—only amongst long-term friends, I must add. We did not tag along to all the card-game sessions, since we had a live-in baby-sitter, Beatrice. Gambling was the only absolutely selfish thing my mother ever did for herself. It was like her religion, complete with days of observance and other rituals. I remember marathons that started on Friday and ended when the sun was rising on a Monday morning, when respective husbands joined in the games of their wives. Otherwise, they took place on Thursday afternoons, and were just for the wives. They were cheerful events that never made us lose our shirts. My mother had a separate gambling wallet. Every month, she put a certain amount of money in it. When the money was gone, she simply did not play until my father's next paycheque. Then again, she might not have stopped. I was a child. I was never hungry, I had a home, and I had interesting clothes. I was not counting. Besides, it was good to see my mother in a good mood, once in a while, mostly on Thursdays. When she won, the cheer spread over the rest of the week.

During the holidays, when the husbands returned home from wherever they toiled all year, the mothers' regular card games included the husbands. All of my mother's friends were military wives. Women and men played at different tables, not because there was any rigid gender separation amongst friends, but the stakes were much higher in the men's game. After all, they were the breadwinners. There was only one woman, the wife of an army physician, who was allowed to play with the guys. Her name was Adele. She had access to more money than the rest of the army wives, and she had tomboyish mannerisms juxtaposed over a girly-girl laugh, so the male card players put up with her—maybe, even enjoyed her presence. Adele's laugh was infectious, and got even higher in pitch and volume as the card game progressed. This is also why she was not well liked by the rest of the women; she was a kind of a traitor. Another reason was Adele's husband. Although rich, he was a homely man. The other wives suspected Adele's materialistic motives. They may have suspected the possibility of infidelities, they may have feared losing their own husbands. So, whatever Adele did or said, and wherever Adele went, was carefully scrutinized by at least six or seven of the other wives. Women who lack economic self-sufficiency learn to stake out their territory like female hyenas. These poker friendships, with their ups and downs, lasted a lifetime. If Adele was a heroine in one of the movies of the time, she would have been a character who would have to die—probably in her own bed, since she was only mildly deviant. In real life, Adele got very old, very fast. Her homely husband died, and her only son placed her in an old age home, despite the pro-family norms of the Turkish society. Sophie and her friends criticized the unkind behaviour of the son to no end. Yet, they too failed to visit their old friend. Instead of visiting Adele in her declining years, Sophie and her friends preferred to organize a few extra card games for themselves. This was their way of punishing Adele's girly-girl laugh, and playing cards with their husbands, rather than taking her dutiful place amongst the wives.

Men's presence during the card games changed the atmosphere in another way. Unlike the wives who settled for coffee or tea, husbands drank *raki*, the Turkish alcoholic drink, which is fifty percent pure alcohol, and smells like anise. No beer or wine for these tough military guys. Yet, some of the husbands had trouble handling their booze, their speech became slurred, their eyes blurred, they had to go to the bathroom for long periods of time, to deposit food and drinks from one end or another. Not my father. My father drank with the best of them, but remained perpetually sober, always in full control. I admired him for that. I would not have liked to have a drunken father.

I loved the poker games the men played; they were serious. Each card, played or discarded, was like a real-estate transaction. Men were not chatty like the wives who gambled for pennies and nickels, and who relentlessly gossiped. I could not wait to grow up to play poker, with men. I secretly admired Adele. I knew every poker rule, every trick in the book before I even started school. I knew how to keep a poker face, even when the hand was a royal flush or an absolute bluff. Once in a while, although not as often as I liked, my father went to the washroom and asked me to play his hand for him. He trusted me, and his friends also knew that whatever hand I played would be considered final. My father would never ask to reverse the cards I played even if I had made a mistake. This trust made me feel good about myself, good about my father. Also, my father never asked me to sit elsewhere, even if he was losing heavily. Everyone, including the men, had superstitions about luck or its absence during the games. They asked people, including their own wives, not to watch their hand if they lost twice in a row. Not my father. He could not have imagined me as bringing him anything but good luck. If my mother was slightly biased in her love toward Agnes, my father was biased in his love toward me. His eyes shined with a different glitter, his lips curved with more curvature when I was beside him. I am sorry that he was away for so long, and so often in my growing years. I am even sorrier that he died so soon. He never met Negrisse. Perhaps Negrisse would not have left me if she had had the opportunity to bask under her grandfather's love and greatness.

11.

New Year's Celebrations

I REMEMBER OUR NEW YEAR'S EVE CELEBRATIONS as major gambling tournaments. All the surviving grandparents, mostly women living with their adult daughters, also joined these celebrations. The older ones did not gamble, but sat around the stove, loosely supervising the grandchildren, but mostly criticizing their daughters. Only the mothers themselves could criticize their own daughters. If anyone else tried to talk against a woman who was not her own daughter, the offended grandmother would defend the accused adult daughter with all her might. There were lines that could not be crossed, and few grandmothers ever tried to cross them. However, all grandmothers, in unison, criticized Adele. First, Adele did not have a living mother to defend her from the sharp tongues of other grandmothers. Secondly, Adele's habit of gambling at male tables did not bode well with the grandmothers. Gender-bending was a concept that came into vogue much after all these older women died.

Preparations for the New Year's party started months earlier. First, all those who attended these celebrations year after year agreed upon the place. The men were mostly away during the negotiations, and besides, they rarely cared about the location anyway. If they had cared, they would not have left the decision to their wives. Once the place was identified, the division of labour had to be established. The division of labour, especially in terms of preparing the food, was not based upon equity or equality among the women. It was based on expertise. Sophie always got the baklava, a buttery, syrupy desert with a walnut filling which adds thousands of life-threatening calories to one's diet. Normally, women made baklava from only forty sheets of dough, a deed that would challenge any professional cook. My mother's baklava boasted sixty sheets, yet it was not any thicker than the ordinary forty-sheet productions, due to her exceptional talent. Her sheets of dough were unusually thin, a mighty skill and source of pride in the history of baklava making. This was before the time when philo-dough appeared in long, frozen packages. This was a time when women laboured in the kitchen for countless hours. Sophie was also entrusted with another pastry, this one filled with cheese or meat. Again, many sheets of dough were rolled paper thin, individually boiled, stacked on top of each other and glazed with melted butter. After a dozen sheets or so, a thick layer of crumbled cheese, eggs and parsley mixture was spread, followed by more buttered layers of dough. None of the families had ovens then, so these glorious pastries had to be baked patiently over the coal stoves that warmed our homes. Grandmothers and kids also helped during this part of the preparations, by slowly rotating the trays over the top of the stove. The trick was to regulate the heat distribution. Sophie's pastries had to turn out perfect. If there were mishaps—like burning in one corner—we had to eat the deformed version, so that Sophie could create another one from scratch. Self-imposed standards are so hard to reach when one is a perfectionist.

We always had a turkey for the dinner, with rice and giblet stuffing, jewelled with pine nuts and black currents. The New Year was a big deal, and no effort was spared to make it a festive occasion. The two indices of festivity were food and poker. Around November, peddlers brought their live turkeys to the cities. Both the turkeys and the peddlers walked, sometimes incredibly long distances. The turkeys gobbled, and the farmers shouted out the price. Each peddler carried a long stick, gently poking at the scattering animals as they walked through the narrow city streets. Peddlers were not gentle because they were animal rights activists; they were gentle so that the skinny turkeys would survive the long journey in one piece. Customers were choosey; they did not want a turkey with a broken leg or a broken wing. The gobbling that went on with each passing flock was something to be heard. Each year, we would go out to the street and try to pick the biggest turkey with the reddest comb and the bluish outgrowths around its beak and neck. These signs were considered to be an indicator of the turkey's good health, at least, until the poor creature was destined to meet with the knife. My mother would ask the turkey peddler to catch a few that she would inspect carefully before she made her decision. Sometimes, she would just decide to wait until the next peddler came along, and the next, and the next. Each time was endless fun for me. I liked the part when the turkeys flew around making tremendous amounts of noise while the peddler was trying to catch the one my mother pointed to. Sometimes, they caught the wrong one and offered a good deal, just to avoid repeating the entire process. What I would now consider as cruel was in those days simply a normal part of life. Much later, Negrisse taught me that mass production of turkeys in turkey farms where thousands of birds are crammed into a warehouse is more cruel. Those creatures die without ever seeing the natural light. At least, the turkeys of my childhood were allowed to roam around.

Once the selection was complete, we kept the turkey in the back yard. Beatrice called this the cleansing process. She wanted to make sure that everything that those "dirty peddlers" might have fed the poor animal passed through its system before we ate it. Also, we tried to fatten it a little, since they almost always looked terribly thin no matter how carefully my mother chose them. At the end, the turkeys we ate were a good size, but always tough, and muscular. Walking around on the streets for days, sometimes for weeks before they were sold was definitely not good for the tenderness of their flesh Our turkeys were like body-builders, more muscle than flesh. It took a lot of basting to make them edible and tasty, but the excitement of the whole process made it worthwhile. At the end, I always experienced the mild sadness of having devoured my short-term pet. Although turkeys do not possess endearing personalities like dogs or cats, they do have a life that I am sure they would rather keep than give up. So, I was more than ready to repent my sins when Negrisse asked me to become a vegetarian.

The New Year preparations did not start and end with food, although festive food was one of the major axis of our lives. The preparations also included entertainment. Sophie's creativity was utilized in this regard as well. One year, she wrote a long poem for my sister and I to recite. Each verse was dedicated to a person who was going to attend that year's party. Each verse made fun of someone, either for something he or she did, or said, or wore, or experienced. Each guest knew one another very well; there were few secrets, and the incidents touched upon in the poem were funny, not mean. Each verse ended with a repetition: "We have so many one-of-a-kinds among us." Indeed we did. As we recited the poem, Sophie accompanied us with her *cümbüş* (a kind of a banjo). So, the poem she wrote was transformed into a song of some sort, and generated much congenial laughter.

Sophie also made special outfits for Agnes and I, for the recital of the poem. Both outfits were black and white. My sister wore black pants and a white shirt, and I wore white pants with a black shirt. We read the words, in a carefully practiced way. In the repetitious choral parts, Sophie joined in. She had a crystal clear voice that my father loved. Yet, my mother avoided singing just for my father, since he was only interested in military marching songs. She reserved her beautiful voice for larger audiences. At the end, Agnes and I received hearty applause for our ability to recite this long poem, but the real glory belonged to Sophie's creativity. Although she was miserly when it came to showing love, Sophie generously showered our lives with her immense creativity.

Flashbook: Anna at age seven

It is one of the rare mother-daughter outings that I remember where Sophie and I went shopping without Agnes. Now, we are on our way back, taking the ferry from the European side of Istanbul to the Asian side. Istanbul is the only city in the world that straddles two continents. Just as we are walking over the temporary wooden bridge thrown over the side of the dock and the side of the boat, Sophie remembers that there was just one more item she needed to buy. Since the ferry is about to leave, she does not have time for long explanations. She tells me to go on my own. The hastily concocted plan is that I should go to her best friend's house, which is about a fifteen-minute walk from the ferry docks, and she will come to retrieve me when she finishes all her chores.

I look back at my mother with bewildered eyes, but she does not waste any time. She turns around and disappears in the crowd. I do not have the address of my mother's friend written down. All I know is that she lives in the tallest building, a few streets above the seashore, and many streets on the left side of the ferry docks. As the ferry lurches on the choppy sea, I try to locate the tall building

I am supposed to go to, and find a little comfort when I spot it in the skyline. However, when the ferry reaches the Asian side, and all the passengers get out, I find myself engulfed by the crowd, and in a panic. The shoreline is low, and I am short, so I can no longer see the horizon. I used to know, but no longer remember the street or the apartment name. I do not remember which floor she lives on, except that it was one of the higher-up floors. I am horrified.

I start walking along the shoreline, hoping something will trigger my memory. I know I have to walk for a while, and turn right. I vaguely remember that the street that goes toward her apartment has a sharp incline, but all the streets I pass on my way have sharp inclines. So, I start to cry, and crying makes me feel even more hopeless. At this point, I have no confidence that I am ever going to find my mother's friend. I am not even sure that I am going to see my mother again. I am lost in a sea of people.

A gentleman walks toward me, and asks me if I am all right. I burst into more tears, and tell him that I am looking for my mother's friend's house. I tell him I do not remember the address and that I do not even remember the woman's last name. My childish fears have capsized my childish memory. I tell the nice gentleman the only thing I remember: the tallest building in the area. So, he holds my hand, and we start asking passers-by whether they can direct us towards the tallest residential building. From where we stand, there is no way of seeing the skyline. Some direct us here, others direct us there, but the gentleman never loses hope. After about an hour, we find the building, and only then he lets my hand go. I thank him again and again, because without his help, I know that this would have been a much more traumatic ending. For all I know, he could have been the kind of a man who took lost children to his own home.

I still have to figure out which floor Sophie's friend lives on. I don't know if she will be at home. It is a tall building and it has close to fifteen floors. So, I take the iron-framed elevator to the fifth floor, and then take the stairs up. At each floor, I carefully check each of the doors to see if I could find a clue to trigger my memory. At last, I reach the floor she lives on, and identify her home from the shape of the doormat in front of the threshold. I ring the doorbell, and she opens the door. Her jaw drops when she notices that I am all alone, and my face is streaked and my eyes are reddened with tears.

She says "My dear child, where is your mother?" I tell her it was all my fault, that I just could not remember. It does not occur to me to blame Sophie for her recklessness.

Sophie arrives after a couple of hours, satisfied and happy with her purchases. Her friend tries to tell her about the scare I had, but it does not register. I say nothing. I do not want to be called "stupid" again. Neither one of us brings up this issue again, but getting lost plays a major part in my nightmares, for many years.

12.

Beatrice's Death

ALAS, CARRYING THE BURDEN of her sad memories for years was too taxing for Beatrice. Years that seemed so easy on me, as a child, caused an escalating corrosion on her. By the time I was ten years old, Beatrice was an eclipsed version of herself, having lost interest in just about everything. The sole exception was her cigarettes, which she smoked with a renewed ferocity. Even her stories lacked some of their vibrant colours, their cliff-hanging quality, and their magical allure. I still loved them, and begged for new ones, knowing that they were mere shadows of their predecessors. Somehow, Beatrice's heart was no longer in these stories, although her heart was still beating to please me. It was also during this time that tensions between Sophie and Beatrice multiplied in leaps and bounds. Sophie had always complained about the "dirty air" invading our home. A non-smoker all her life, my mother was a legitimate and forceful accuser. It is also true that Beatrice occasionally complained about my mother's card game marathons. Generally, the card games were benign, a bunch of housewives taking turns to host a game in their own homes. None of the housewives had that much money to spare, so the games were played for nickels and dimes. The issue was that if my father and the husband of the hostess of the game were out of town, the afternoon games had the potential to spill into the evening. Then the younger children like myself who came home would not have a snack, and may not even have a decent dinner. Although Beatrice always provided loving supervision, she was too old and too fragile to cook our dinner.

In earlier days, both Beatrice and Sophie avoided making a big deal of their complaints, since they knew they had to continue living together. At the time, in my country, there were no retirement homes to deposit grandmothers in. The elderly lived with their adult children, mostly daughters, since generations were eternally locked in loyalty. Although this pattern made things predictable for the elderly, the system also had its shortcomings, especially in creating crushing obligations. I cannot even imagine settling in Negrisse's home in my golden years, which I am sure are not likely to be that golden. I cannot imagine it, since I know for sure that she would not take me in. When the time comes, I will have to make my own old age and funeral arrangements. For the latter, the silver lining is that I will get to pick the colour of the flowers: I will pick buttery yellow roses.

When Beatrice's health sharply declined, the personal pride and cultural controls that held together the mother-daughter relationship disintegrated. Well-hidden resentments of earlier times and the newly developing troubles found many cracks from which to surface. For the first time, I heard Beatrice openly yearn for her glory days on her rich farming lands. For the first time, I heard Sophie bitterly remind her that those days were over, and she had to be grateful for her bowl of soup and her clean bed. I now think that Beatrice's longing for her previous lands was a symptom of her ailing health; it was not lack of appreciation of Sophie's efforts. Like an aging elephant that senses her imminent death, Beatrice yearned for her ancestral burial grounds, to complete the spiritual circle of her life and her pain. Sophie took her request as vindictiveness and ungratefulness, and in turn, that increased her own hostility toward her mother.

As Beatrice lost both her physical and mental powers, Sophie harvested more and more power. Yet neither found peace. Beatrice became increasingly quiet, distant, and ever more fragile. Her bare bones protruded from the shroud of her wrinkled skin, her eyes became smaller, and turned as milky as her eternal cigarette-smoke clouds. My Nane was decomposing right before my eyes, but I was too young and too full of love to see the inevitable. Sophie missed the seriousness of the decomposition as well, for her own reasons. She was irritated by the spilled tea, the scattered crumbs, the forgotten cigarette butts, and the spilled ashes. Beatrice started getting served her bowl of soup after we finished eating our own meals, as if she were a maid. She was not able to eat much anyway, so her body consumed itself. Her personal grooming also showed a marked degeneration. The tight bun that had always harnessed her sparkling white hair went out of control. The shirts she wore got larger and larger on her, as she got thinner and thinner. They were either partially unbuttoned or buttoned out of sequence. She kept looking for one of her slippers, when she was wearing both, or shuffled herself into the bathroom with no slippers on, which was against Sophie's rules. Ironically, she no longer searched for the crackled picture of my grandfather. Maybe she forgot that she had the picture, maybe she forgot the man who had stared back at her with his liquid eyes. Beatrice never forgot my name though, and when I called on her to come for her evening soup, she always mumbled "Thank you, Anna, my dear child." Then she forgot what I had called her for, and went back to sleep. I had to wake her up again, and escort her to the table. I often sat with her as she ate, since I could not bear her increasing loneliness.

Eventually, Nane's bedroom got moved from the larger one attached to the living area to the one at the back of our house. Her new room was dark and small. The only window in it faced a dreary wall. Once the clumsy old bed was placed in it, there was little room to move around. No other furniture cheered up the room, and no decorations warmed the barren walls. We even forgot to put a picture of me to keep her company when I was at school, to ease her solitude.

At the very end, Beatrice walked with much difficulty. Sophie and I dragged her out of her bed for breakfast; she ate a little bread soaked in lukewarm tea or milk. Rarely, she asked for some feta cheese or a few black olives, but it was hard for her to chew. We stopped giving her olives because she choked on the pits. She soon forgot to ask for them, or anything else. She sat at the table, staring at her food, until we took her back into her room. I yearned for the woman who told me the best stories anyone can imagine, and it became excruciatingly painful to endure her stoic presence. My Nane turned into a shadow, an empty space that I could almost see through. Most amazing of all, she stopped smoking, but continued to smell like cigarettes despite the baths we gave her. The life-long ingestion of nicotine had seeped into her bones.

Towards the end, Beatrice spent all day and all night in her clumsy bed, totally oblivious to the back room's claustrophobic nature. Her only remaining activity was going to the bathroom, with our help. She accumulated black and purple bruises from the difficulty of moving around, and the confined space made matters worse. She always thanked us and blessed us for taking her to the bathroom, but did not quite know whether she still had to go, or she had already gone. She always murmured "Anna, my dear child."

I remember the New Year's preparations, just before her death. I was naïvely hoping that the seasonal excitement in the house would bring back some of Beatrice's vitality. Instead, her health declined further. On New Year's Eve, my parents, Agnes and I were invited to a house party, which was our accustomed way of ushering in the New Year. There was always plenty of food, drinks, toys and games for the children, and more potent drinks and card games for the adults. Unlike the other years, however, Beatrice had to be left behind. There was no way to take her anywhere in her present, listless condition. Sophie made sure that she was fed, bathed and comfortable before our departure. Sophie and I took her to the bathroom although her bathroom needs were few in those days, since she was eating so little. Each of us, in our own ways, wished her a Happy New Year before we left. She had no response to give.

The party was lots of fun. I felt happy, and content, and soon forgot about Beatrice's absence. I was too excited, the festivities too many, the food plentiful, and the friends, games and gifts too numerous to remember what was missing. What was missing was Beatrice.

It was well into the first day of the new year when we returned home. The sun had risen, the sky was clear, and we were happy, tired, content, and stuffed with food and drinks. As soon as my parents turned the key, I remember being the first one to push open the door. I was exhausted, eager to go to sleep, eager to re-experience the festivities in my sweet dreams. The door hit Beatrice. She had somehow dragged herself out of her bed, crawled around, and collapsed on the floor. My parents had to carefully and gently lean on the door to push her aside, in order to be able to gain entry. Their faces were wearing masks of fear. My face was already covered with tears. Beatrice was curled in a ball; one side of her mouth curiously distorted and wet, one side rigid and no longer capable of movement. She was eerily white and cold, a ghost from the years passed. Her milky eyes held no blame. All alone, Beatrice had suffered a major stroke.

Our family doctor was one of my parents' closest friends. In fact, he was the one who was married to Adele. They were with us at the just-ended party. He came to our house shortly after he was called, but the long festivities of the night, and too much food and drink had significantly dampened his professional enthusiasm. He seemed eager to return to his home, to his own bed. "Age," he said, "Age. We will find her a hospital bed tomorrow," and he left.

I remember the following morning when my mother and I gave Beatrice her final bath in our home. I remember how small and dry her body had become, how severe the curvature of her spine was. Sophie cut her hair short so that she wouldn't be hurt if anyone tried to comb it at the hospital. With the moving side of her mouth, Beatrice was trying to say Anna, without being able to complete it with "my dear child." Beatrice was carried out to the ambulance on a stretcher, as I touched her freshly cropped hair, still damp from her final bath. In response to the well of tears in my eyes, Sophie lied to me for the first time, and said that Nane was going to get well. For the first time, I knew not to trust my mother.

I went to the dark room after the ambulance left. Her bed was still warm, the fragile contortions of her body still imprinted on the lumpy mattress. The room was outright malevolent without her in it. Beatrice never came back, and Sophie was visibly relieved. My heart was broken though; the only consistent source of warmth had been taken from my life. My father also loved me, but he was mostly away. I am sure Sophie loved me too, in her own way, but her first choice was Agnes. Besides, she was not that good at this occupation we call mothering.

Decades have passed, but Beatrice's memory is fresh in my mind. I still remember bits and pieces of her stories, although I can no longer recall a complete one. She still visits me in my dreams. I can still hear her say, "Anna, my dear child." Her dignity still transcends the conditions of her sorrowful death. She still radiates meaning into my life. Sometimes, in the wrinkles of my own face, I see a fleeting resemblance to Beatrice. With the exception of her targeted feelings of ethnic-group hate, I miss everything about my Nane.

13.

My Father

MY FATHER WAS THE PERSONIFICATION of human dignity. I looked up to him as a child. I respect him even more now. Like his mother, Mavis, he was orphaned as a child. The family chatter told me that he was only nine when his father passed away. The chatter did not say why my paternal grandfather died. At that time, death must have been a more integral part of life; people were expected to die, with or without a reason. The trouble was that Mavis was considerably younger than her husband, maybe as much as twenty-five years, and she was left behind with four little children. Mavis must have been hard-pressed after her husband's death. My paternal grandfather never left a picture of himself for me to see.

It must have been a mammoth task for a young woman, in times when women had absolutely no political or legal rights, to remain alone without being quickly escorted into a remarriage. But Mavis was a survivor, and somehow, she had beaten the odds. She raised my three aunts, until each married a respected and accomplished man. The husband of my oldest aunt was a military physician; the husband of my middle aunt was an engineer. However, it was my youngest and the prettiest aunt, Angel, who had won the jackpot. She married an Arab Sheik who was rumoured to be richer than the city budget of Istanbul of the time. Wealth may buy happiness, but it does not buy life. Within six months of her gold-studded, fairy tale marriage, my beautiful aunt died. Sophie said it must have been the heat of Arabia that killed her. Some blamed the food of a foreign country, while others thought that she missed her family back at home, and had stopped eating. Whatever the cause, Mavis lost her precious youngest daughter, and did not even get a chance to attend her burial. It was before air travel, and the coal-powered trains only went part of the way. Having to tend for my young father and her own huge house, Mavis neither had the time nor the money to venture into the Arabian Peninsula in horse carts and camel caravans. Mavis shed her burning tears as Angel's body was buried in the scorching sands of her husband's land.

After the loss of her husband and then her youngest daughter, Mavis decided to send my father to the prestigious military academy in Istanbul. Mavis's decision was wise, and served two purposes: first, the military provided a decent career for men, through absolutely free formal education. Second, Mavis wanted some male leadership and modelling in my father's life, since he no longer had a father to provide much desired male leadership. So, my father started his honourable but also demanding, lifelong military career when he was about nine. His military academy life is well documented with pictures, all black and white, many crackled, and yellowish by now. In each picture, my father appears larger than life, almost always occupying the centre of a crowd. He must have been very popular, and maybe, also well liked. He was exceptionally bright. Many decades later, when Negrisse scored 160 on her IQ test, I immediately knew where her gift came from. That kind of brilliance certainly did not trickle down from Randall's side.

My father looked like Paul Newman in his youth, and if you ask me, that is pretty damn attractive. From the photographs, the impression I get is that he must have engaged in every sport that was available in his school. The pictures show his chiselled body playing football, which North Americans erroneously call soccer. However, I like in the photos of his diving and swimming competitions the best. There are also pictures of him in rowing competitions. His boat was Number 13, one of many out-of-the-ordinary choices my father made. Number 13 was considered to be unlucky by almost all. His choice was practical. When asked, he explained that none of his peers wanted the Number 13 boat, so it was always available for practice. Many years later, he taught me how to swim, and he was my first coach when I started my own swimming career. I even managed to set a few records, mostly to make him proud. Like my swimming career, my records in 100 and 200 meters freestyle were short lived. Yet, they managed to make my father exceptionally happy and proud.

At his military academy, my father's nickname was "The Blonde." This is noteworthy because not many of my country's people are blonde. Turks have a reputation of having relatively dark olive skin, brown eyes, and straight brown hair. Generally, my country's people are not very tall either, probably an artifact of many years of eating and drinking the wrong things during surges of war. However, my father had green eyes, and before the white set in, his hair was indeed blonde. His skin however, was a dark olive colour, turning a rich dark brown every summer. My father was beautiful; he looked like the Greek war god, and my mother knew it, though she never openly admitted it. Her possessiveness of my father was probably unconscious, mostly well hidden behind a shallow, nonchalant shroud.

For others, who did not know or like my father as much as I did, he had three shortcomings: He was short-tempered, he was a vegetarian, and he could not hear in one ear. My mother openly complained about the first two, but only when my father was not around. We were never allowed to mention the third: his deafness. Let me start with the first weakness.

After so many years of reflection, my conclusion is that my father was a very sensitive man behind a granite-like appearance. He got hurt easily, but he did not know how to express his gentle side, his military upbringing was too macho for that. Rather than showing his vulnerability, he got angry. Often his anger passed quickly, and he never held a grudge. Moreover, he never raised a hand to his family. Yet, there were a few occasions when he slammed his fist on the table. In one particular occasion, he threw a plateful of food to the wall. The plate was full of beans cooked in olive oil, his favourite dish, and I remember their glistening tumble across the floor. I had also seen my mother drop a bowl of beans on the floor, so I was familiar with beans rolling on the floor. And my mother was good in scrubbing the oil out of the wooden floors. The point is that, although his rages were few and far between, we all feared my father as much as we loved him. In those very rare occasions, when his anger bristled and roared, Sophie softly asked Agnes and I to leave the room. Our cat voluntarily followed us. In that land, in that time, fear of one's father was as desirable as obedience, respect, and loyalty.

My father's temper was well known, and greatly exaggerated by those who knew him well. Sophie's rendition of his moments of anger also exaggerated the truths and contributed to the myths, so my father became inaccessible to most. Over time, he took on a mythic existence, like Zeus sitting on top of Mount Olympus. I still think his infrequent temper tantrums were a camouflage for his very gentle inner self. Most of the time, he would write the most beautiful poetry, which was about love, yearning, and pain. He deeply loved his family, especially me, and he missed our presence in his day-to-day life as he was away most of the time, like other military men of war years, who were called upon to sacrifice so much for their country.

When I was only eight or nine years old, I wrote a poem for my father, and sent it to him by mail, without Sophie's help. Although I long lost the copy of what I said, the poem was about his long absences. My father's answer to me came back as a poem, which still brings tears to my eyes. He wrote:

My dreams are shining and bright,
because they are full of you, Anna,
You call me "daddy" and approach me, smiling and merry,
I hear your steps toward me
I want to hold you, and embrace you
My arms fold around emptiness,
And you disappear!

A sacred struggle, a sincere wish,
Warmth in coolness, heat in cold,
As long as I live and as long as you wish,
My arms will remain open to embrace you.

My dreams are shining and bright because they are full of you, Anna,
You call me "daddy" and approach me, smiling and merry,
I hear your steps toward me
I want to hold you, and embrace you
My arms fold around emptiness,
And you disappear!

This was the father I knew: gentle, loving, and comforting. A man who sometimes feared his own gentleness. My father wrapped his gentleness within a rough exterior, only allowing us the occasional glimpse.

According to Sophie, the second shortcoming of my father was his refusal to eat meat or anything that had remotely touched it. This was not due to an awareness of animal rights, which many years later transformed Negrisse into a vegetarian, and me into a guilt-ridden meat consumer—for a while. My father's choice was not driven by health consciousness either. In those days, parents insisted that their children ate sweets and meat, for what they called "good calories." The reason behind my father's vegetarianism was simple: the sight and smell of meat nauseated him.

When he was a little boy, even before his father's death, he had choked on a piece of chicken bone. Rather than working through his fears, it seems, his fear of meat was reinforced. Sophie's version of the story was that Mavis had shown him a chicken bone each time he had done something wrong, reinforcing the association of meat with unpleasant events. Then again, my mother strongly disliked my paternal grandmother, thus, this version of the story might have been just a figment of Sophie's imagination to put Mavis down. Family loyalty, in Sophie's world, did not extend to her in-laws. My paternal grandfather was exempt from her strong aversion since he was already dead. Mavis and my remaining two aunts were not that lucky.

The short of a long story is that my father was a vegetarian, and my mother despised it, and blamed Mavis for it. She complained endlessly that she had to cook everything twice, with meat for us, and without meat for my father. Fish was our saviour, and the Black Sea provided the best. The next shared taste revolved around many kinds of pastry dishes that gave my mother an edge over other housewives. In the creation of sophisticated foods and pastries for the New Year's parties, she was the queen. She also demonstrated her talents during other holidays when my father came home. For the rest of the year, we had nutritious, but not imaginative soups and casseroles.

During my father's visits, I loved tasting the food on his plate, no matter what else I was served. He would start with whatever we were eating—minus the meat— and end up with something much more delicious. A pinch of salt, a shake of pepper, a sprinkle of more exotic spices like cumin, lemon juice and whatever else he sprinkled onto his plate, made his food tastier than ours. He liked to share his creation on his plate, and I was his most loyal customer. Maybe his food simply tasted better because it was his, and offering some to me made us both glow with happiness. When I looked at my father, I saw a majestic eagle, so powerful and omnipotent to the outside world, so loving to me. I felt warm and safe growing up under his protective wings. All other men in my life failed miserably in comparison to my father. They were never a match for his strong character, his uncompromising honesty and morality, his equally uncompromising loyalty and love. I felt very lucky to be the beloved daughter of such a great man. I was also unlucky to start with a role model who would be so hard to live up to. As it turned out, Randall never came close to my expectations. My other lovers were also shadows in varying degrees of paleness. When you stare at the sun for so long, in the image of your father, all other men start looking like collapsed stars, dark and hollow.

The third characteristic that Sophie considered a weakness was that my father did not hear in one ear. I think he had trouble hearing with the other as well, but this is just a guess. Being deaf was his greatest weakness, at least, in his own mind and in Sophie's. Because of his razor sharp intelligence, he had developed and refined many strategies to cover up his disability. For example, he read lips. He was also brilliant in deciphering meaning from a few loose words he actually heard. It was like a form of audio speed-reading for him. He always wanted people to face him when they talked, and he got upset if they did not. In our home, we all talked relatively loudly, even when we were not addressing my father, so that he would not feel left out. The trouble was with strangers and acquaintances who did not know our ways. In situations like those, we had our own little tricks to help him out. For example, we recapitulated what others had said, a little louder and facing my father, which the original communicators might not have done in the first place. Often, I sat on my father's lap, and provided a simultaneous re-account of what was being said. Yet, the trick had to be carefully executed, not to offend his feelings. It was a tight rope that we all learned to walk, since my father despised being dependent as much as he despised his disability. His inability to hear, at least in his mind, was as debilitating to him as Beatrice's hump was to her. However, like Beatrice, my father carried his disability with utmost dignity, although this effort took a lot out of him—and us. We never said the word "ear" in our house. In our house, we acknowledged four rather than the usual five legitimate senses: see, taste, touch and smell!

Many years later, after many technological advancements were made, my family was able to afford a hearing aid for my father. The gadget cost a fortune. The mechanical part of the hearing aid looked like an unusually thick frame of eyeglasses. The sides that went over the ears were thicker than a fountain pen. Like an octopus, a semi-clear tentacle went into my father's ear. Although the machine we purchased would not have won any beauty contests, it did accomplish miracles. Through reclaiming most of his hearing, my father became more relaxed, less fearful of showing his gentleness, and even more loving than before. He developed a new sense of humour that we were not familiar with. We even started cracking jokes about ears in our house, the target of our jokes being my mother's hefty ears. During his short-lived retirement, my father taught his two pet canaries to perch at the sides of his hearing aid-eyeglass concoction. Those were the happiest times in my life, when my family was complete; my father was within reach, and our home was in peace.

Since then, through death, through divorce, through separation, and eventually, through Negrisse's painful self-inflicted absence, my family has been ravaged and splintered. In the chapters of this book, I am trying to collect and reassemble the scattered pieces, give them shape, preserve their meaning and contain them within two covers, before they too turn to dust. This artificial containment of my memories is the best I can offer, an illusion, much like my dreams. The past is like a Monarch butterfly, colourful and beautiful, but also fragile and dusty.

Flashback: Anna at age six

We are taking a long bus trip, to or from somewhere. I am not clear about our reasons for taking the trip, but the bus we are on is crystal clear in my memory. It is a relatively old bus, narrow and long. It has a long nose, under which the engine is located. It clanks and puffs black smoke and diesel fumes on the road, but most busses of that era are like that, so I am not particularly worried. Besides, I am sitting on my father's lap, in the single passenger seat beside the

driver. I love this long journey on my father's lap. I love spending
such a close time with my father. I also get to look around, as the bus
ascends and descends mountainous terrain; the view is breathtaking.
My father gives me an ongoing geography lesson about the lakes,
streams, and mountains that come our way. Sophie and Agnes are
sitting on the two-seater seats behind us. I bet Agnes is furious with
me, since I get to sit on my father's lap and she does not. This is one
of the very rare occasions when I have an advantage over Agnes. I
am younger and light as a feather.

There are few rest stops along our long way, mostly tarpaulin
covered huts constructed over a deep hole in the ground. In most
places, there are two huts, one for women and one for men. As a
universal truth, there is always a longer line in front of the women's
facility. They have more clothes to fumble with, and they are also
responsible for their children's personal hygiene. Men unzip/zip, and
they are done. These are the places our bus occasionally stops to let
the travellers relieve themselves. There are no scheduled stops. The
driver shouts at the top of his voice that one of these tarpaulin huts
is approaching, and asks if anyone is in need of a stop. There is no
microphone. If some of the travellers shout back, the bus rumbles
to a stop. If not, the driver forges ahead.

We are in one of these relief spots, and we just took our turn to
visit the quite intimidating washroom. The smell is something, not to
mention the scary size of the hole we have to crouch over. Anyway,
I badly needed the stop, so why complain? Because we got out from
our front row seats first, we are finished way before the others. My
mother passes around one of the soapy washcloths she has prepared
for this purpose, and we each carefully wipe our hands. Our family
washcloth goes into the bag of used washcloths, again prepared for
this purpose. Then, my mother unwraps one of the family meal packages she has prepared. We all have cheese sandwiches, some dried
fruit and a yogurt drink called ayran. While I am eating my tasty
sandwich, I put my hand between the doorframe and the open door
of the bus. My father immediately pulls my hand back, and warns
me of the danger of what I did. He tells me someone may push the
door closed, and my fingers may get crushed. I continue eating my
sandwich, but soon forget the important warning. I place my hand
again between the doorframe and the door, while I balance myself

on my father's knees. By this time, all the passengers are back, and the driver asks my father to close the door on his side, so that we can be on our way. My father obliges, and I give an unearthly screech. The top of my ring finger on my right hand is crushed.

Amongst my own yelps of pain, I hear shrieks from my mother and some other passengers. My father does not shriek or cry, but his complexion has turned into chalk. His eyes are flashing; his normally green eyes have taken a much deeper shade. He immediately reopens the door, and releases my wounded finger. On the top, up to the first knuckle, it looks like a pancake, but there is no blood. He grabs a clean washcloth from my mother's basket of travelling equipment, and starts re-shaping my finger. With each manipulation, I weep and wail, but he continues. His whole face is covered with sweat. I remember the time when he plucked the leblebi I had inserted into my nostrils. The memory takes away some of my pain.

The bus takes off again, with the promise to stop at the next health dispensary. According to the driver, there are no nearby hospitals. So, my father re-shapes my finger, and wraps it in one of my mother's silk scarves. By this time, my whole finger is swollen, and badly bruised, but my finger no longer resembles a pancake.

About an hour later, the bus stops at a roadside health dispensary. It is an underequipped place, but they manage to bandage my finger a little better than before. The bus waits for us as there are no strict schedules to keep. None of the passengers complain about the delay, they seem to be more concerned about a little girl than getting to wherever they are going. We are in after-war Turkey, and life is laid back.

On the way back to the bus, I hear my father whisper to my mother. He says "If I had my gun with me, I would have shot myself." I love my father even more for loving me so much. Since I had been aptly warned, the accident was my own fault. Yet, my father never forgave himself for slamming the door on my finger.

Part IV:
Siblings as Daughters

14.

Agnes

AFTER THEIR UNEVENTFUL DIVORCE, I heard my ex-brother-in-law refer to Agnes as the "dragon lady." Although harsh, this label was not used in malice, since Agnes and her ex remained friends. Yet, the label reverberates with a keen perception since it is based on a kernel of truth. Every single woman in my family has a dragon in her, and the most distinguishable of all dragons lies within Agnes. So, everyone present, including Agnes, laughed at the "dragon lady" label. The mutual laughter was a cover to hide the accuracy of the description, as known by those who are close to Agnes. She is colourful, beautiful, strong, loud, and somewhat ferocious.

Agnes is my older sister. She was the one Sophie fussed over the most, or as the Turkish saying goes, she was the "light of our mother's eyes." Agnes was bright, stubborn, domineering, and manipulative when she was a child. As an adult woman, she specialized further in all her earlier talents. The perplexing thing about Agnes is that she could also be nice, caring, dependable, protective, and warm, if and when she wanted to be. Her amazing capability to switch from the warm and caring mode to the cold and crushing one, and back to warm again makes her unpredictable. Thus, for the naïve and uninitiated, Agnes could be dangerous.

For me, the combination of her caring and intelligent side versus the cold and manipulative side made her into someone I loved and respected, but also feared and despised, all at the same time. I had never heard of sibling rivalry in my childhood, so I had to deal with my conflicting emotions all on my own. Many times, I felt good and proud of my older sister. However, I also felt anger and guilt for my inability to banish my negative feelings towards her, and wished that I loved her without qualifications. In my family, and on the surface, we were to only feel love, respect, and loyalty for our family members, so I had no working category for my competing and contradictory feelings. Overtly, I showed love and respect for Agnes, which I did, in part, really feel. Covertly, I hid my fear and distrust of her, even from myself, until recently. Agnes is a wild card in my family, the hardest to love, the easiest to abhor. Her unpredictability has been the source of her greatest power over me, and most of our lives, she has basked in this ominous power.

To say the least, Agnes had an unshakeable willpower, even as a young child. Although I was too young to remember, Sophie often talked about her iron will, which reached obduracy. Sophie also talked about Agnes's legendary temper tantrums. According to Sophie, the only way these tantrums could be stopped was to send Agnes to her bedroom, and ask her to stand facing the wall for fifteen minutes. This time-limited isolation has worked to cool her down, and bring her back to her senses. However, according to Sophie's narrative, Agnes would not leave her solitary position facing the wall, even after Sophie announced an end to her punishment. She would continue to stand alone, facing the wall for at least another fifteen minutes after she had been dismissed. In a way, and even as a small child, Agnes had to exercise control over everything that surrounded her, even to the degree of exerting some control over the punishment she had received. The need for control, which was obviously present early on, spread to almost all aspects of Agnes's life and relationships over her adulthood. This obsessive need for control came to define Agnes, and also became the main force tainting all her relationships.

As children born during and just after the war years, Agnes and I grew up without many toys. We did have a porcelain doll that had blond, porcelain hair and blue glass eyes. I have no clue of her pedigree, although I know that she was a doll beyond my parents' modest means. It is possible that she came to us through one of Beatrice's wealthy relatives. It is also possible that she would fetch a pretty penny in today's doll collector market, if Agnes allowed it to come out of the curio in her house. The doll was out of the reach of most of our peers. She sat on the dining room buffet, dressed in one of several fancy outfits made by Sophie. For the New Year's celebrations, the doll appeared as a transgendered Santa, with a red smock and cotton hair and beard. She had no name, since we were not allowed to establish any childish intimacy with her. She was like the crown jewels that you could see and admire, but all hell would break loose if you tried to touch.

My first recollection of Agnes is in relation to a dispute about two blow-up toys one of my father's subordinates had brought to us from Japan. His name was Norm. Norm was a veteran of the Korean War, who looked intact on the outside, but was mangled up inside. He had been imprisoned and tortured by the North Koreans, and had miraculously found a way to escape. Maybe, he had been rescued. Sometimes, Norm would drink himself to sleep in our home; at other times he would cry himself to sleep. Although my father had no tolerance for drunks or sissies, he tolerated Norm. After all, both were soldiers, knowing full well the long-term destruction war unleashes upon even manly men. For me, Norm was just a source of childhood curiosity. He was a man so unlike my own father, that he formed an antithesis.

Of the two plastic blow-up toys we received as a gift, the one I liked the most was a yellow and brown giraffe, which had a floppy butterfly on its tail. The other one was a baby deer, tan in colour, and with a handful of white polka dots scattered on its back and sides. The baby deer was not adorned with a floppy butterfly. Instead, it had a small plastic bell attached to its collar. During a time when alternate toys were nowhere to be found, both toys were a rare gift for us, so we thanked Norm profusely. However, with my childish enthusiasm, I wanted the giraffe, and with her older-sister privileges, Agnes refused to let me play with it. As usual, Sophie took Agnes's side, although there was no objective reason for her to hoard the giraffe. So, I had to settle for the baby deer. I disliked the little bell that adorned its collar and I wished it had a floppy butterfly like the giraffe. Both toys had the texture and smell of a discarded chewing gum. For most of our early and late childhood, Agnes controlled what I could or could not have and I simply could not have that giraffe.

Come to think of it, I do not recall a single game Agnes and I played together. She was an older sister who did not have the time or patience for a younger one. On very rare occasions, Agnes would join in the games I was playing with other children, closer to my own age. Each time, Agnes would abruptly change the established norms and rules of our childish games. For one, the rules would become tougher and more complex. According to Agnes's new rules, some of my friends got excluded, some started to cry. I never won anything in the games Agnes organized, whereas I was pretty good in holding my own amongst my peers. Yet, I was always happy to see her join in, her presence was like an affirmation of my own existence. It was like the warrior goddess of Athens descending from Mount Olympus, and fumbling with human affairs like those that caused the Trojan War. Agnes seemed to have an invisible sword, which could transform me into a semi-goddess, or cut me up into little pieces, and scattering my remains to the vultures. I looked up to Agnes in awe, and in trepidation. I tried to guess from which direction she would be blowing on a given day. Most days, it seemed as if she blew from the North Pole ... and not bringing gifts like Santa! I also recall Agnes in a substitute mother's role, caring and comforting me. Maybe it is because of these feelings of warmth and trust I felt for her in my earlier years, that the negative feelings I also harbour were so threatening, so hurtful. During the years when we still rented out Beatrice's wheat, onion and watermelon fields, Sophie and my father would go away for a week or two to settle the accounts with the farmers who worked our fields. I dreaded those weeks of parental absence, since I had this horrible and irrational fear that I was never going to see my parents again. My fear was not a fear of abandonment. Instead, I thought that my parents might die in an accident in their travels. Maybe, this was one unfortunate result of having listened to too many of Beatrice's stories. In those stories, loved ones died, especially when they wandered off. When I was little, the fear of abruptly losing my parents was insurmountable. When I was in the grip of these childish fears, Agnes was the warmest parental substitute in the whole wide world for me. She was older, and unlike me, she was not prone to irrational fears. She talked to me gently; assured me that our parents were all right and that even if something happened to them, she would take care of me. She tucked me into bed, only on those days of my mother's absence, because it was not Sophie's habit to tuck anyone into bed.

Agnes's unwavering confidence in herself made things appear okay, for a while, until my irrational fears seized me up again. Each time my parents were away, I felt weak. Agnes was strong. Each time I was down, Agnes pulled me up. Each time I needed help, she provided it for me. It is in times when I am not down, and I am not weak and I do not need help that she can be cold and dismissive. In times when I do exceptionally well, she can turn into the dragon lady and show her fangs ... or not. Agnes is a mystery; she still keeps me guessing.

Agnes always managed to set the standard for me to follow, but I don't think she could have managed it all on her own. Sophie perceived her as the best role model under the sun, the north star of the night, and naturally, demanded that I follow in her footsteps. Sophie was a perfectionist, she wanted me to reach for perfection, and Agnes personified the perfection she wanted. I did my best, but I did not, could not, duplicate my sister. If I ever reached perfection at all, in anything, it was my own brand, and I treasured its uniqueness with or without Sophie's nod of approval. My goals were emotional, feelings-related most of the time. I was never successful in accumulating tangibles, which Agnes excelled at. If I sound bitter, it is because mostly I am, but amazingly, I understand Sophie. Her feelings toward Agnes are no different than those I felt for Negrisse since the first time I held her in my arms. No one else ever came close to evoking such powerful feelings of adoration. I did not have additional children. If I had, I might have also expected them to become clones of my first daughter. Even worse, I might have made them feel inadequate unless they duplicated Negrisse to get my approval. That would have been a disaster, another notch in the mother-daughter conflict scale that is already overburdened in my family. Fortunately, I stopped at one daughter.

Perceived from another angle, my early childhood might be considered an easy one. I had a living example of what I was expected to be: Agnes the II. I dressed in similar clothes, her hand-me-downs, even if they were made to look a little different through Sophie's ingenuity. I was sent to the same American school as my sister. As prestigious as it was, it was not chosen specifically for me. I always wanted to go to a German school. I don't exactly know why I wanted a German school. Perhaps just to be different, just to have a say. At school, a whole slew of teachers also used my sister to compare and contrast me with. I had to get A's because Agnes was an A student. I had to run for the student council, because Agnes had been the president of the council. I had to get a leading role in school plays, because Agnes played leading roles in the previous years' performances. I did keep an A average, but I also became a problem student for a while. Too many rigid expectations are not good for anyone's development.

For a while, I even enrolled in the field Agnes had chosen for herself at the university: economics. I hated every minute of it. My mind did not work well in calculating tangibles and making profits. I also married Agnes's best friend, another economist. Randall eventually developed time and motion studies for everything in our lives. How many minutes to the grocery store, how many minutes back; how many minutes to vacuum the floor, how many moves to put away the groceries, how many minutes to go to the bathroom and to wipe oneself. Sure, I am exaggerating a bit, but I felt as if this is exactly what he did. I felt that our life was a ticking clock, counting the seconds and the minutes of each of our actions.

For a while, I also worked part-time at the same bank Agnes was a supervisor at. We had lunch together every day, as unequal colleagues, as unequal sisters. It was the "chosen" route, and I struggled to earn people's approval, to earn Sophie's approval, by stepping into each footstep left by Agnes as she boldly walked ahead of me. On rare occasions, I rebelled, and tried to be different. During my rebellious moments, the shit hit the fan, at high speed.

I was always expected to be the mediator, since Agnes had the dominant role. There was no tolerance in my family for challenging the established pecking order. On top of the ladder, sat my father, the loving patriarch. Then came Sophie and Agnes. Beatrice and I formed the lowest rungs. It is no wonder that Beatrice and I loved one another so much.

Agnes is indeed bright, probably much more so than most people I know. Her memory is like a steel trap, once captured, things are never released or forgotten. Yet, Agnes's memory is selective; she prefers to remember the events that shed a positive light on her. She also demands a selective memory from others, so they too remember events that reflect positively on Agnes. She will leave the room, or throw a tantrum if memories surface that she would rather forget. She would swear that certain things never happened, and accuse me of concocting memories that have no basis in reality—in her reality, that is. In contrast, I have a more abstract wisdom, more creativity, and more tolerance. Although I do have a bit of Agnes in me, my dragon side, I am still better with people. I relate to the students

I council, I try to see events from their point of view rather than imposing my views on them. I am glad I discontinued my studies in economics, and chose instead a career that required reaching out to others. I find solace in listening to and offering suggestions for the growing-up related confusions of the students that come to me. In my adult years, I found my own strength, whereas in my growing-up years, I was constantly made aware of my shortcomings.

In our early years, things came easily for Agnes. For example, she studied very little but made the annual honour's list. She made many friends, and had few foes. I had to work very hard just to reach par with the high standards she so effortlessly established. My accomplishments were considered as normal and expected, my deviations utter failures. Sophie took note of my failures; she was observant and vigilant. As a child, I often shrunk under her critical gaze.

The mostly hidden, but stressful relationship I had with my older sister was not totally her fault, just like it was not totally Sophie's fault. I also played a passive-aggressive part in the game. Agnes reached the beautiful age of flirtation much before I did. She became a teenager and developed an interest in spending time with her peers, and talking about or hanging around with boys. Sophie had strict views about dating and all other activities deemed "dangerous" for girls, so she often summoned me up to serve as a chaperon to my older sister. I was not required to do anything, but just be around so "things did not get out of hand" as Sophie put it. I did not quite understand how my presence could keep things in proper order, but I enjoyed the special and rare privilege the chaperonage bestowed on me. I also got to exercise my passive power within the newly designated role. Agnes had to take me along if she wanted to go out with her friends. I am sure she absolutely hated my presence amongst her friends. I, on the other hand, loved having access to the world through Agnes. I had my own heartthrobs amongst the crowd, even though to them I was probably just a nuisance. Yet, boys understood that they had to tolerate me if they wanted to be around my older sister. My sister's friends seemed to have a bit more freedom than she did, since they did not have to drag along their younger sisters like Agnes was required to do. Maybe, they did not have younger sisters to tag along. Thus, I learned about teenage angst much before I myself became a teenager.

Agnes's flirtatious occasions were mild and platonic, as considered absolutely crucial for "good girls" of the time. At most, the co-ed opportunities were to go to the beach, and maybe, just maybe, touch hands, stare in someone's eyes, or smile with an unspoken promise which could never be delivered. All such innocent teenage activities took place in public places, in full sight of other people. The younger chaperons like me were an added safety measure, in case all else failed and all the beach patrons started copulating on the same day, or something. A long walk along the beach, around the time of sunset, when the weather was balmy and the hormones boiling, was considered a date. The sea would be enchanting, making every young heart pound in every teenage chest. Teenagers strolled along, their emotions flashing through their pimpled cheeks, occasionally touching hands under the watchful eyes of many others. I played my part well, giving as much freedom to my sister as possible by pretending to be deaf and dumb. Occasionally, I turned mean if she crossed me. Under such occasions, I refused to go for the usual stroll with her, depriving her of the possibility of holding hands with the sweetheart *de jour*. When I stayed at home, she had to stay home too. For the first and the last time, in her teenage years, Agnes had to give up some of her power over me.

Like their adult mothers, daughters also lacked freedom in the Istanbul of my childhood. The only way to "catch" a suitable man was to remain a virgin. Women and girls were taught to distrust their bodies as "things" that had the potential to create chaos. All forms of sensual excitement, such as kissing and necking were forbidden. Daughters had to preserve the social seal of approval, and not take any chances that might "break" their physiological packaging. Mothers, like Sophie, were the self-designated executioners of female sexual oppression, in which, they themselves were also victims. Agnes went through this brainwashing before I did, and resented it.

Yet, when her own daughter reached her teens, Agnes attempted to control her sexuality just as much as Sophie had attempted to control ours. Agnes too, had swallowed the paternalistic bait, and had internalized the double bind. Agnes, like our mother, became the executioner of patriarchal controls over women's bodies. Once, I bluntly asked her in relation to Darion, my niece: "Are you afraid she is going to wear out?"

"How can you say that? She is a girl!"

"What if she becomes a career woman? Why can't she make her own individual choices in every dimension of her own life, including her own sexuality?"

"She will fall! She will become a loose woman! No one will marry her!"

"What if she finds a partner who sees her like an equal and respects her as a total person rather than an unused vagina?"

"Please don't say those types of things to me! Let's end this conversation."

So we did. Agnes kept on controlling her daughter's life and constructing barriers against her sexual freedom. In many ways, Agnes turned into Sophie. The emotion that turns daughters into their once-despised mothers is fear. They fear the sensuality of their own bodies, they fear bearing children they cannot support, and they fear losing their eligibility to be chosen as a marriage partner. Women in my growing years existed within patriarchal rules they did not make themselves. Men loved hoarding wealth, and they wanted to control that wealth even after they were gone. They wanted offspring they could identify as their own, so they controlled women's sexuality, earmarked as wives. They exploited other women's sexuality, marked as unworthy to become wives. So, mothers tried their best to keep their daughters in the eligible pool, a.k.a. virgins. This cultural pattern dissects women into two and objectifies them as sexual parts rather than total human beings. Women end up being classified as good or bad, or used or unused, marriageable or unmarriageable, keepable or discardable, all on the basis of the intactness of their hymen. I was raised in a strange world where women had become the most animated protectors of their own oppression. I played my little role, albeit assigned, of oppressing my sister's freedom. She, in turn, oppressed my freedom until I got married, and then, deprived her own daughter from exercising her freedom. If I had been given a chance, I might have done the same thing to Negrisse. After all, we learn to enact the ways of our mothers, just like they have learned to enact the ways of their own mothers. Negrisse left my house before I could do so, and maybe that is the silver lining of all those black clouds.

15.

Mavis's House

INICKNAMED MY PATERNAL GRANDMOTHER "Cotton Candy," but I never called her that name to her face. It was not proper for children to give nicknames to their elders, especially to those who were light years older than themselves. My paternal grandmother had lots of baby-fine white hair, which never stayed in a tidy bun as Beatrice's. Instead, on her sun-drenched skin, Mavis's white hair shimmered, like a dissolving, untidy halo, or a cloud of cotton candy.

Mavis lived in the huge house that my grandfather had built for his family. The house, crouched on a hillside, was built of stone at the bottom, and wood at the top floors. There was a massive garden in the front. To accommodate the incline, the garden had three tiers. After Mavis's death, my own family lived in that house. Thus, in her absence, Mavis's home, and especially her garden, played a significant part in my childhood dreams.

Mavis was a very private person. Up until the day she died at the amazing age of 83, beating most life-expectancy odds for her peers, she lived independently. Singlehandedly, she took care of the huge house and its big garden. It seems she was the source of the granite-like qualities in my father. I believe that I also possess some of these granite-like qualities, although in my case, they were dormant for a long time.

My memories of Mavis are distant, cloudy, and filtered through my mother's negative feelings towards her. In short, my own feelings are not warm or pleasant either. The strong detestation between Mavis and Sophie was obvious even in those rare occasions when they addressed one another. Sophie called Mavis "lady mother." This was a concocted, distant term, which no one else used. It hummed with a passive aversion and resonated with alienation. Mavis, in

turn, never called Sophie by her name. Instead, she called her *gelin*
(daughter-in-law). My mother's status as an attachment through
marriage rather than through blood was thus emphasized each time
she was summoned. Yet, their mutual dislike never reached a pro-
portion where it was translated into a deed or action. My father had
not allowed any overt hostilities between the two women.

Sophie's dislike for Mavis was probably an overreaction to my father's deep love and respect for his mother. In her later years, he also
contributed some money towards her support. This financial support,
albeit minor, was a sore point for Sophie, although she never openly
complained about it. My father was a loyal, responsible son of an
ageing widow. No argument from my mother would have changed
that responsibility. Sophie kept her resentment in check; she knew
her boundaries. My father also kept his generosity in check, not to
aggravate Sophie's aversion.

An additional factor behind my mother's resentment was that
Mavis did not like Agnes or me, at least, not as much as she loved
and doted on the children of her daughters. In her eyes, we were
contaminated, diluted in heritage through our mother's presence.
Sophie herself had no qualms about treating her own two children
differently, and later, even her own grandchildren. Yet, she hated the
fact that Mavis also had her favourites. Mavis worshipped her only
son, my father, but she was partial to the children of her daughters.

When Mavis was alive, every year we spent a full month in the
great house. She never visited our house. Maybe, this was because
our home changed location because of my father's various military
appointments. We often ended up in inconvenient parts of our country,
and lived in inadequate types of housing. Also, maybe, Mavis did
not want to lose control by coming too close to Sophie's territory.
So, one month a year was the only occasion the life of Mavis crossed
our own, on her own terms, in her own territory. During that month,
we also saw my older aunt, and her daughter, and my plump aunt,
and her son. My plump aunt had huge breasts, was cuddly, and
perspired a lot, so I tried to keep my distance. Like Mavis, she also
called my mother *gelin*, which assured that she was also despised
by Sophie. Because of the substantial age difference between his
sisters and my father, and because of the age difference between my
father and Sophie, my two cousins were closer in age to my mother

than to Agnes or I. This age difference as well as Mavis's partiality, exasperated the jealousy between the children of the three siblings. It also underscored Sophie's marginality within the family. The family boundaries were demarcated as Mavis, her two daughters, and their two children versus Sophie and her two children.

Even during those annual trips, my father would be absent most of the time, leaving Sophie, Agnes and I at a discernable disadvantage. Sophie's childish behaviour and frequent pouting did not do much to improve our standing in Mavis's eyes. Beatrice was always absent from these annual visits. Her outspokenness would have further complicated the already tense in-law relationships.

If it weren't for the hidden resentments I mentioned, these annual gatherings could have been special for me. After all, they were the only occasion where I actually experienced a sense of an extended family. Otherwise, my family consisted of Beatrice, Sophie, Agnes and I: a family of two women and two girls. Occasionally, my beloved father joined us, but too soon he would have to leave again to fulfil his obligations for his country and for the army. Obligations and loyalty were the paramount requirements of being a man in post-war Turkey. They trumped sentimentality.

Mavis's house was built on a hillside. One had to descend (or ascend, on the basis of where one was going) through three tiers of the garden to reach a wooden gate. The gate was tall, and opened out to a narrow, cobblestone street. A thick, stone wall buttressed each side of the gate. When opened, the tall gate hit a bell, dangling from the top of its frame. This is how Mavis could tell that some-one was on his/her way to the house. Mavis had plenty of time to prepare as the intruder belaboured the incline toward the house. There were few intruders on Mavis's privacy; I guess we were some of those few. Otherwise, the street as well as the house was mostly empty. The street was so narrow that only horse carts and smaller vans could pass through, and only on extremely rare occasions like someone's death, or moving in or out. Deaths occurred more often than moves; Mavis's neighbourhood seemed frozen in time. The once affluent neighbourhood had long refused to advance forward, even according to the slow ticking time of ancient Istanbul.

Despite its obvious drawbacks, the cobbled street, the large house, and everything about the garden were absolutely beautiful. All three tiers of the garden were filled with wild flowers and vegetation that could give any botanist a month's worth of overtime. There were hundreds of tulips that religiously opened their cheerful heads amongst this natural chaos. The tulips were white and red, and mostly followed the path wedged between the garden gate and the house. A few derelict tulips added colour to the remaining, mostly green parts of the garden. In this antiquated neighbourhood, lawns would have been considered an absolute waste. Lawns would have been sacrilegious. The three tiers of the land were distinctly separated from each other by additional stone walls. The heaviest wall separated the lowest tier from the narrow street. While holding the weight of the garden behind them, the stone walls had bulged over the years. I always had the feeling that they were going to come down and crush some poor soul who dared to approach the house. Amazingly, they never tumbled, only bulged out further. They outlasted Mavis, and they also outlasted our long stay in the house after her death. When I went back to the house some thirty years later, I found the house mostly renovated and replaced, but the garden walls were intact, only more pregnant and more overwhelming than before.

Mavis's house was decorated before my grandfather's death, at a time of considerable affluence. Maybe because of my grandfather's once-upon-a-time wealth, or maybe everything was purchased such a long time ago, it seemed that everything in the house was of a precious antique quality. There were heavy velvet drapes, cascading down from twelve-foot ceilings to the floor. They were pulled back and gracefully tied with silk ropes thicker than my skinny arms. The furniture was in various shapes and sizes, mostly hand-carved ebony, mostly covered in lush velvet or shimmering silk. The south-facing parts of the house were done in warm velvets, especially for winter use. The north-facing sections of the house were done in light coloured, cool silks for spring and summer use. There were semi-circle marble tables, sitting on long, gracefully carved legs. Priceless ebony tables supported carved ebony frames that housed bevelled mirrors. The combined height of the tables and the mirrors almost touched the twelve-foot ceilings. Some of the mirrors were clouded and streaked with age, but the magnificently carved furniture only gained more glory from its apparent age. I always felt dwarfed by the elegant furniture in Mavis's house. The bevelled mirrors kept an eye on my behaviour, just like Mavis had done with her cool gaze during her life.

I never saw what was under the black silk shroud that covered one of the heavily gilded frames that hung on the wall when Mavis was alive. It was only later that I learned that the black drape hid a picture of my father's sister, Angel, who had died within the first year of her marriage to an Arab sheik. The wealth of the sheik was still a main conversation topic long after my aunt's death. Angel's covered picture was like my father's hearing disability. We all felt the pain it caused, but we never mentioned a word or acknowledged the fact that this mishap existed. After Mavis's death, I saw my aunt's picture for the first time before Sophie got rid of it. Indeed, Angel was dressed in a dreamy white dress, the curls of her lush hair sweeping down her shoulders. She looked like an angel, and was stunningly beautiful.

Two other things I remember from the early years of our visits were the old-fashioned toilets of the house and the old-fashioned kitchen. The two toilets, one on each floor, were solid marble from the floor to ceiling. The marble was white, with varying shades of grey striations, permanently enclosed within the marble's dense layers. The floor was also solid marble, with two slightly elevated platforms to place the feet on, and a hole right in the middle. The marble surface was ingenuously crafted to ever so slightly slant into the direction of the hole, with the exception of the two raised platforms. There was a metal—possibly tin—flap that covered the hole. The flap opened downwards with weight when we did our business in the bathroom, and flapped back into place when we were done. There was a plastic barrel with a rudimentary faucet, in the toilet part, and another one at a marble sink at the entrance. These barrels had to be manually filled each day, since Mavis's home was constructed pre-running-water. The whole thing was not as comfortable as the western toilet bowls that we take for granted now, but it was just as functional and possibly more sanitary. We did not sit on anything, so there was no fear of contamination from toilet seats. All one had to do was put on the specially designed wooden shoes, which were called *takunye,* over one's stocking feet or right on top of slippers, walk to the platform, turn around to face the door and squat. In most houses, *takunye* were carved as a wooden sole, with a thick rubber band to accommodate the largest feet in the household. At Mavis's house, these wooden toilet shoes were pieces of art in their own right. They were inlaid with mother of pearl and other semi-precious stones. Once in the room, equipped with the wooden slippers, it was very easy to learn where to crouch, so that one never missed the hole. Little deviations did not matter either, thanks to the smooth polish of the marble and just the right angle of the decline. Every day, the whole bathroom floor was washed with some kind of an acid that hissed and bubbled furiously on the marble surface. Probably, this acid treatment would have gouged holes in our delicate ceramic fixtures of today, if not continue to pierce right through the floor. Instead, the daily acid scrubbing added beauty to the marble, and also served as a tool to teach consideration and respect for others. Each user poured a little water into the hole after he/she was done, made sure that the tin flap was clean and in its place, walked to the door on one's wooden shoes, went out with one's socks or slippers, placing the *takunye* outside the door, and facing in, for the next person's easy access. At Mavis's, shitting, like other things, was an experience in restraint.

16.

Mavis's Kitchen

MAVIS'S KITCHEN IS THE SECOND PLACE I remember distinctly. Roughly, it was the size of a half tennis court, and covered almost half of the ground floor. The rest was divided into a dark pantry, two bedrooms, one long hallway, wide stairs to the upper floor, a huge entrance, and one of the marble toilets. Mavis rented these quarters, but shared the kitchen. When we inherited one third of the house—two thirds going to my surviving aunts— we also inherited the privilege of living in it for as long as we wanted. We also inherited the tenants, who were an older couple with an older son, and a much younger daughter who was my age. Sophie was not the only woman who had trouble controlling her reproductive powers. Our tenant had acquired her daughter at an unusually late stage in her life.

In the kitchen, the floor tiles were a shiny burnt-red. We had to walk gingerly when they were wet since they offered no traction. A door as wide as three regular doors connected the rest of the house with the kitchen. Another, much narrower door opened into the coal shed at the highest tier of the garden, which in turn, opened to the garden. A third door went into a very dark corridor, which we were not allowed to enter. I often imagined that the third door lead to a world beyond this one, not necessarily scary, but definitely different, dark and damp. I imagined that the dark space was occupied by a dragon, large, colourful and scaly, the resident protector of the house. Thanks to Beatrice's tales, I had a wild imagination as a child.

Since the main door to the kitchen was huge and heavy, like the door to a monastery, it was always left open. In winter, Mavis dangled a padded curtain made like a comforter from the ceiling, to serve as a flexible door and insulation. Due to my late grandfather's occupation, there were plenty of comforters in the house, each an exquisite piece in its own right. Otherwise, the house had no insulation. No fluffy pink fiberglass panels between the walls either. Mavis thought that cold strengthened the character, and in winter, her house got cold enough to rattle our bones. The huge window frames were not properly sealed either. On many occasions, Agnes and I woke up to a thin blanket of frost on our heavy blankets. Although the commonly occupied rooms had fireplaces, bedrooms had no source of heat. If Sophie was in a particularly good mood, she let us take a hot water bottle to our beds. If not, which was the norm, Agnes and I had to shiver in our separate beds until we managed to get warm. After such a rough start, the mornings seemed to arrive much too soon.

We used to keep a change of clothes on our nightstands, and dress up while still under the warmth of our blankets. To my knowledge, nothing much has changed on that particular cobbled street with its bulging stone walls. Current lives are still as serene as they were in my grandmother's time, but also full of hardship. Although I heard that the houses on that street now have running water and flush toilets, I very much doubt the availability of central heating.

In between the door to the kitchen and the one to the shed, there was the gaping mouth of an underground cistern. This cistern whipped my wildest imagination while at the same time contributing to the richest nightmares of my childhood. Somehow, I always associate Mavis's cistern with Beatrice's stories. On the corner diagonal from the mouth of the cistern, there was a walk-in fireplace, which was the original stove and bread oven of the house. In the era I remember, it was used only on washing days, when we had to boil the laundry water in large cauldrons. Our regular cooking was done on a gas-pump stove, which in fact burnt oil, and which was then considered a mind-boggling technological advancement. In fact, the gas-pump stoves were not very reliable, and we would hear about women who were blown to pieces or maimed for life when they exploded. Yet, the pump-stoves were the lifeline of the kitchen, both in Mavis's final years and for the duration of our stay in her home after she died. We then graduated to compressed natural gas, which came in stubby iron containers. They too were prone to explosions, and they too hurt and disfigured women. After many decades, our kitchens are much safer, give or take a few carcinogenic chemicals we still use. The dangers in kitchens today are the toxic additives to our food, rather than temperamental stoves. One way or another, women continue to be at the mercy of their kitchens.

When Mavis was still alive, her kitchen was an enchanting place for me. This was not because of its beautiful tile floors, or the ominous mouth of the cistern, or the walk-in fireplace, or even its twelve-foot ceilings. What fascinated me most were the long shelves that housed hundreds of little jars of Mavis's jams, pickles, and rose-syrup concentrates. Mavis spent most of her adult life, including her later years, making these little jars of preserves and delicacies. The ingredients were lovingly grown in her garden, including the pickling spices she used. The fruits were from the assortment of fruit-trees she tended, which yielded bushels of fruit. The seals for the jars were made from melted paraffin, which formed a perfect seal when it cooled down.

Mavis's rows and rows of jars had dozens of colours, textures, and aromas of her preserves. They shined like jewels. They tasted even better. Agnes and I were not allowed to touch these jars. We were not allowed to choose the ones we wanted to taste. Mavis made all those decisions for us during our visits. Although Agnes and I were far from starving, and although Mavis did allow us to sample a few kinds, I often felt deprived. It seemed that the jars that had the brightest colours, the jars that contained the rarest fruits were saved for the other grandchildren: the children of Mavis's daughters. This slight unfairness drove Sophie crazy, and this is probably why we felt distant from Mavis, even when we were guests at her house. I still associate inequality with food, and over-stuff my own pantry to compensate for my childhood.

When Mavis died, the only pain I felt was the pain of my father. At the time, we were renting a small, dark apartment, not in one of the choice areas of Istanbul, just because it was convenient for my father's work. Even then, he had to wake up before 5:00 am every morning—except Sundays—and come home well after the sunset. Protecting the motherland was a gruelling business. I was not quite school-aged yet, since our primary schools start at age seven. My sister was still attending an elementary school, and had not quite advanced to the fifth grade. We heard that Mavis had suffered a heart attack while visiting my oldest aunt who lived in another city. Mavis was gone in less than a few minutes, a clean and dignified departure, most becoming to how independently she always lived. Almost all my blood relatives died because of heart attacks, electrifyingly quick and final. The exceptions are Beatrice and Sophie, who endured long durations of convalescence. In each case, they also endured the indignant outrage of their caregiving daughters. As they say, life is a drama that repeats itself, although the players change each generation. So do the mother-daughter tensions.

My father brought Mavis's body back to Istanbul. Given the transportation limitations of the day, this was a formidable task only a loyal son could accomplish. When he returned from his journey, I had trouble recognizing my father. He had aged, appeared tormented, and was many kilograms lighter, all in the span of a week or ten days. I never saw my father cry, but I am sure, the death of his mother made him cry in his dreams. He was the only son of a devoted single mother, in a part of the world where the term single-parenthood was yet to be invented, let alone accepted.

After his mother's burial, and before my two aunts' bickering for the inheritance started, my father started reading what Sophie called "awkward" books. Although my father was the most equity-conscious person I have ever known, and I mostly take after him, greed runs fairly deep on both sides of my family. My two grandmothers are the only exceptions.

The books my father read after the death of his mother were about miracles, death, reincarnation, spirits, and spiritualism. He became a deeply religious man, without being bound to any specific religion. A way to understand my father's religiosity required an understanding of far Eastern religious philosophies. Through the years, I also developed a respect for Eastern religious and philosophical systems, and learned to respect my father even more through them. My father read extensively about the Yogins and Fakirs of India, and Buddha, Tao and Zen. He read ferociously about rebirth and "official-looking" accounts of rebirth. I suspect that he might have tried to establish a spiritual contact with his mother during that time, but I am just guessing. If he did, I hope he was able to find some peace.

Maybe, my father was one of those people who missed the opportunity to say how much he loved his mother, while both were alive and well. Maybe, my father was crushed under the burden of unspoken gratitude after losing his beloved mother. In my own adult years, I think I sinned in the opposite direction. I told Negrisse I loved her so many times that my words lost their meaning for her. Negrisse escaped at the first chance she got, possibly because she was tired of my endless expressions of love, and possibly, interpreting my love as a chain. Negrisse could never know the magnitude of the wound she caused by her departure, just like my grandmother could never know the void her death created in my father's soul. My family has troubled mother-child bonds. They are broken often by death, but sometimes by cruel choices.

Many years later, when I could read fluently and when my vocabulary became adequate to deal with the depth of the subject, I read many of my father's books on spirituality. I was astounded, thrilled, scared, and tongue-tied about many of the stories in these books. Above all, I felt really close to my father, close to his emotional life, which had not been visible to me then, and was definitely not visible to Sophie or Agnes. Even in my adult years, I feel a special bond with my father, on both an intellectual and spiritual plane.

On the side of more earth-bound matters, I spent most of my days in Mavis's garden when we were there. Among the dense covering of weeds and wild flowers, I discovered numerous fruit trees and shrubs. I learned to climb these trees, just as easily as I walked on the ground. Each season, there were succulent fruits to be devoured, and I loved them all. There were red and green plums, pears, miniature and full-sized apples, quinces, black, pink and white mulberries, two persimmon trees, one pomegranate tree and of course, half a dozen fig trees. We also had passion fruit, and some grapes. The only thing that surpassed the culinary delights in Mavis's treasured preserve jars was the fruit that ripened on her trees. Sophie did not preserve anything, but joined me in devouring the fresh fruits. She climbed trees well, but I could climb higher since I weighed less. My family also depleted all of the preserves we inherited from Mavis when she was no longer around to tell us which ones we could eat. However, it was not the same. I wished she were the one who offered her delicacies to us rather than our raiding her shelves after she was gone.

17.

The Cistern

I VIVIDLY REMEMBER THE COOLNESS of Mavis's house even under the blistering Istanbul sun. The house also had a strange, moist smell that was not at all unpleasant. The major reason for both was the great cistern built within its foundation walls. Even on the hottest summer days, when the sun could boil an egg in a few seconds, Mavis's house was naturally cooled to perfection. The way the cistern worked was simple, but for a very young child, mind-boggling. All the eves of the house, which were carved out of hardwood and lined with tin sheets, were directed into a very large metal pipe. The metal pipe toggled between two possible outlets: one went directly into the well in the garden, the other came right through the ceramic-tiled wall of the kitchen at the ground floor level, and into the open mouth of the cistern. Above ground, the cistern looked like a huge potbelly stove made of concrete. The actual cistern, which we could not see, was as large as the kitchen itself, roughly the size of a half tennis court. The mouth was covered with a tight fitting small-holed sieve, then a larger holed sieve, and a largest holed sieve, stacked in that order. Mavis lined the layers of sieves with as many layers of white sheets, specifically used for the purpose. The cloth liners were in the shape of shower caps, snuggly fitting each metal sieve. Since neither air nor water pollution was an issue at the time, the only filtration that was deemed necessary was the filtration of the organic debris from the roof. Since the house towered over the three-tiered garden, there was little organic debris to filter out.

In principle, the first three hard showers of the spring were directed to the outside well. Mavis believed that this process cleaned the air, and washed the roof. When the fourth hard rain came, all the water that the eves could gather were directed into the mouth of the cistern, already dressed in its white sheets. It was an eerie feeling to watch all that water gush into the house and get swallowed by the cavity. It was even eerier to hear the water fall approximately six feet, down to the cistern floor. For me, the feeling was as majestic as my first visit to the Niagara Falls, many years later. However, my second and subsequent visits to the Falls enraged me. The Falls were degraded by tons and tons of chemical waste, bubbling, boiling and tarnishing the otherwise pristine shores. I felt as if someone desecrated my grandmother's immaculate cistern, which provided all our drinking water in my childhood. The water from the cistern was always ice-cold, soft and tasty. It smelled like the clean air after a spring shower.

The cistern also equalized the climate within the house. At the end of September, when the water was almost gone and before the major rains started again, a man (never a woman) was lowered into its depths to scrub the tiled walls and the floor. The man worked for the whole morning, using only a gas lamp to see what he was doing. Mavis's cistern was the heart of the house, almost revered, and kept meticulously clean. It provided all the water needs of the household, and never once ran out. For me, the cistern also provided ample food for imagination. I imagined water-dwelling murderers, electric blue and green dragons, marine-beings with tentacles, all hiding in the cistern, each following meticulously developed plots to get me, or to get members of my family. Sometimes, it was Beatrice's enemies, like the Greeks or the Russians, who were prowling in the depths of the cistern in their diving suits. Sometimes, I imagined huge spiders, bats or other terrifying creatures living in the cistern's depths. I think my active imagination about what the cistern might have hidden is partially responsible for my eternal infatuation with horror films. The other reason is, of course, Beatrice's intriguing stories that were always larger than life.

18.

Mavis's Fruit Trees

A S FAR AS THE FRUIT TREES WERE CONCERNED, figs were my favourite. I almost pity non-travelling Canadians who have never seen a real fig tree in their lives, or get to taste a fresh fig from its branch. The shrivelled and dried figs we find in North American supermarkets are a very poor approximation of this fruit, a delicacy of the gods. Adam's choice of a fig leaf could not have been random; he must have adored the fruit as much as I did. However, I do not envy Adam's choice of underwear. Fig leaves are covered with a coarse surface. When severed, the leaves also bleed a milky substance that causes skin irritation. Adam must have been the first human with an intense itch, way down there, even before the middle-ages epidemic of herpes or gonorrhoea. The milky-white excretion immediately turns into a dirty brown colour and is hard to scrub away. Children who are fig-tree dwellers are distinguishable from other children by the presence of these sticky, brownish markings. They are the shapeless Rorschach tattoos of fig lovers.

As far as I am concerned, people should not be considered adults until they have learned to climb fig trees and consume an ample amount of figs. In Mavis's garden, there were dark purple, dark pink, and light green figs. One particular tree, just across from the front door, was referred to as the camel's foot. Camels have large, fleshy feet. The size of the figs this particular tree produced was close to a good-sized orange. The other trees gave less impressive looking fruit, but their fruit was just as sweet. Fig trees are a far cry from other fruit trees that I have seen. First, they are never straight, but mostly contorted into the oddest shapes. Their smooth, greyish bark covers a multitude of strangely twisting and turning branches. In dusk, fig trees look as if they need an exorcist. The tips of the branches are shaped like the poisonous arrows of some ancient Aboriginal tribe. I often wondered why Steven King never wrote a horror story about a fig tree. In early spring, little fuzzy, poison-green buds appear in this parade of convolutions. The buds eventually turn into the hand-shaped leaves that are rumoured to have covered Adam's private parts. Eve was smart enough not to adorn herself with these scratchy leaves. Better to go naked than get a nasty itch.

In mid- to late spring, pinhead-like growths appear among the rough leaves. The growths are very dark green in colour, and as hard as rocks. In male trees, these growths never make it to the luscious fruit stage. They only grow to the size of hazelnuts, and lack the millions of round seeds regular figs encase. The fruits from male trees are not edible, but are gathered to make one of the most desired jams in the Middle East. They have to be collected, peeled, and repeatedly boiled in water, until the sticky milk drains from the white flesh of the fruit. Women who make the jam suffer from a rash on their hands for weeks, the vengeance of the male figs that never ripen and never get to produce seeds. The prepared male figs are then cooked in heavy syrup. Eventually, they turn into bite size gems reminiscent of emeralds. If the bite-size droplet of this emerald is cut in half, one can see a cavity full of hardly visible filaments that have been gorged by the syrup of the jam. Female trees produce the real fruit. In the womb of the female figs, millions of tiny seeds mature in the sweetest of all fruit pulps. Female figs do not need human intervention to taste like jam; they drip with their own honey.

Mavis's fig trees were all females, with the exception of one in a corner, convoluting towards the neighbour's garden. I was a fig-eating machine in my childhood. I liked them the most when they ripened and burst their outer skin. In perfectly ripe figs, the very bottom of the fruit cracks, oozing out a honey-coloured syrup in the shape of a teardrop. The syrup is sweeter than honey though, and much denser. It oozes and glistens until a fig lover like me relieves the tree from its exquisite burden.

Those who cannot climb fig trees had developed other ways of reaching the fruit. First, they would get a very long, smooth cane, the longer the better. Then, they would slice one end into four sections, by making two crisscrossing cuts. The cuts need to be approximately eight inches long. Then, they would wedge four pieces of twigs among the sliced tips, thus creating four segments bracing the cut end. They make sure that all four segments remain joined at the lower end of the cut by reinforcing the joint. What this process produces is a long stick with a funnel-like opening on one side. From then on, all one had to do was to reach for the fruit with the stick until the fig sank into the funnel-like opening, and twist. The stick-users had one disadvantage though: the largest and the ripest figs did not fit into their primitive gadgets. Trying to enlarge the mouth of the gadget was useless since it always broke the neck where the funnel joined the stick. So, the best figs waited for tree-climbers like me. The figs waited, bearing their oozing syrup, crackling their already cracked skins, and sweetening their flesh loaded with millions of perfectly round seeds. I picked and devoured these marvels of mother nature with complete adoration and childhood greed.

The three mulberry trees Mavis had were my second favourite. They ripened before the figs did, so I naturally moved from one type of beloved fruit to another. The black one was a colossal tree, which not only fed my family and myself, but also satiated a whole lot of neighbourhood children. These children systematically raided its outstretched branches, which transcended the boundaries of Mavis's garden. We did not mind sharing the abundance, as long as the neighbourhood children did not break off the branches. Even when I was very young, I was a self-appointed protector of nature. I considered hurting trees or wildlife sacrilegious, with the exception of snails. After rain showers, I collected snails by the bucket, from the crevices of the stone walls that framed Mavis's garden. Then, I delivered them to my father's always greedy chickens. Before their death by pecking, the bucketful of snails profusely slimed and glided over one another's outstretched flesh. They shimmered like oily pasta with mushrooms that has suddenly come alive. Hundreds of translucent antenna stretched and retracted, the bulbous eyes at each end trying to make sense of their predicament. My protection of the nature did not extend to these creatures since they devoured the red and white tulips I loved.

The white and the purplish pink mulberry trees were small, and provided only a small yield. So, I spent most of my culinary energy on the black one. The ritual surrounding the mulberries was as follows: I would climb an eight-foot ladder to bypass the huge trunk that was devoid of branches. Then, it was a quick step to the system of branches that were heavily laden with the black fruit. The berries painted my fingers, nails, lips and especially my tongue a dark purple colour. The purple eventually turned into a dark grey, moody like storm clouds or an aging bruise. Repeated washings somewhat helped, but the bruise colour never left my skin for as long as the mulberries were in season. Sophie was also a good tree climber. She shared my enthusiasm for raiding the trees for their fruits. At the peak of the mulberry season, she would invite friends to join in a process called "mulberry shaking." Four people would each hold a corner of a clean sheet, while a fifth climbed the tree and shook the branches. The terrestrial quartet would follow the arboreal member from above, as the tree-climber changed her location amongst the branches. I say "her" since only Sophie and I climbed trees. The rest of my family always remained firmly planted on the ground. So, as we shook the branches we were on, mulberries and an occasional earwig would shower onto the stretched-out sheet, yielding bushels of clean, juicy harvest. Stray mulberries would bomb the volunteers holding on to the corners of the sheet, which was a slight occupational hazard. At the end, the terrestrial quartet looked like "purple-people-eaters," a song that became wildly famous during my early teens.

Agnes never had the courage to climb trees. The best she could do was to climb halfway up the ladder, and beg Sophie or me for a few pieces of ripe fruit. Her next best option was to stay on the ground, and collect the ones that fell as Sophie and I moved among the branches, pursuing our own delights. The trouble was that Agnes had to compete with the chickens for the fallen goods, a competition the chickens often won. There were many more of them, and they were more agile than Agnes. To see her chasing the two-legged creatures, and in turn, getting chased by them was one of my childhood delights. As I balanced myself among the lush branches and delighted in eating the fruit bursting with flavour, I felt some power over my sister. Most other times, Agnes had power over me and I did not win contests with her as often as the chickens did. If she didn't win one of our eternal arguments, Sophie stepped in and solved the quarrels in her favour. In our household, entrenched inequalities were called a lesson in respecting one's elders.

So, Sophie's naked biases had a cultural cloak to hide behind. As it turned out, Agnes did not learn how to respect other people's ideas and wishes, and when the years eroded Sophie physically and mentally, Agnes extended her full power over our mother. Eventually, the mother and favourite daughter pair got locked into a reversed child-parent relationship, each hating the other's role, each hating the role she found herself to play. The sad truth is that the mother-daughter conflict does not vanish through time; it just takes on an ironic twist when the mother turns into the child. Sophie treated Beatrice badly, knowingly or unknowingly she infantilized her, and deprived her from making decisions on her own behalf. In turn, Agnes became the best ally but the worst nightmare of Sophie's declining years. She did provide Sophie with food, clothing and medical care. On the other hand, she treated her like a five-year-old child. More than once, I heard Agnes shouting at Sophie: "You are not going to think for yourself, I am going to think for you!" I would see tears shimmering at the corners of Sophie's eyes, but she did not protest her infantilization. At the time, she was experiencing a decline in her mental capabilities, but not to the degree that she had to accept unquestioningly the control Agnes was holding her under. Yet, she no longer had the power to challenge Agnes, instead she became even more dependent. Why is it that each generation loves and hurts, and hurts and loves?

Of course, none of these questions occurred to me when I was still a child. I simply took delight in the semi-dwarf pear trees, starting on the fruit when they were as hard as rocks. I don't think Mavis's pears ever reached full maturity when I was around. The kinds of apples and the quinces Mavis had fared a little better, since they were less juicy and more conducive for cooking than raw consumption. I still remember taking a few bites off each, just to make sure that they were as inedible as I remembered them to be. I even took small bites off fruit without bothering to pick them. In the years we lived in Mavis's house, there were many violated fruit, still hanging on their stems, like broken ornaments on a Christmas tree. The trees eventually rejected their compromised offspring. They came tumbling down to be consumed by our voracious chickens that devoured everything in sight. In their free time, which they seemed to have a lot of, they even scratched the bare ground and pecked at stones and pebbles.

The two roosters we had also pecked at one another, as they fought over their shared harem, until my father ordered the loser to be killed and boiled for supper. My father had no pity for losers.

The other fruit trees in Mavis's garden also received my undivided attention, and my undivided appetite. I made natural earrings out of the flowers of the pomegranate tree. Pomegranate flowers are unique. Brilliant, orange-tinged, shiny petals burst out of a darker, leathery jacket that is fire engine red. Like golden tassels, yellow stamens complete the ball of fire. As a child, I wasn't that crazy about the final fruit, since the stony seeds of the pomegranate did not make it suitable for mass consumption. Only half a century later, a result of their antioxidant content, did pomegranates become highly desirable fruits. In my childhood, they were just pretty fruit, which required chewing and spitting.

The two persimmon trees were even less desirable in my ranking of the fruit desirability. The fruit first appeared as a small, green acorn in the midst of a buttercup shaped dark brown holder. The acorns eventually grew into the soft bulb of the fruit, and took on a deeper orange colour resembling the colours of the sunset. In this transformation, I never knew when the fruit was at its best. When the orange was lighter in colour, the flesh would be hard and relatively tasteless. It would also leave a strange, tingling sensation in one's mouth, as if someone washed one's mouth with soap. Unripe persimmons are like freezing wearing off after heavy-duty dental work. When persimmons get too ripe, however, they turn into shiny orange sacs filled with sweet mucus. They would drop from the tree, like small bombs, and cover the yard with a slimy blanket. Pigeons, chickens, bees, wasps and flies were the ones who enjoyed this feast. Now, when I see persimmons, heavily oiled and individually wrapped, lounging decadently in their cartons for North American consumers, I can't help but remember the mounds of oozy, unwelcome decay in Mavis's garden. Of all the fruit trees I raided as a child, persimmons were the ones that repeatedly failed to tempt me.

19.

My Father's Chickens

AFTER WE MOVED INTO MAVIS'S HOME, my father came up with the brilliant idea of raising purebred chickens. My father was always the idea man, but his ideas often required hard labour someone else had to do. In this case, we had a man as hired help who did the dirty work of the garden. When he was not around, it was either Sophie or me that did the heavy lifting. Agnes, like my father, never lifted a finger. So, to bring my father's brilliant idea into practice, we got pure white chickens, and reddish brown ones from a supplier. The white ones were for producing eggs. They had slender, muscular, aerodynamic bodies, canary yellow feet, and tall, bright red combs. The combs on the rooster would stand up, like a fleshy Mohawk, but the more delicate combs of the hens would tilt to a side, like a French twist. The reddish brown chickens were fat, puffy, and clumsy, not egg layers but good for eating. They had dirty red combs and deep voices. They ate and shit at an alarming speed.

Upon my father's specific instructions, we let the chickens roam around in the three tiers of the garden during the day. They quickly turned the wild jungle of growth in Mavis's garden into a barren landscape. The only portion of the garden that escaped their razor-sharp beaks was the flowerbed on the upper tier, and the patch of red and white tulips along the path to the outside gate. Our chickens were like lawnmowers, they devoured everything: fallen fruit, the flies on the fallen fruit, and a million and a half kinds of bugs that lived in the crevices of the stone walls. My father wanted to grow show-quality chickens, in a land where centuries of inbreeding had resulted in pretty ugly looking creatures that hardly weighed a couple of pounds at full growth. Indeed, our chickens became the pride of my father, with their shiny feathers, crazy combs, and bright yellow legs that were as thick as good-size tree branches. They did not win any prizes; there were no prizes to be won by anyone's chickens in my childhood. My father's ideas never translated into any kind of a business either, but remained as one of his hands-off hobbies. Yet, our chickens provided plenty of aromatic eggs. We also ate the one's which did not satisfy my father's visual or moral expectations. The docile roosters got eaten. For after-war children like us, a high-protein diet was like winning the lottery. This was long before I learned about animal rights, and stopped eating all land animals, small or large. I have Negrisse to thank for—or blame—for this transformation.

My father was an experimenter. The diets he experimented with turned our chickens into small vultures. Of course, he himself did not touch the chickens he was only the "brains" of the project. He was a vegetarian, so he did not consume any of the two-legged creatures. The hired help as well as Sophie put in the necessary labour to keep up with the chickens, albeit reluctantly. I also put in a lot of work, but for me the work was pleasure. I adored my father, and shared his enthusiasm. My father asked us to grind eggshells, and combine the resulting meal with the chicken feed, which we also prepared. The feed consisted of scraps from the neighbourhood butcher, leftovers from our daily meals, grains from Beatrice's farm, surplus fish from the fishing boats, and earthworms and snails I collected after a hard rain. The latter two, Agnes and I handpicked in bucketfuls. At the time, we heard rumours that French people considered these slimy nuggets of flesh a delicacy, something we could not even conceptualize. Our own snails were either pecked to death or went right into the crusher to fatten up the chickens.

Due to my father's idiosyncratic concoctions, coupled with the steady carpet of over-ripe fruit on the ground, our chickens grew to unheard of sizes. The white ones laid eggs every day, some more than once a day. It became common for us to harvest eggs with double yolks. Occasionally, I remember eggs with triple yolks. Even the red chickens, which were mainly kept for their meat, started laying eggs, while their flesh became tough and less than desirable. Our chickens were much too fat, much too muscular, and started smelling too much like the concoctions they devoured. They became unruly, and roamed around like a street gang. They kept watch over the long incline that connected the outside gate with the house. They attacked sales people like the milkman who tried to come to our door. Sophie had to accompany our guests from and to the garden gate so that they would be safe from our bandit roosters. They also attacked me going to and coming back from school. I started carrying a long stick to shoo them off as best I could. By that time, we had almost stopped eating chickens. Sophie refused to buy dressed ones from the butcher shop when we already had so many at home, but we no longer enjoyed eating the ones we had. Moreover, considering the size and the ferocity they reached, catching and killing them would have required a specialized butcher. The hired hand refused to carry out such a dangerous task, and although Sophie complained, no one really blamed him.

Thus, my father's experimental chickens became permanent fixtures of our yard, getting fatter and more languid by each passing day. They pulled out every single blade of grass as soon as it appeared. I think, the roosters stopped having sex with the hens, so the hens no longer produced baby chickens. It seems my father's dietary concoctions disrupted the harem life of the roosters. I did not know that chickens had a sex life then. Even inquiring minds like mine were kept in total darkness about sexuality, whether it concerned chickens or humans. So, eventually our chickens lived as fat and quite aggressive pets, and eventually died of old age.

After Mavis's home, when we moved to one of the resort towns of the Black Sea, I had the exceptional pleasure of creating my own zoo of all kinds of creepy-crawly creatures. To her credit, Sophie let me keep all kinds of small creatures in my bedroom, as long as they were prevented from venturing outside of my door. I had silkworms, caterpillars, grasshoppers, frogs, salamanders, and once, even a miniature snake. Some were confined to boxes and jars; others walked, hopped, and crept at will. I collected each and every one of them from our garden, which sloped into the beach. We did not have the luxury of buying our pets. I was also allowed to have an indoor/outdoor cat with the condition that it never soiled Sophie's house. His name was Bambo, and he was truly magnificent. My love for cats began with Bambo, and I have had a lifetime pleasure keeping cats for company.

My love for cats was unconditional. They did not get scolded when they broke a vase, or soiled my carpet, or scratched my furniture.

The cats in my childhood had to, however, suffer consequences if they did not meet Sophie's rigid expectations. For example, if she caught them doing something they were not supposed to (i.e., if they relieved themselves on Sophie's carpets), they went right back to the vicinity of the butcher shop they were originally retrieved from. Don't get me wrong, butchers did not kill cats, and Turks never eat the flesh of meat-eating animals (with the exception of fish). But, the neighbourhood butcher shops attracted a huge number of street cats, and the butchers always fed them with scraps of meat left over from their daily sales. So, street cats were born, lived, mated, and often died close to one or another butcher shop. When women made their weekly meat purchases, they often walked through a crowd of cats. Some picked the best-looking kittens to bring to their homes. So, amongst such crowds came our various pet cats.

20.

The Disease Without a Name

SOPHIE HAD A VERY LIGHT, almost milky complexion, a highly desirable characteristic among Mediterranean peoples with their sun-drenched skin. She had black eyes, where the pupil and the iris were almost indistinguishable. Sophie was a very beautiful woman, until she came down with the skin disease without a name.

The skin disease followed Agnes's marriage to her heartthrob, Lynford, a man my mother did not approve of. Frankly, I think Sophie would have had difficulty in finding any candidate on this world appropriate for her precious daughter, Agnes. Unfortunately, the Rockefellers or the Kennedys were not lining up at our doorstep to ask for Agnes's hand. Sophie's rejection of Lynford was *not* because he was a "bad" person. He just did not hold a graduate university degree, whereas Agnes did. Sophie, like most of my family members at the time, was an intellectual elitist and had an obsession about higher education. My father had also sacrificed himself by living most of his adult years away from his beloved family, so that my sister and I could attend the best private school in Istanbul. Without hesitation, my parents had paid the backbreaking tuition fees for the two of us to pursue higher education. Maybe, an incongruity between religion and ethnicity would not have been as hard to take for them as the discrepancy in educational attainment. So, Sophie openly complained about, and showed resentment toward, the fact that Agnes was marrying "a high-school graduate." Sophie used the term "high-school graduate" pejoratively, and saw Lynford as a pariah.

Sophie's stubborn reaction and blatant rejection of Agnes's marital choice was funny at first, since her logic was so convoluted. However, all of us understood its corrosive implications, once we realized that my mother's prejudice was much more than a transient reaction. Moreover, the magnitude of Sophie's negative feelings and disappointments unleashed a psychosomatic ailment that almost took her life and permanently altered our lives. Sadly, Sophie openly held Agnes morally responsible for her suffering. And, in turn, Agnes never forgave her for reacting to Lynford the way she did. The fragile mother-daughter relationships that generally afflict my family reached new heights of dysfunctionality with my mother's serious illness.

Ironically, Sophie's obsession about higher education partially stems from the fact that she herself had none. She was bright, probably much too bright for her own good, and certainly much too bright for a woman confined in the patriarchal society of her time. As she put it, she was "given away" (married) at the age of sixteen, and had given birth to Agnes at seventeen. There was no time for schooling, and not too many opportunities for an extended formal education for women of her generation who grew up in a society ravaged by numerous wars. Besides, Sophie knew my father for many years and was quite fond of him, so her marriage was not necessarily an "arranged marriage." It was just that she was spoiled rotten as an only child and she had a natural inclination to complain about most things. Her relatively affluent family, especially before her father was captured and became a much-abused POW, had pampered Sophie. Thanks to Beatrice's substantial assets, and her willingness to sacrifice all for her husband's safety, my grandfather was eventually released. But the family had lost most of their fortune. So, when Sophie expressed interest in a higher education, her parents may have cajoled her towards a stable marriage. My father happened to be an eligible candidate, so they were married. Thus, Sophie's craving for a university education was never fulfilled, but appeared in full force as a prerequisite for her daughters, and of course, her sons-in-law. For Sophie, her own creativity, keen intelligence, and perfectionism meant nothing without a piece of paper to affirm it. So, she did everything in her power to live her educational dreams through Agnes's and my own achievements at school. She saved, sold property, and did without many necessities in her life to keep the two of us at the most expensive, and most prestigious American school in Istanbul. At our school, the curriculum was in English, and the teachers were imported, which most people could ill afford. Sophie basked in our reflected glory, and she thus harboured many stringent requirements for men who would marry us.

Looking back on those years, it now occurs to me now that Sophie's obsession about higher education was not as an end in itself. Higher education was a means to an end. She did not necessarily dream about either Agnes or I becoming independent career women. The fact that we both were was incidental. She wanted us to have the best education possible so that we could "catch" best of all possible husbands, and live happily after. Sophie had naïve, almost childish expectations about happy marriages, and erroneously equated them with education (and wealth). Strangely—but not inexplicably—I also developed an obsession about Negrisse's formal education many years later. We quarrel with our mothers, but whether we like it or not, we make similar mistakes. In my case, my reasoning was different. I wanted Negrisse to be an independent woman, a self-sufficient woman. I never wanted her to face the economic difficulties I faced when I became a single parent. I did not want her to be dependent on a husband's (any husband's) paycheque. To her credit, she did become independent and self-sufficient, but she also learned to resent me for my intellectual elitism.

A few other short-lived and totally platonic attachments aside, Agnes did fall in love with Lynford. He was good-looking, extremely bright, multilingual, funny and generous. The two first met at a bank where they had part-time jobs. Years later, I also held a job in the same bank when Agnes's own position had become permanent and marginally important.

When Sophie found out about Agnes's relationship with Lynford from a friend who spotted them holding hands, she hit the roof. Sophie turned into Colombo, chasing the two of them around, and ferreting them out while they were holding hands walking over the Atatürk Bridge, or in the public ferry. Sophie engaged my father in this "preservation of family-name" business. The two of them arranged a meeting with Lynford's parents to put an end to the relationship. But, Sophie's strategy to break-up my sister's infatuation with Lynford backfired. Rather than breaking up under Sophie's pestering, they chose to get married instead. The funny thing was that once the marriage decision was taken, my father switched sides. He developed and showed a real liking for his new son-in-law. They played chess together, talked about politics, and drank *raki* (our national drink) until the late hours. I too, was very fond of my brother-in-law, who treated me like his own little sister. Lynford turned into the brother I always wished I had. So, Sophie found herself alone, burning up with her festering disillusion and disappointment.

Sophie's implosion was quick and complete. The disease without a name started like a rash, like the ones people with sun allergies get. In a couple of months, however, the blistering spots covered all of her body and face. The itch and the burning were visibly unbearable, but not the worst of the symptoms. Sophie also swelled up like a balloon. The swelling, especially in her face and neck, made her look fat and bloated. In reality, she was losing weight. Some days, she couldn't see through her eyes, when the swelling shut down even her pupils. On other days, she could not eat any food, the swelling having closed her oesophagus. The rash on her body multiplied and enlarged, and shone like an oil spill on a white beach. The rash had a mind of its own, and looked as though it was churning in front of our eyes, like moody clouds before a hail storm.

At first, neither my father nor the family doctor understood the seriousness of Sophie's illness. They hypothesized about the kinds of food that may have disagreed with her system. The expectation was that the rash would go away soon, hopefully as quickly as it had descended. It didn't. And the fast pace of the progression of the disease took everyone by surprise.

Sophie was referred to a hospital, where the gravity of her condition became apparent. The interns at the hospital who carried out the initial and routine treatment of in-coming patients were totally baffled. They ran out of the room to call their supervisors. The supervisors contacted the highest rungs of hospital care and administration. Sophie suddenly turned into a famous guinea pig. The doctors tested liquids, solids, powders that contained cobalt, cortisone, penicillin and a million other possible treatments. Ambulances ricocheted Sophie from one hospital to the next, for tests, biopsies, and skin grafts. With each touch, with each needle, with each scalpel, her diseased skin was further tortured.

Eventually, renowned professors of medicine from neighbouring countries were invited to study and write papers on my mother's case. The sheer number of photographs that were taken of her body and face could have put Marilyn Monroe to shame. I do not know how many medical dissertations were eventually published about my mother's unique illness, and how many aspiring health professionals received huge research grants. What I do know, is that despite all medical efforts, Sophie swelled up more, the rash went deeper and started eating up her flesh. Large sores appeared on all parts of her body, and she began to stick to her clothes and bed sheets. In the mornings, we literally had to scrape her off, despite her pain, in order to change the sheets. The mother that I knew who was a bundle of energy was soon reduced to a blob on a wheelchair. Her disease attacked her muscles and caused muscle deterioration. Helplessly, I watched my mother burn like a candle, from both ends.

During all these tragic months, which were in their way to turning into years, my recollection of Agnes is fuzzy. She was newly married, recently promoted in her bank job, and she and Lynford had a new place to furnish and take care of. Probably, Agnes was totally exhausted. To their credit, she and Lynford frequently visited my mother after their regular work day. To their credit, she and Lynford supervised my mother's transfers from one hospital to another, as many times as it was necessary. I also remember the two of them trying to cheer up my father, who preferred to stay home and sulk. But, for my mother's day-by-day needs, like changing her gown, changing the sheets, feeding her small quantities of water or juice, waiting until she had the courage to swallow, was left to me. Sophie was in so much pain that she allowed no nurse or caregiver to touch her, only me.

The nameless disease took on an even more foreboding tenure, in its second year. The general swelling remained, but in addition, temporary swellings developed just like a tornado touchdown. One minute, Sophie would be lying flat on her back, which was the way she now spent her days, and the next minute, a large balloon appeared under her arm or in her neck or between her legs. The timing or the location of the balloons was unpredictable, so was the timing of their disappearance. Doctors, who were desperately trying to help her, found themselves miserably impotent against the ravaging disease. Even the specialist lost hope. They warned us that if one of these impromptu swellings hit her throat, or her lungs, there would be nothing they could do. Whatever unearthly churning we could see from outside was also tormenting her interiors. Within two years of the start of her troubles, Sophie turned into a monster people were afraid to look at. Like someone suffering from leprosy, she lost chunks of flesh.

It was during the height of her disease that I grew the closest to my mother. At the time, I had just started attending the University of Istanbul. At the end of my classes, I always rushed to the hospital to visit her. I always found a way to be with her, despite the fact that they shifted her from one hospital to the next. I brought with me peeled and pureed fruits, freshly squeezed juices and soft puddings. By then, she was not able to consume any solid food, and she despised the hospital soups, for good reason. But our growing closeness extended to a deeper level than my edible offerings. It involved her diseased flesh, which gave her excruciating pain. She allowed no one but me to actually see her unsightly sores or touch her body. Like Beatrice, Sophie was a proud woman. She did not want to people to view her with disgust, then turn their heads. Besides, even the gentlest touch brought her unbearable pain. She said that I was the only one who did not hurt her as much.

So, I became her constant companion before and after school. I also became her private caregiver, although she was in residence in some of the best hospitals in Istanbul. Even before I went to school, I would help the hospital personnel change her sheets. Then came the most difficult part: spreading the medicated balm her doctors concocted all over her face and body. The balm came in a small bucket. The smell and the texture of the balms changed occasionally, since the doctors were trying different things. These bucketfuls of balm did not cure Sophie's ailment. No one knew how to cure her. Yet, the balm did prevent her flesh from falling off more than it did. So, I religiously spread the medicated balm every morning, trying my best to let only the balm touch her body rather than the weight of my fingers. The process sometimes took an hour, and had to double as a bath. The doctors never allowed me to wash Sophie with water since she went into convulsions if water touched any part of her skin. The effect of water on her inflammations was similar to sprinkling holy water on an unholy being, like we see in horror movies. The droplets sizzled and burned. Then, I dressed Sophie in a soft cotton gown, which immediately soaked up some of the oils from the balm and clung to her flesh. On my after-school visits, I took the soiled gown home, to be washed, rinsed, and rinsed again, then dried for the next visit. We did not have a clothes dryer at the time, so I had to depend on the cooperation of the sun.

Sophie's illness roughly coincided with my father's retirement. He no longer had to go out of town repeatedly, like he did throughout his military service. Suddenly finding himself in the role of a single parent, since I was still living at home, he learned to cook for the first time in his life. Neither he nor I did much cleaning; we were both exhausted with worry and our other respective responsibilities. During the worst period of Sophie's illness, which was in its third year, my father rarely went to visit her. I am sure this deeply hurt Sophie. I think his avoidance of visiting my mother was not because of a lack of care. On the contrary, I think my father avoided visiting Sophie precisely because he cared too much. I think, he was afraid of breaking down in front of her, and in front of me. I think he was afraid of getting shattered, and not being able to pull it all together again. His entrenched and internalized military self-image was not able to tolerate such a public show of weakness. Instead, he opted for projecting a granite-like exterior, a solitary mountain, strong and ominous. Sensing his well-disguised sensitivities, I tiptoed around my father as gently as I tiptoed around my sick mother. I hoped and prayed that this ordeal, this trial by fire for my father and I, and trial by flesh for Sophie, would end soon. I feared that none of us would be able to muster the necessary strength to survive much longer.

To his credit, my father did everything in his power to enable me to spend long hours with my mother, every day. He gave me money to buy her flowers. He sent her letters and poems that he wrote for her during sleepless nights when he sat at our balcony, waiting for the sun to rise. I read my father's letters to my mother, which were full of kind, encouraging, and loving words. She preferred to save the poems for later, hoping that she would be able to read them herself. I do not know what she did with them, since she could hardly move, but I respected her privacy. I respected *their* privacy. During this entire conundrum, I never saw tears in my father's eyes, but I am sure he shed them when I was not around. My father loved my mother much too much to see her suffer the way she did. Yet, I wish he had openly shared his own suffering with me. Instead, each of us suffered in different ways, in our lonely emotional silos. He was also, I believed, much too hard on himself, since he suffered a fatal heart attack shortly after my mother's miraculous recovery.

Sophie's illness, which confined her to one or another hospital over a three-year period, did two things for me. One, I grew up and matured well beyond my chronological age, although I was still a teenager. Secondly, I bypassed the period when teenage daughters are allowed to feel angry, and try to resolve their growing-up conflicts with their mothers. This important period when the teenage daughter learns to separate herself from her mother did not happen to me. In a way, and with no fault of anyone in particular, I was catapulted into the role of an adult, without sorting out any of my own growing pains. When I felt the urge to dissociate myself from Sophie to find my own self, when I felt the need to challenge some of my mother's beliefs and convictions in order to determine my own comfort zone, my mother was too sick, too weak, too dependent on me and too lonely to be challenged. Exactly when I was ready to detach myself from Sophie, I found myself more and more attached to her.

My mother and I talked a lot in those days when she was confined to a bed. We talked more than ever before, and more than ever since. Although she never told me in so many words, I sensed that she was afraid of dying. I also sensed her possibly irrational fear that my father would remarry right after her death. She wondered what would happen to me. In the grips of a disease that was devouring her flesh, she was helpless, insecure, and very lonely. Obviously, my father's physical absence, despite his letters and poetry, was fuelling her fears and insecurities. She was afraid of losing my father's love, and she was afraid for me. In a way, her illness was like a mirror, reflecting the complexity and the depth of her dark and sad emotions, which lay beneath the surface. I felt great pity for Sophie. My heart hurt as I saw her multiple vulnerabilities. Therefore, my teenage conflicts with my mother were further delayed.

The exceptional closeness that Sophie and I developed during her illness incrementally dissolved after she got well. Our conflicts came up with surprising force, possibly because they were suppressed for the duration of her illness. What also contributed to the growing distance between my mother and myself was my father's death shortly after Sophie's recovery. Sophie exchanged her dependence on me and on my father over her illness for her newfound subordination to Agnes. After my father's death and her own mortal struggle with her illness, my mother collapsed in on herself, and regressed into a child. She relinquished all her power to Agnes, and symbolically left me without a mother. In a way, I lost not one, but both of my parents.

In reality, Sophie did not die. She was alive and well for my wedding to Randall many years later. Her cure was miraculous, and even spooky. The miracle took place when the last hospital that was looking after her ran out of cures, options, alternatives and hope. They had tried everything that any doctor or specialist could think of, and failed. So, under the auspices of the approaching religious holiday, they sent her home in an ambulance. They said it would be good for her morale, but I think the real reason was they gave up on her. They wanted her bed back to accommodate a different patient they could actually help.

Sophie came home, with a few extra buckets of ointment, disturbingly swollen and literally emaciated. Even after the religious holidays were over, the doctors were reluctant to readmit her. She did not want to go back to the hospital anyway. I think, by that time, she was ready to die at her home. So, neither her morale, nor her condition improved one bit. I still made numerous trips to the hospital to replenish her buckets with medicated creams. Each morning, I still tried my best to spread the cream on her body from head to toe. Her diseased flesh and the cream mingled together somehow, and tried to resemble a human shape. Each evening, I washed her used gown, and rinsed, and rinsed and rinsed.

It was during such a time of despair that one of my father's ex-soldiers showed up at our door to pay his respects to my father. My father was always protective of the conscripted soldiers under his service. He went out of his way to protect and preserve their rights. He made sure that they were given plenty of food, had appropriate clothes to wear, and learnt how to read and write during their military service. His care was noteworthy, since at the time, none of those services were standardized. He also helped them find reasonable jobs after they were discharged. In a society built on loyalty and honour, my father's good deeds were appreciated and never forgotten by his subordinates. So, it was not unusual that one or two showed up at our door from time to time to show their respect.

The young man who showed up at that time was from a particularly deprived background. His civilian clothes were washed for the holidays, but much too big for him. They were faded and patched at different spots. He did not keep eye contact with any one of us, and spoke in a barely audible voice while staring at the floor. He did not allow himself to sit in the presence of my father, and chose to stand the whole time, with folded hands. He spoke with a vocabulary consisting of a few dozen words, all revolving around his respect, loyalty, and gratitude to my father. He was obviously very poor, simple, but genuine and totally devoted. He even brought with him a box of candy, which must have cost him a week's worth of groceries, and eventually, a few new patches on his worn-out clothes.

My father's devotee, who arrived at our house so unexpectedly, muttered a few words of sympathy and grief from his limited vocabulary when he saw the condition my mother was in. Having seen her once or twice during her days of perfect health, the young ex-soldier was in awe at the startling change. What was also incredible was his insistence that he had seen the same disease before. He claimed that his own mother, in his remote village, had suffered from exactly the same disease, which almost claimed her life. He was so animated and so persistent in his proclaimed knowledge of the disease that my father could not help himself but laugh. Even Sophie found a place in her swollen mouth to smile at the ex-soldier's enthusiasm. We were from a yet-to-develop country, but my family belonged to the enlightened class where reverence to "science" was entrenched. So, if the whole medical community had tried their best but failed to help my mother, who was this wretchedly poor man to claim that he had knowledge about my mother's ailment? Thus, without further ado, my father thanked him for the candies he brought, showed his appreciation for his loyalty, and showed him the way out as quickly as possible. But before our loyal visitor left, he announced the elusive "cure." He advised my mother, whom he addressed as *abla* (older sister), to dissolve a cube of "blue-rinse," commonly used to rinse clothing, in warm water and drink it for a month. He advised occasional follow-up with the same remedy thereafter. We all said thank you, but immediately dismissed him as a fool.

Meanwhile, Sophie's desperation was total, and her health was getting worse each passing day. Her discharge from the last hospital obviously did no good, except to kill the last glimmer of hope she might have had. Every morning, I was surprised to see her still alive. Every morning, she even surprised herself for having clung to her suffering for yet another day. Those were the doomed conditions under which she decided to give the blue-rinse a try. She was at the end of her rope and she had nothing else to lose. None of us had the heart to tell her that her decision was ridiculous.

So, I bought a fresh box of blue-rinse, which looked like cubed sugar, only cobalt blue. It cost only a few pennies. I dissolved the cubes, one a day, in warm water, and served the scary looking blue liquid to Sophie, every morning before breakfast. At first, the only difference was the awful taste in her mouth, and the increased amount of gas in her digestive system. She said drinking the stuff was comparable to drinking water from a dirty toilet. Otherwise, there was no visible change in her appearance. She still stuck to the sheets; she still ballooned on the most unexpected occasions and in the most unlikely of places. Yet, I had the sense that her excruciating pain seemed to subside a little. Occasionally, she even asked me to comb her hair, or whatever patches were left of it. Yet, just as our young visitor had promised, at the end of the month, her swelling was starting to come down. Her open sores were also showing some marginal improvement. For the first time in the last three years, I allowed myself to believe that my mother was going to make it.

To this day, I believe that the blue-rinse cured Sophie! Maybe her illness was just psychosomatic, but who cares. The truth is that, she almost died, but came back. Of course, the deep scars from the numerous biopsies, and the more numerous scars from her once ravaged flesh remained. Neither did her skin ever regain her milky white complexion, or peeled-egg texture. The parts of her body that had served as an arena to the most atrocious battles with her disease remained wrinkled, shrivelled, and scaled like a reptile. But, Sophie did survive, and she did regain her mobility. After exactly three years of letting nothing but cream touch her skin, she even started taking full baths without being scalded by the water. The curse was over.

The top medical people in Istanbul hospitals and their foreign colleagues, who had flown in and out to see the progression of

AYSAN SEV'ER

Sophie's disease, were stunned. After the initial shock of witnessing
the miraculous recovery, they tried their best to appear in control.
Some even had the audacity to claim that they were the ones who
spearheaded the successful treatment by their ointments. The only
logical conclusion they could draw was that the cure must have been
a delayed reaction to their own medical efforts. Some said that my
mother was already on her way to recovery when they released her
from the hospital, which was totally false. None of the medical doctors we talked to believed us when we tried to explain what really
happened. A few shunned us for the rest of their medical careers,
just like we had initially dismissed my father's devotee's ideas. So,
Agnes took it upon herself to send the brand of the blue-rinse my
mother drank to a private medical laboratory, and paid for the tests.
They found minute traces of cobalt in the rinse, which is generally
considered toxic, but not much else. My mother's cure was very
spooky, and remains without explanation, scientific or otherwise.
What is undisputable is that, the tribulations we went through
changed all our lives.

21.

Randall

SHORTLY AFTER MY FATHER'S DEATH, Agnes developed a strategy to see an end to my relationship with Aron. Aron was my boyfriend for the last four years. He was exceptionally bright, and he was from a highly accomplished and relatively affluent family. I was in love with him, and most certainly, my feelings were not one-sided. We were not lovers, at least not in the technical sense, but we were very much in love. However, Agnes decided that I should stop seeing him, and convinced Sophie that barring me from seeing him was the right thing to do, given the fact that I was a young woman who had just lost her father. Agnes claimed that my dating Aron was going to taint the good name of our family. So, Agnes relentlessly worked on Sophie's fears about "what would others think." Soon, there were curfews that did not allow any breathing space for me, other than my trips to school and back. Although Aron tolerated the tightening grip on my life for a while, he was not Job. Soon, we officially parted, since I was never allowed to be a part of our former social life. If I had lived in a society other than the Turkey of my youth, I would have left my home and established my own independence. But I was in Turkey, and respectable young women did not leave their families before formal marriage. I do not know what would have happened between Aron and I, if Agnes and Sophie had not taken it upon themselves to tear our relationship apart. Probably, I would have married him, and possibly, we would have been divorced by now. But, that would have been due to my own choice, rather than due to Agnes's dictatorship.

Shortly after my forced break-up, Agnes introduced me to her friend from the university: Randall. The sad truth is that I had to forfeit the love of my teenage years to escape Agnes's crushing control, and

Randall just happened to be there. Originally, Randall was from a small agricultural town. He was the older of two shadowy brothers. I say shadowy, because they were very quiet people. To notice their presence on any occasion, one had to literally come face-to face with them, even if they had been in the same room for a long time. Randall had a crowded ancestral tree of relatives. Aunts and uncles and their respective offspring increased their numbers geometrically, by annual production of more children. I did not bother to learn the names of most new arrivals, since I could never keep up with the influx. Most of these people were kind, hard-working and generous, but poorly educated peasants. The only two who had broken the cycle of manual farmland work and managed to rise above the crowd were Randall and his brother. Their parents, despite their own limited income and Spartan living conditions, had found the resolve to send their two sons to Istanbul, to be educated at two of the best universities the city had to offer. University education in Turkey was free at the time, but the entrance requirements were exceptionally tough. Since then, capitalism has also seeped into the educational system of Turkey, and hundreds of so-called private universities have cropped up. Now, all one has to have to get accepted is an eye on top of one's head, and another eye somewhere above the belt, and a whole pile of cash. No brain is required.

It seems Randall and his brother had done their best to secure a much-coveted slot in higher education, at a time when higher education was hard to obtain. Their mother had rented a bachelor's apartment for the boys to live in. Their mother made by-monthly trips from their village, to cook for them, to wash their clothes, and to make sure they were not fooling around and neglecting their studies. The brothers worked hard, got acceptable grades in all their courses, and the parents had toiled and troubled to buy their books, and to keep clothes on their backs.

At first, I interpreted Randall's parents' dogged commitment to push their sons out of lifelong rural life as a sign of altruism. Many years later, when I asked my mother-in-law what made her sacrifice so much for the education of her sons, her answer was simple and practical and had nothing to do with altruism. She said, "So they will look after me in my old age." So, as in other parts of the world where old-age security programs are woefully lacking, the parent-son relationships were mostly, and blatantly material-based. Parents did their best to raise their sons well, so that the sons would reciprocate after they established themselves. Traditional families like these rarely invested so much in their daughters, since daughters were considered as "someone else's property." What is ironic is that, usually, it is the daughters who eventually take care of their aging parents, not the sons. Randall's parents had no daughters. It was my side of the family that was blessed—or cursed?—with generations of female offspring.

As it turned out, Randall and Agnes had met in one of their university courses, and had become good friends. Agnes was good at sniffing out who might be of value to her, and Randall was very good at taking notes. He knew shorthand, which was the equivalent of owning a laptop computer at a time when laptops did not exist. Randall had also tutored Agnes in preparation for the tough final exam in accounting. Ironically, Agnes passed and Randall failed that particular exam. Agnes appreciated selfless giving in others, since she was not much of a selfless giver herself.

I first met Randall at my sister's house. By that time, Agnes was happily married, and both Randall and Agnes were gainfully employed, which was the first requirement of eligibility for a prospective husband. Randall always brought carnations, five of them, when he was invited for dinner. He also had the irritating habit of kissing women's hands, like a gentlemen in nineteenth-century France. He looked awkward when he did this; women whose hands were targeted also felt uncomfortable, but were strangely amused by this unnecessary display of gentility. Randall's brother also kissed hands, having watched his older brother's gentile ways. When both were invited for dinner, they went around kissing hands like antiquated toys. They often caught Sophie washing dishes or preparing food. She had to quickly wash her hands and then submit them for the ritual. She smiled at Randall and welcomed him, but showed her annoyance after he left. I think the brothers were over-compensating for their rural upbringing, but the gentile ways they had acquired had a distinctly artificial flavour, like plastic tomatoes.

After Randall got his university degree in business management, he landed a well-paying job in an automotive plant. The plant was one of the technological stars of the newly industrializing Turkey at the time, producing a total of fifteen trucks a day. To celebrate his success, Randall bought two dress shirts for himself, one a light blue, the other a subdued green. He also bought two dress shirts for his brother. So, the two peas in a pod clad in their new shirts, arrived for dinner, kissing hands as usual. From his initial pay-check, Randall made the first payment on a dishwasher for his mother. When the dishwasher was paid in full, he asked me to marry him. I accepted, since I did not have anything better to do at the time. Moreover, I was under Agnes's constant supervision, which I deeply resented. After my father's death, she had declared herself the honorary patriarch of our home, with Sophie's full blessings.

Randall was Agnes's friend. He was a hard-working and polite man who had her confidence. He was highly educated, and both Agnes and Sophie liked him. At the time, this was the basis of a sound marital selection. There were no fireworks in my heart—not even sparks—but I thought those would appear in time. I was desperate to escape living under Agnes's thumb.

The way Randall asked me to marry him was not memorable in and of itself. The only thing that came out of it was a badly burnt pot. The two of us were sitting on the balcony of my mother's apartment flat, which was in the process of being subsumed by Agnes. It was springtime, and the balcony had a partially obstructed, but still a breathtaking view of the Marmara sea. I was warming some milk in a saucepan in the kitchen to make some hot chocolate for the two of us. By the time Randall's marriage proposal speech was finished, the milk had boiled over, and the pot was irreparably scorched. We had to throw away the pot, but there were celebrations on both sides of the families.

Nevertheless, Agnes expressed some concerns about my marital choice—mostly after the fact. She said our backgrounds were so different that our marriage was going to start on a shaky ground. Knowingly or unknowingly, Agnes was covering herself for all possible outcomes. She wanted to reserve the right to say, "I told you so!" if things did not work out. After all, Agnes was the matchmaker, since Randall was her friend. If things turned sour, Agnes could say she warned me about the incompatibility of our backgrounds. Agnes said Randall had a "civil-servant" mentality, emphasizing the "servant" part. According to her, Randall lacked the initiative and the ingenuity that her own husband, Lynford, possessed. The bottom line was that my choice was not as good as hers, an acknowledgement that gave her a sense of superiority and comfort. If I had married one of my earlier boyfriends, whom she could not tolerate, she would have been deprived of these feelings of superiority she cherished so much. An old Turkish saying reminds us that no matter how much you shake it, the oil will always rise to top of the water. My family's oil was Agnes. She always found a way to rise to the top of events.

22.

An Uneventful Marriage

OUR MARRIAGE PREPARATIONS went quickly and smoothly. Each side did what they were supposed to do—more or less. After all, there are centuries old norms and guidelines for these kinds of situations, therefore, Turkish women do not need wedding organizers. For example, Randall's mother took me shopping, generously spending what little my husband-to-be had managed to save from his recent employment. One of the things she bought for us was a huge barrel of butter, fearing a "city girl" like me would force her precious son to eat margarine. I think that barrel of butter lasted us as long as our marriage did, well give-or-take a couple of years. Randall bought the wedding rings, eighteen-carat gold bands, no diamonds. I got mine melted down after our divorce.

God bless her, Sophie did her share and more. She paid the dressmaker for the hand-embroidered satin wedding dress I designed for myself. At the time, this was a small fortune. She also bought most of our furniture, not the best, but surely well above the average. The list was as follows:

- A six-piece bedroom set, ivory formica, very fashionable at that time, but cold and sharply angular.
- Two-piece living room set, moss green with black armrests.
- Black formica dining room set, eight pieces in all.
- Two solid coloured rugs, one green, one beige. We placed the green one under the dining room, to pick up on the colour of the living room set.
- Two comforters, ordered to specification, one green, one orange.
- Two blankets, both real wool, with green and orange in them.

•Orange bed spread, taffeta and silk, hand embroidered with fake pearls.

•Two sets of sheets, pure cotton, both white and hard to keep clean. The top sheet had buttonholes all around its edges, to match the buttons sewn all around the comforters. Changing sheets was a task that took an hour, but once done, the comforter was securely encased. At the time, zippers were expensive; they did not get wasted on duvet covers.

•White china with real gold trimming. Complete for eight.

•Silverware, complete for twelve, including hostess serving sets.

•Crystal glasses, four different kinds, complete for eight. Regular glasses for daily use.

•Fridge and stove, very small ones compared to North American standards, but appropriate for the apartment. A washer with an automatic wringer, a celebrated invention of the times. No dryer, the sun did the job throughout the year.

•Two sets of sleep wear for me, both white, frills over frills, flowers on flowers.

•Brown pajamas, real silk, for Randall. A silk belt with matching silk tassels.

•Terrycloth bathrobes, bright pink for me, grey/white/navy stripped for Randall.

•An exquisite pearl necklace, completely natural, not cultured, as my personal wedding present.

•Gold cufflinks for Randall, which to my knowledge, he never wore. His cuffs had regular buttons.

Although the thought never occurred to me at the time, I guess, all the things Sophie provided was a form of dowry. The list of what Sophie did not provide for me was much shorter:

•Any knowledge of human sexuality.
•A real choice.

Sophie did not help me with these because she never had them herself. She could not give me something she had never known. How can I blame her for that?

Our wedding took place in Istanbul, on the windiest and the rainiest day recorded in the last century. Many of our guests were not able to attend, some came in late, and all were soaked and shivering. Fortunately, the civil judge assigned for such matters showed up, and so did the two witnesses, so we managed to sign on the required dotted line. Once the signing was over, our guests rushed back to their homes, fearing the bad weather might turn even worse. Randall and I went back to our single-bedroom, tastefully decorated apartment, thanks to Sophie's efforts. He did not carry me over the doorstep, although I was as trim as a seaweed. I walked through the door on my own two feet. We were wet and cold, and bewildered. The norms which specified what should be bought, in what quantity, for whom, and when, did not extend to guiding us through the first night of our marriage. If there was any magic to be had, we totally missed it.

So, I changed into one of my frilly and virgin-white lounge sets, a little itchy in its newness. I sat in the armchair of our green living room set, equally new, equally itchy, and equally alien. Randall did not even allow that much comfort for himself; he sat in his dark blue suit, dark blue tie, crisp white shirt, all freshly purchased for the occasion. We sat, not knowing what to say or do, for hours. We talked about the weather, since it was bad enough to talk about as an excuse. I wondered why we were not going to bed, now that our contracts were signed and sealed, and my ownership legally transferred to his name. I did not have the courage to ask. I waited for him to initiate the move towards the bedroom. After all, I was socialized to think that husbands knew such things better than their wives, but Randall was as naïve as a high-school teenager.

It was well past midnight, and the severe discomfort had worn us down to a pulp when Randall asked me to go to bed, calling me "his wife" for the first time. I liked the possessiveness implied in this label; I felt "owned," thus protected. Nothing else was that memorable that night though, and nothing much else for the years that followed. No wonder that in some primitive tribes in New Guinea, brides spend their first night with an experienced older man, the groom's uncle or a witchdoctor in an established patriarchal role. Thus the first night is not wasted on an inexperienced groom and an inexperienced bride. In the west, teenage or young adolescent sexuality takes on this educative function, so at least the bride or the groom—or both—have sufficient experience by the time they arrive at the marital bed. However, my childhood and youth was spent in a society bristling with norms against pre-marital sex. So, the first night of marriage was often left to the blind leading the blind. Even after the disaster of the first night, sex was an obligation on one side and a right on the other. We had no models to emulate about the exquisite mutuality of human coupling, when done right, and many couples were not creative enough to invent it for themselves. For me, it took many years and Greg's arrival in my life to allow myself to truly enjoy the exquisite sensations my female body possessed.

The morning following the wedding, I wondered around in the apartment that was now my home. I made two jars of jam that day, from an exotic fruit someone had left in our fridge. Thus, the first day of my marriage to Randall was punctuated by an exotic jam. I was well trained for and eager to perform my wifely duties.

Did I like Randall? Most likely I did. Was I proud to be his wife? Most likely I was. To be fair, Randall was an intelligent, hard-working, polite and considerate man. He had no bad habits for me to complain about, not that that stopped me from complaining. He did not smoke, and he did not drink with the exception of a single beer or a single glass of wine when we had company. He seemed to appreciate all the food I cooked, although some meals were only barely edible. He was not sharply handsome, like my previous teenage boyfriends had been. Nothing about Randall was sharp or outright. On the other hand, he did look pretty good when he was dressed up, and he was a reservoir of knowledge, especially knowledge of the Trivial-Pursuit type. For example, he would know the names of all candidates running for an election, regardless of the length of the list. He would know the names of the actors and actresses in any given movie, including those who had relatively minor roles to play. Randall would know the daily weather report, the schedule of the ferryboat, the exact name of the font of the newspaper headings. He was neither generous nor stingy; he was a man of mediocrities.

23.

In-Law Conflicts

DESPITE HIS EVEN-TEMPERED OUTLOOK, we had many conflicts. Our original conflicts were not about Randall's idiosyncrasies, like gargling out loud, or like drying every single toe separately, like polishing silver spoons, after he took a shower. They were not about my own idiosyncrasies either, although presumably I had many. What we started to quarrel about was our families. During the early years of my marriage, my family kept very close contact with us, which obviously bothered Randall. In those years, Randall was never infuriated—only mildly bothered. My family called at least a couple of times a day, sometimes more, to see how I was doing. They wanted us to visit them every weekend, and attend all social functions as an extended family unit. Since Agnes was a close friend of Randall's, I thought he would enjoy this close proximity to my family, but he didn't. He just appeared to put up with it, until he saw an opportunity to uproot us, and move me as far away from my family as possible. At the first opportunity, we immigrated to Canada.

Our conflicts about Randall's family were more blatant. His family infuriated me, and unlike his more passive aggressive interaction strategies, I complained bitterly and loudly. The sources of our conflict had much to do with the differential cultures we were raised in. For that, at least, Agnes had hit the nail on the head. For example, I had different expectations than Randall about the sanctity of one's home. Although my family visited us many times, and we visited them even more often, it was never without a courtesy call before we actually showed up. In his rural upbringing, time must have been a much more flexible commodity for his family. For example, his parents showed up without our prior knowledge, or stayed for a week when they said they were just going to drop by. They were nice to me, and my mother-in-law always helped with the cooking and washing the dishes. However, I knew that they saw their son's home as if it were their own, and their proprietary attitude made me insane. The way I saw it, it was my home, not theirs, and they should not show up at the door whenever they so pleased. Looking back on the whole thing, I can see how unfair I must have been, but that is water that has long gone under the bridge.

Randall's mother was a very wise woman. She carefully covered up her lack of formal education by speaking very little, and observing a lot. In addition, she had a rich reservoir of practical knowledge. She knew how to say just the correct words to please someone. Although I cannot say that I ever loved Randall's mother, I can honestly say that I did respect her in many ways. Randall's father, on the other hand, was a different story. He almost never talked, and on those rare occasions when he did talk, he only uttered single-syllabled words like "yes," "no," "come," "go," "good," "bad." He communicated through so few words that he could have been multilingual, within a few hours, if he so chose. All he had to do was learn to say "yes," "no" in another language. Randall's father never kept eye contact, although he had amazingly beautiful blue eyes. He was an enigma, and I absolutely dreaded being alone with him for not knowing what to say. I was never one for prolonged silences.

Of the three, I disliked Randall's brother the most. He was the walking/talking personification of everything I disliked in Randall. If there was a problem of any kind, he would blindly take his brother's side. When he was in our home, I felt silenced, outnumbered. Randall's brother had a distinct vision about what his beloved brother's wife should look and how she should behave, and his vision was in complete conflict with who I was.

To be brutally frank, I mostly resented the economic dependence of Randall's parents on their sons. Since Randall was the older son, he took on the lion's portion of the responsibilities. I looked at this dependence as an unfair competition for the things I wanted to do in my new marriage. For example, I wanted to start a family; I was dying to be a mother, but Randall told me we had to wait. If it were up to him, we would not have had Negrisse. Despite all my troubles with her, and despite all my heartache across the past decades, I cannot imagine a life without knowing that Negrisse is located somewhere in that life, even through her absence. Although she chooses not to be a physical part of my days, weeks, months, years, she still laughs and cries, and still calls me "mom" in my dreams. For that alone, I am grateful for my otherwise humdrum marriage.

Part V:
The Fourth Generation

24.

Negrisse

I ALWAYS LIKED CHILDREN when I was young. I spent hours taking care of neighbours' children. It never occurred to me to ask for money. In my culture, and at that time, it would have been inappropriate, if not altogether rude, to ask for money for work that was considered neighbourly. Besides, children's company was a privilege, not a burden for me. There were times when my parents, half-jokingly, expressed a fear that I might produce a dozen children of my own. In reality, I only had one, and adored the one I had. It was only during my young adulthood that I developed an intolerance for young children. Although I take full responsibility for this unfortunate transformation, I also think Negrisse had something to do with it. Let me tell my story of her, so that you, as the reader, can serve as an informed judge. Keep in mind that where Negrisse is concerned, I am biased both in my love and in my pain, so take my words with a handful of salt.

Before our marriage, a desire I never fully expressed to Randall, was the desire to have my own children, preferably a boy and a girl, or two girls. Talking about something that involved a carnal act was not considered appropriate at the time, so women did not talk about having children even with their future husbands. Sexuality was considered a taboo subject, even amongst the to-be intimates. I assumed that Randall, soon to be my husband, would also want children, shortly after our marriage.

My assumption about the path to youthful parenthood did not materialize. Instead, after our wedding, I found out that Randall had no desire to move into the role of fatherhood anytime soon. He thought, and probably rightly so, that we should wait until we established ourselves a little. Maybe, he was just sick of children, since women in his extended family were inclined to give birth to multiples of children. This incongruence between our respective desires for children bothered me immensely, but I did not complain about my husband's delay tactics. At least on the surface, I kept up the pretence that delaying children was a mutual decision. On a deeper level, the level at which my youthful weaknesses and irrational desires lurked, I felt rejected. I wanted my baby, and I wanted him/her soon. Randall, the man who called me his wife, was depriving me from the ultimate goal of my life. Thus, the first seeds of resentment towards Randall were planted in the early months of our marriage. Throughout the years, this resentment had many occasions to feed on itself, and it eventually devoured the remaining shreds of our mutual existence.

Holding up to the deferential role expected of a wife, I did not openly quarrel with Randall. Instead, I found a clerical job in the bank Agnes worked at. It would be more accurate to say that my sister found the job for me. Like many of my female peers, I worked for eight hours, and then, came home to cook and clean. I made jams and jellies, pastries and tarts, soups and meat dishes. I prepared our lunches for the next day, making sure that they looked as good as they tasted. I also embroidered, sewed, knitted, and even made stained glass windows to decorate our one-bedroom home. I ironed all our laundry, including Randall's briefs and socks. Housewifery was what I had prepared myself for, and I played the role to full tilt. Doing endless tasks did not leave me the energy to question the mundaneness of what I was doing, not even once. Besides, all the excitement of my marriage was in my jams and pastries; the part between the sheets lacked luster. Our sex life was as appetizing as cold, congealed oatmeal.

It was about then, that I started fainting. It started when I collapsed in the ferryboat one morning on my way to work. Fortunately, Agnes was with me, so I did not lose my purse to purse-snatchers. I had always been a very healthy person, so the fainting spells were a new experience. It seemed as if all the weight from my shoulders lifted for a few seconds, and I was enveloped by a friendly darkness. My fainting scared Agnes and all other friends from the bank taking the morning ferry to work. After I came to, I also scared the hell out of myself.

Randall showed a polite interest in my fainting spells, similar to the politeness he showed when listening to other people's conversations. He showed no discernable emotion, however. After all, his own mother was a hypochondriac, claiming heart problems, bowel problems, and nerve problems on a daily basis. Randall had learnt to ignore women's health-related complaints, whether they had legitimacy or not. However, he never questioned the legitimacy of his mother's various ailments. For my fainting spells, his response was mostly a quiet resignation. At the time, I had yet to grasp his avoidance of all feelings, and all problems, until they hit him right between his eyes. As a newlywed, I was scared. I expected some emotion. I expected some kind, comforting words. Instead, Randall basically went through our marriage like a robot, doing the right thing when the correct button was pushed. He did not take initiatives on his own. Even amongst robots, I would say that Randall was an early prototype requiring much tinkering.

When they heard of my fainting spells, my in-laws thought that I must be pregnant with their first grandchild. I wasn't. I was just exhausted, busy playing the role of the perfect wife, busy satisfying the wants and the needs of others. When my morning spells continued, and spilled into afternoons, I quit my job and I quit my pursuit of higher education. I was relieved. I hated the study of economics. Besides, not having to go to work meant that I could cook and clean to my heart's content. Shortly after stopping work, the fainting spells stopped, and Randall got a promotion. The company even let him drive the company car once in a while, which put stars into his otherwise starless eyes. We did not miss the little bit of income my bank teller's job used to bring in. It was then that I was really ready for my baby, which Randall still resisted. Probably, I was craving for love, which Randall was incapable of expressing.

I know for a fact that I got pregnant in November. I remember the cold and rainy night where we found some warmth in our bed. Besides, I had conveniently "forgotten" to take my pills for a few days, and we had to rely on a more crude form of birth protection. Only for a single night, we were less careful. This is the very first time I dare to admit my subversive role in what Randall considered an accident. The accident was that I got pregnant. Randall did not like the news one bit; he just shouldered it, as a convict who was just told that he was sentenced to the electric chair. Randall did not hug me, he did not look at me, and for a very long time, he did not even touch me. Maybe, he thought, I was contaminated. Maybe, deep down, he sensed my insubordination, and he was punishing me. He was right, I had orchestrated my pregnancy, and I had done it for myself, not for us. It was only many years later, after our bitter divorce, that Randall found the devoted father role pleasant. In my view, his devotion was suspect since it came so late and after such a long period of rejection of me.

I was only a couple of months pregnant when New Year's Eve arrived. Randall suggested going away, rather than the alternative of staying and celebrating with my family. My in-laws did not celebrate the New Year's anyway; they saw it as the invention of heathens and agnostics. So, I agreed to go away for a few days, to a farm that had been transformed into a rural spa. It was known as the Polish Village, and Polish immigrants to Turkey ran it for city folk like us who wanted to re-connect with their more innate side. So, we went for walks among verdant fields, thinned out woods, and free-grazing farm animals. The clean air helped with my morning sickness. I took delight in petting cows, sheep and horses, and watched with some trepidation the pigs and piglets wallowing in their own feces. When we were served pork sausages for breakfast, I politely refused, and opted for cheese and olives.

In this rural venture, like during many other times, Randall and I pretended to be the happy couple, expecting their first child. After the New Year struck, and those who were not expecting had their share of bubbly drinks, Randall and I retired to our chalet and slept in separate beds. That was the second saddest New Year I remember. The first was when we walked into our home after long festivities, and found Beatrice's body wedged between our front door and the wall.

25.

Delivery

WITHIN THE BOUNDARIES of my controlling family, my gynaecologist was predetermined just like my clothes or my school, or my marriage to Randall were. His name was Henry Duller, and he was also Agnes's doctor. He was a tall, dark, and cheerless man with less than a friendly demeanour. He had extremely large hands, which scared me during my monthly check-ups. Yet, I was assured that he was the best in his field. After all, Agnes would not have gone to the second best, would she? Every month, my check-up costs us more than the money I spent on our groceries. Every month, Henry Duller told me that my pregnancy was as normal as a textbook case. I guess, by providing a great compliment, he felt justified in collecting his hefty visitation fee.

In the first few months of my pregnancy, I was extremely sick during the mornings. After that, the only thing that was unusual for me was that I craved quinces. I had them on my dresser, in the kitchen, in the bathroom and even carried slices wrapped in cellophane in my purse. I devoured their relatively dry, choking flesh as if they were the juicy figs in Mavis's garden. Not before and never since, have I ever liked quinces, although I like the quince jam Sophie used to make.

Other than the obvious expense, there was one other catch to going to a private doctor in my country of origin. Henry Duller's practice was expensive. Moreover, he also expected the delivery to take place in a private clinic. Yet, given the relative poverty of the State, and the sparse availability of medical doctors for its large population, the government had made it mandatory for each physician to work at a public hospital for at least one day a week. So, like all physicians, Henry Duller was also expected, by law, to serve one day at a State hospital, for mediocre pay. State-run hospitals were free for the populous, and served literally millions of the poor and the desolate portion of Turkish society. Duller's conscripted service period started from 12:00 am on Wednesdays until 8:00 am the following Thursdays. He instructed me not to start my labour on a Wednesday, as if I had a choice. Guess what? I went into labour on a Wednesday afternoon, the first week of August. So, the lonely and mostly isolated days of my pregnancy were punctuated by yet another unfortunate outcome: having to go to a State hospital which was known to deliver babies, more or less like McDonald's delivers standardized hamburgers.

It was during an afternoon visit by Sophie, Agnes, and Lynford that my labour started. I was in the process of serving hot tea, a cultural must, when I felt the unmistakable pain of contractions. I kept serving the tea and the torte, like the gracious host that I was, expecting the next bout of pain with trepidation. I also felt great excitement, since the time I was going to hold my baby in my arms was approaching. The sharp pain came, so did a succession of others. Each time, I bit my lower lip.

After the tea was served and re-served, and the torte eaten, all but the last piece that I saved for Randall, I announced my condition. It was Wednesday; the day Duller did not want me to deliver since he would not be able to collect his hefty private clinic fees. All those who were present laughed and joked, and laughed some more. My brother-in-law left, and came back in a taxi. None of us owned a car. My things were already neatly arranged and packed, so it took us only a few minutes to jump into the cab, and head towards the State hospital where Duller worked on Wednesdays. The only one who was not there was Randall.

Randall arrived after work, upon reading the note I left him amongst the already washed and dried tea set. Apparently, he first devoured the piece of the fruit torte I had also left for him, before he set out for the hospital. He sat beside my bed, like a total stranger, as I sweated and shook with increasing bouts of pain. He felt out of place, he was out of place. He had not been in the emotional picture throughout the entire nine months of my pregnancy. At 8:00 pm, Randall excused himself and went home, probably hoping to arrive to an already delivered baby the next day. Maybe this is not really true, but I always had the feeling that he was glad my labour started on a Wednesday. The difference in the fees of a private clinic and a State hospital were huge, and Randall was a miser.

During the early hours of my labour, I had a lot of confidence about the power of my body to deliver, and just as much confidence in the strength of my baby to find her way out. After all, my baby had stuck with me when I felt so alone in my pregnancy. We had slept together, ate together, walked together for the last nine months. My baby had let me know through her forceful kicks that she was there, and that she was strong. Henry Duller had also told me that my pregnancy was as normal as a textbook case. Now that the time had come, all my baby and I had to do was to push a little.

Although I was at a crowded State hospital, Duller had his pull. I was given a spacious room that had two beds in it, one for me and one for Sophie, who kept vigil. Although Duller helped with the room arrangements, he appeared extremely disappointed that I started my contractions on a Wednesday. He told me that although I was given a nice room, he was going to treat me like one of the crowd, because we were not in a private clinic, and here, he was not my private doctor. He also told me that he was going to leave the hospital at 8:00 am sharp, in the morning, whether or not my delivery was complete. I said I understood, but I went into a silent panic. My panic grew in leaps and bounds when I saw the crowd of women he was talking about, when he took me, to what was called the delivery "arena" for my first internal examination.

It was shortly after Randall's departure, long after the afternoon tea at my home, and long after my first experience with contractions that Duller decided to examine me. It was exactly 12 hours before the end of his shift. He had announced to the members of my family who brought me to the hospital that the delivery was going to be in the morning. After this announcement, Agnes and Lynford left. Randall had come and gone, since fathers were not expected to engage in any form in the birthing process. My culture considered the simple donation of sperm worthy enough for fatherhood. Moreover, my baby's father, up to that point, was particularly a reluctant one.

A nurse ushered me through endless corridors into a huge, public delivery room. Despite my strong contractions, I walked behind her. Wheelchairs were a rare commodity; you either went on a stretcher or walked. That night, I chose the latter. At least, I thought I did;

maybe I had no choice. The cavernous delivery room presented the most horrifying scene that I had ever seen in my life. There were more than a dozen delivery tables just like chopping-block counters at a professional meat market. About eight women, give or take a few, occupied these delivery tables, some shouting, some crying, and others just gazing up at the ceiling until their next gut-tearing cramp made them join in the grotesque opera. Most of them were totally naked with a stained sheet barely covering them; some were wearing loose hospital gowns on top. All had their legs up and spread wide open. Two women had not-yet-detached cords dangling down into a bucket.

It was then it hit me that the ones quietly gazing at the ceiling had just delivered. There were buckets full of afterbirth and pools of blood on the floor. They had delivered their babies in this house for the poor, without much individual care and without a bit of privacy. It was also then that I noticed that the empty table that Duller was gesturing for me to lie on had a yellowish brown cockroach scurrying around it, although the white sheet that covered it was absolutely clean. It was then that I completely panicked and knew deep down that I would never be able to do what those other women had just done. I could not deliver my baby here, not among this crowd, not among buckets of afterbirth, not in the presence of cockroaches.

After the first examination, or what I would call a walk in terror, I stopped dilating. Although my contractions increased in strength and frequency, my body just refused to open up to let my baby through. Sweat covered my body, pain ripped my innards and tears choked me. By the time I went back to my room, leaning on the nurse that I had followed to the delivery room, I was a shrunken woman. I cried and told Sophie that I was not going to be able to deliver in this hospital. My mother was not much help, since women rarely have the power to alleviate other women's suffering. The only ones who could help were Duller, my greedy doctor, or Agnes. In our family, Agnes was basically an honorary patriarch since my father's death. As for Randall, he had not participated in the process of my pregnancy, at least not willingly, so I did not expect him to rush to the hospital with a solution.

After listening to my fearful sobs, Sophie said I was being silly. When the time comes, she said, I would deliver. Once it gets in, she said, it always gets out; the "it" she had in mind was my baby. She was wrong. I never gave birth in that hospital. I just stopped dilating altogether and struggled with the contractions enclosed and confined in my body. I was trapped in that horrible hospital room, just like Negrisse was trapped in my belly.

I walked in the room all night, sweating, crying, and moaning. To her credit, Sophie stayed awake and kept me company. I was escorted to the delivery room two more times, and got confronted with more or less the same number of women. As the hours progressed, there were definitely more cockroaches. Each time, I was told that I had dilated only one inch, the same as when I entered the hospital. I could have told them that. My backbone ached so much that I thought I might implode. My morale was shattered. My body was a fortress that housed my own pain and incarcerated my baby.

At 7:30 in the morning, Randall showed up at the hospital. He was all set to greet his offspring, freshly washed and powdered. He was not expecting to be greeted by me with tears flowing out of my eyes, sweaty, horrified, and still carrying my huge belly. Through my tears, I begged him to take me out of this place, I told him that I would die and my baby would die here, with me. He did not know what to say or what to do. He just mumbled something like I was going to be all right. By this time, Agnes and Lynford had arrived. They took one look at me, had a five-minute consultation with Duller, and we were on our way to the private clinic. Duller was also in the cab Lynford had fetched; he had seen the benefit of hitching a free ride. He might also have been afraid. Recognizing his negligence in the matter, my brother-in-law threatened to ruin his career if anything happened to me or my baby. Of course, this threat was a bluff. In Turkey, individuals do not have the right to sue their doctors, even for blatant forms of malpractice.

Once his private clinic fee was assured, Duller immediately became an active physician, maybe too active for my baby's sake. Definitely too hurried for my own safety. He called his wife, right from my private room, to inform her that he would be busy until lunchtime. Then he gave me injections, every fifteen minutes, to re-start my halted dilation. At that point, I was much too weakened to walk on my own, so they placed me on a stretcher.

The money we ended up paying bought me a private delivery room in which I cried and screeched like a wounded animal. I would have rather died many times over, if it were only for me. But, my death would have also meant the death of my baby, so I bit my lips, and continued ripping the sheets that covered my body. The dosage of medication to speed up the delivery process tore my insides out, buckled my backbone out of shape. Duller used no painkillers. Through the talons of pain, I was awake, but felt less than human. It felt like a pack of hyenas were tearing into my body. I wished for the comforting blackness I experienced in my earlier fainting spells, but could not faint.

Negrisse came to this world, around lunchtime, just as Duller had informed his wife over the phone. Randall had gone out for his lunch when the delivery took place. Maybe he was not able to deal with my inhuman cries; maybe he just didn't want to miss his lunch. Who knows? My husband was not one to get emotional about life events, whereas he could always be rational about his food.

I saw Duller slap my baby's buttocks with his large hands. Negrisse had a bruise on her bottom for more than a week. She also had a bump on her head, which didn't go away for six months. It seems that corner of her head had been in the birth canal when I stopped dilating. Duller's greed could have killed her. She was lucky; she escaped with a small bump. I escaped with much deeper wounds, both literally and figuratively. But on that day in August, I was exceptionally happy.

Duller sewed me up, yet I no longer felt pain. I was elated, accomplished and glorified. All the pain, all the suffering was gone, and I was left with a baby who was more beautiful that even the ones I had caressed in my dreams. When they brought Negrisse to my room, she was swaddled in white, washed and powdered. She had about an inch-and-a-half of pure black hair. Her hair was wet and neatly brushed to one side. The bump on one side made her hair slightly stick out. It was then that Randall showed up with a bunch of pink carnations. I did not like carnations any more. Yet, I was much too happy to get upset. I let him kiss me lightly on the cheek, and we started to play the game of a happy family instead of the happy couple everyone saw us as. I was a mother after all, and for that, I was grateful. I wanted to be the best mother in the whole wide world.

26.

Parenthood as Sudoku

B EING THE PARENT OF NEGRISSE was exhilarating, but also
difficult. I guess all parenthood is difficult. We have rule books,
licenses, and permits for almost everything we do, including
digging in our gardens, replacing plumbing, removing large trees,
fishing or driving. Astonishingly, no permits or licenses are required
for the most important responsibility of one's life: being a parent.
So, men and women have sex—or make love—anywhere, anytime
they like, and if they are careless—or if they choose—pregnancy
follows. Many men stay, some walk away, but women's choices are
a lot more limited. Unless they take the extreme measure to abort,
which may not be a viable alternative for many, they gestate, and
lactate and find themselves swaddled by the expectation to become
a good parent. Most societies, including many so-called developed
societies, still equate women's biological capacity for pregnancy with
their not at all biological capability to parent. Amazingly, however,
this haphazard gendered social arrangement works in the majority
of cases, since most kids grow up to be okay, rather than turning
into a menace to themselves or to the societies they are a part of. In
Negrisse's case, and without too many reasons I can pinpoint, my
parenting labours crumbled and collapsed.

Once, I heard myself say that parenthood is like Sudoku, and I
immediately liked the simile. Sudoku is a popular arithmetical puzzle. It consists of a 3 x 3 table, creating nine large cells. Within each
large cell, there is a smaller 3 x 3 table. The grand total of all cells
in Sudoku is 81. The trick is to use numbers from one to nine, only
once, within each of the smaller cells, in a way that in each row and
in each column of the larger matrix, numbers from one to nine also
appear only once.

Sudoku game tables come semi-constructed, with a few numbers already scattered in the matrix. The player has to solve the puzzle by filling out the remaining numbers in each of the smaller cells, without breaking the rules of the game. Sudoku players use pencils rather than pens, since many different placements of the numbers will be required before the unique solution is obtained. There is only one solution to each game, and many players give up way before they find the ultimate solution. The misleading part of the game is that the tried-out numbers seem to work for a while, and yank the player to go forward in placement of other, contingent numbers. Yet, the whole arrangement crashes when two numbers of the same value end up appearing in the same column or in the same row, forcing the player to re-work the entire puzzle with a different set of numbers. A single error in the placement of numbers immediately multiplies and generates many more errors. Sudoku is lots of fun, but it can also drive one crazy.

Parenthood is like Sudoku, with infinitely more cells than the 3 x 3 x 3 x 3 arrangement in the game I described. A few bits of information are provided, here and there, but each parent must find the unique solution that works for his/her child. Unlike Sudoku players, parents cannot use pencils, where errors can be easily erased; new and novel solutions may not be easily available. In parenthood, to locate an error and erase it is also challenging. Since personal or social actions are infinitely more complex than simple numbers, to locate and remedy one's errors require more sophisticated skills than matrix algebra. Moreover, in Sudoku, the game board is an inanimate object, but in parenthood, the child is a living, breathing, active agent. As the parent adjusts or changes his/her game play, the child also adjusts or changes his/her reactions. At the end, one cannot give up and toss the game into the garbage bin. As a parent, one has to endure, regardless of the circumstances. So, unlike Sudoku, the unique solution in the resolution of the parenthood game is to be able to retain love, respect, and communication without succumbing to socialization errors that may have tainted the relationship. The keys to successful outcomes are not restricted to a finite set of numerical inputs (1-9), but are infinite.

Negrisse was the most beautiful baby girl in the whole wide world. At the very least, that is how I perceived her. I dressed her up in beautiful clothes, most of which I personally made. I loved to place her in her luxurious baby carriage, and parade her in playgrounds, shopping areas, or at gatherings of family and friends. Total strangers approached me and commented on what a beautiful baby she was. She seemed to bask in this attention, smile and gurgle to delight her adoring audience. Eventually, she transformed those baby sounds into spoken words, and over time, her words got sharpened, and polished, and became poisoned like pre-historical warriors' arrows. Over time, Negrisse became a master of language use, and her skill extended to the four languages she taught herself with ease. The only language she refused to learn was her mother tongue: Turkish.

If and when she desired to do so, Negrisse attacked the vulnerabilities of people around her, and wounded them with only a few spoken words. At other times, Negrisse was an orator, bestowing carefully measured splendour and awe on her audience through her magical use of the languages she spoke. It appeared that most of her 160 glorious IQ points were concentrated on the language centres of her brain. Whether personally hurt or glorified, no one dismissed Negrisse. She loomed larger than her five-feet-two stature. But, all of these developments came later. At first, she was just an adorable little girl.

I was mesmerized by my daughter's honey-brown eyes, her perfectly smooth skin, wavy chestnut hair, and rose-coloured cheeks. Amazingly, the dark hair she was born with was replaced by much lighter brown hair within the first few months. I loved to watch her when she slept; she resembled the most beautiful of angels. I got up many times during the night just to check up on her, and listen to the rhythm of her breathing. When I held her in my arms, I felt that she was part of me, and I a part of her, merged together in total harmony and unity. Yet, it would be complete falsehood if I told you that our early days were easy. By no stretch of the imagination can I say that Negrisse was an easy baby. To be fair, neither was I a relaxed mother. For example, even before she was born, I had made the decision to breastfeed my child. As if to honour the choice I made, and within minutes of her birth, my breasts swelled up with milk. The rush and the volume of my milk were intense; I felt like the facsimile of the Borden Cow commercials. Milk gushed through me, and squirted out, soaking my underwear, pajamas, and housecoats. Since Negrisse was born in the sweltering heat of August, the sticky feeling of my clothes and the smell of my own body did not bode well with my high standards of bodily hygiene. To regain some control over my leaky body, I showered numerous times a day and repeatedly changed my clothes. Under the unaccustomed pressure, my breasts hurt and my nipples cracked. Despite being something I had longed for, breastfeeding became a time of pain, rather than a time of serene pleasure I longed to share with my little daughter.

Looking back, and given the level of intelligence of my daughter, I have no doubt that Negrisse reacted to my discomfort, and compounded the existing problem with her own discomfort. Within weeks of her birth, she refused to take milk from me. As a naïve first-time mother, I took this rejection personally. Although my body was manufacturing enough milk to feed at least half a dozen infants, my own daughter was refusing to take a single drop. Thus, each feeding session became torture, with the physical pain of my breasts, and the symbolic failure I felt in my inability to provide nourishment for the most precious being in my life. I lost weight, and although no one identified it as such, I fell into a deep depression.

In tears, I visited Henry Duller once again, telling him about the hopelessness I felt. His diagnosis was casual and simple. He told me that given the intense pressure and the volume of my milk, Negrisse was instinctively afraid of drowning. Rather than trying to feed her directly, he told me to pump my milk and give it to her in a bottle. He must have been correct because pumping my milk and feeding it to my daughter with a bottle worked for a little while. However, it also reduced the quantity of milk my body produced and once my abundant milk thinned out, pumping became more difficult. Negrisse continued to refuse the milk from my breasts, as she had gotten used to the ease of the bottle. Feeding sessions were filled with stress. As usual, Randall was nowhere to be found during the feeding sessions. With the mounting pressure, one of my breasts dried up completely, leaving the other one alone to fend for my daughter. I felt ugly and misshapen with one breast shrivelled back to its pre-birth size, and the other still mountainous, cracked and painful. I felt like a cartoon character. I felt like I was a failure.

When I look back on it, this early struggle laid the grounds for many other struggles to come between my daughter and myself. Like my botched experience of breastfeeding, each of the struggles I had with my daughter deeply hurt and scarred me. Worse, our struggles also scarred Negrisse. She was never content as a child, and I very much doubt that she became a happy, easy-going woman. For her sake, I hope I am wrong on both accounts.

Flashback: Negrisse at age two

Negrisse just started eating some solid foods. She is exceptionally picky. Meal times are continuing to be a problem for her, and for me. Just when I think she has swallowed a mouthful of food, she spits it out. She has also learned to hide food in her cheeks, like a squirrel or a chipmunk. She spends hours holding the food in her cheeks. She takes a nap, wakes up, food still stored in her cheeks. I honestly do not know how to deal with this problem.

Despite mishaps in feedings, Negrisse's physical body, as well as beauty, grew throughout her childhood. Yet, what impressed me most, and all those around her, was her razor-sharp mind. She had learned how to read by the time she was three, and she read everything and anything she laid her eyes on. Her breakfast started with reading all the information on the cereal box, the milk carton, or anything else that happened to be on the table. The day continued with her reading the headlines and the comics in the daily newspaper. She had books of her own, those that said things like "run, Sam, run" or "the little train that could," but she rarely bothered to spend time with them. Negrisse was more interested in the daily headlines. She had memorized the words to every Christmas carol ever written, before she reached the age of four.

Flashback: Negrisse at age three

Negrisse is playing in the backyard. She is wearing her hand-knitted bikini. She is adorable. She has her little splashing pool, but she is not in her pool. Instead, she is totally engulfed in the nature that surrounds her. She picks up leaves and examines them like a bota-nist. She watches caterpillars chomping on newly sprouted carrots I planted. I am hanging the clothes that I finished washing on the outdoor wash line. The sun is warm; there is not a cloud in the sky. The day is glorious.

Negrisse picks up a rock the size of a Ping-Pong ball. She is turning it over in her chubby hands, examining each contour. She loves rocks. We have a large rock collection in her bedroom. In a split second she throws the rock in the air, and moves directly under it to watch it come down. The rock comes down on her right eye. Her eye swells up, and turns eggplant purple within a couple of minutes. Negrisse does not shed a tear, but I cry hysterically. She has a wide smile on her face, like a scientist who just blew up her lab experiment. I scold her. But I am angrier with myself than I am with her. I was right there, but I did not see it coming. I curse myself for my carelessness.

At night, Randall taunts me for letting such an accident happen. He is never there to keep an eye on Negrisse, so he does not have a clue about how quickly things can go wrong. But, rather than challenging his armchair parenthood, I absorb his criticism and I feel worthless. I feel I am turning into Sophie.

Once she was old enough to play outdoors, Negrisse showed a lot of interest in nature. She did not play with dolls, or balls, or skipping ropes. Instead, she collected leaves, bugs, stones, insect eggs and cocoons. Since I also loved the outdoors, I spent endless hours with my little daughter, collecting, naming and categorizing things. We turned one of the empty bedrooms of our large house into a laboratory for our nature finds. From the cocoons, moths emerged, and flew free in the room. Every morning, we brought in fresh flowers for the moths to land and feed on. These relatively short years of shared joy with my daughter also reminded me of the carefree childhood I spent in Mavis's garden. In those years, I did not, could not, have imagined that the bonds Negrisse and I shared were weak and fragile, and could easily be severed ... by her. I thought that our mother-daughter bond was invincible.

Negrisse was not much for colouring in children's picture books. I think the lines that were already on the pages restricted her boundless imagination. She refused to colour within those lines; she did not want to be confined by the dark boundaries of simple rabbits, kitties and horses. Instead, she loved drawing and colouring her own pictures. Around three years of age, she started drawing and colouring bees of her own creation. The bees were yellow and black and had individualized stripes. They were active, doing things. They were not making honey, like one would expect bees to. They were buzzing around, visiting various places, reading books, and carrying furniture to their bee houses. Negrisse's bees had human-like lives, human-like families. Negrisse's bees did not show much emotion, but demonstrated reasoning and logic. Negrisse's bees were like Negrisse.

Suddenly, the bees went away and the dragon phase of her artwork appeared. This was much before the infamous Jurassic Park movies, so I have no clue where her inspiration came from. Dragons, some not necessarily fierce looking, but others with much less than friendly demeanour, appeared on page after page of her drawings. A few had fire coming out of their nostrils; others had long flames coming directly out of their mouths. Some of Negrisse's dragons had green and red scales; some had armour, like the knights of the middle ages. Almost all had long tails and forked tongues. Some had only two, others four, and still others had up to eight legs, all furnished with razor-sharp claws. Yet, there was something very human about these dragons. Some were drawn sitting around, reading books. Like the drawings of bees that came before them, Negrisse's dragons lived in families like clumps.

Negrisse preferred the company of her dragons to the company of friends. Although I tried to invite some of the neighbourhood children to our home to provide some company for my single child, Negrisse found them immature, silly, boring, and stupid. After all, they did not even know how to read books and newspapers, at the age of three or four, as she did. They did not know how to count or do simple math. When it came to drawing pictures, all the neighbourhood children could produce were circles with mismatched eyes and crooked mouths, rather than the sophisticated drawings of ant colonies or dragon families. Negrisse had little patience with her immature peers, who happened to be just "normal" for their age group.

Flashback: Negrisse at age four

Negrisse is four years old. She is beautiful. I dressed her in one of her favourite dresses, one of the ones I made for her. The dress is a dusty rose colour, with a white collar and short, white, puffy sleeves. On the right side of her skirt, I embroidered large, white flowers. Negrisse looks like a princess in this dress.

We are shopping in the supermarket. She is sitting in the front basket of the grocery cart, her body turned towards me. She is looking at the shelves and reading the brand names, specifications, ads. She is reading out loud, and other shoppers who figure out what she is doing are amazed. As usual, Negrisse is delighted with the attention she is receiving.

A very large and grossly overweight shopper walks toward us. She is smiling widely, having noticed Negrisse's beyond-her-age reading. Negrisse turns around and looks at the approaching woman, and shouts: "Mommy, that woman is fat." I freeze and turn red with embarrassment. I say, "Negrisse, please do not shout, and please do not say such things." Negrisse says, "But Mom, she is fat." By then, the woman has stopped and no longer has the wide smile. She is hurt and I am desperate. I am ready to apologize, but how can my apology undo her public hurt? Negrisse continues, "Mom, you told me to always tell the truth. That woman is fat, but you are telling me not to say that. You are not fair."

I hastily push our cart away from the shoppers who have witnessed the event, the target of Negrisse's disparaging remarks amongst them. We come home with half the groceries I intended to buy. This is the very first time Negrisse uses my dedication to truth and fairness against me. It is not the last time. This is the first time Negrisse realizes the power of words to hurt people. In the following years, she perfects her verbal arsenal as a potential weapon. Negrisse learns to win the war of words.

When Negrisse started school, her teachers did not know what to make of her. The school did not know which grade to place her in, since her reading and writing skills were amazingly advanced, but her social skills were pretty much underdeveloped. So, they gave her an IQ test, and she scored out of the charts. I think Negrisse liked school, in her own way. At least, she liked to astonish her teachers by quoting something from that morning's newspaper, or a well-known poem, or a passage from a famous book. It took a few minutes before her teachers grasped the depths of her knowledge; it took a few more minutes before they struggled with the power of her steel-trap of a mind. Negrisse was like a sponge; she sucked in incredible amounts of information, and calculated when to let go of that knowledge to create the maximum impact. She had just turned five.

Around that time, Negrisse started to draw people in her pictures. It is more accurate to say that people were added to her already existing repertoire, since her interest in drawing dragons continued. Maybe she drew people because her teachers expected her to include people in her drawings. One way or another, her new genre of pictures was about families, and many of them were pictures of her own family: father, mother, Negrisse. Usually, our two-storey house appeared in the background, with an acceptable depth perspective more or less. Usually, the father figure was drawn much larger, the mother figure medium size, and the child the smallest of the three. Usually, there was grass in front of the house, and a blazing sun in one corner. Our cat Boomerang, whom Negrisse had named, also appeared in these family portraits. In most pictures, Negrisse was holding Boomerang in her arms. Boomerang was almost as large as Negrisse, possibly showing how highly Negrisse regarded her cat. However, sometimes the pictures showed Boomerang wandering around on the green grass in front of the house. In real life, Boomerang was never allowed outside, since she was an indoor cat. In Negrisse's outdoor pictures, Boomerang's natural brown and golden coat had a poisonous-looking green tinge, as the cat was coloured on top of the brilliant green grass of the lawn.

Within a month or so after attending the first grade, Negrisse was upgraded to the second grade. She still found her classmates immature, but took skipping a grade with stride. The only difference I noticed was in her drawings and paintings. Before she reached the age of six, Negrisse stopped drawing single pictures, and moved into creating picture booklets with distinct story lines. Most of her picture books were still about her family, but now, her father and mother, and Boomerang and herself were engaging in activities, doing things according to the story line. I watched the immaculate details in her creations with pride. As a woman who had dabbled in painting in my earlier years, I was constantly in awe of my young daughter's accomplishments. She indeed had an uncanny understanding of shapes, colours, perspective, and depth.

I was also impressed with the complexity of her story lines, which showed an amazing imagination.

I also felt increasingly uneasy about my own receding role in her story lines. While her stories bestowed a variety of activities and accomplishment on her father, I appeared to do very little. In her picture books, I lost stature, and became smaller in size, whereas Negrisse grew up and occupied more space. In one story, which particularly jolted me, Negrisse had drawn and coloured her father dressed in a suit, going to work, then coming home, reading his paper, washing his car, cutting the grass, watching the news, and playing catch with Negrisse. In this particular story, I appeared on the very last page, standing over the kitchen counter, and making peanut-butter sandwiches. The caption said, "My mother spreads things." Having been reduced to a role of "spreading things" in my daughter's eyes catapulted me to action. That year, I decided to enrol in the local university, and started taking courses in adult and child psychology and education. At the end of the same year, I asked Randall for a separation, which he agreed to grudgingly. For the first time in my life, I was embarking on a journey to find myself and establish a role that Negrisse could proudly acknowledge.

Flashback: Anna at age five, Negrisse at age five

I was a naïve child, and some of my naïveté, I retained as an adult. I am glad to hang onto some awe about the things around me; I would not have liked to be a person who thought she knew it all. I think some childish naïveté, mixed with some adult wisdom, is a healthy combination. As a child, though, I only had the naïveté, and no wisdom.

Some people took advantage of my trustfulness, even little people around my age. I think their predatory behaviour better reflects who they are, not who I am. Some people sold me things that were worthless. One little girl, just a few years older than I was, sold me discarded transfers on the public transit system. I think I paid a total of two cents for the whole bundle. When she found out, Sophie called me stupid, and asked me to get my money back. I was embarrassed and crushed. I did not feel stupid; for me, it was a fair exchange. I liked to collect things, I liked the transfers. When I went to retrieve my money, both the kid who sold me the transfers and I were sad about the way our business venture turned out.

Negrisse is five-years-old, and she also collects public transit transfers. She has a thick bundle of them. She spends time organizing her transfers according to the location of origin, date, time of issue, and other criteria that seems important for her. I give her the transfers I am issued, and happily contribute to her collection. She does not buy them, like I had once done, even though I would have understood if she had. I never tell her about the story behind my own childhood collection. I never ever call her stupid. I make a special effort to point out how smart she is at every appropriate occasion. She is smart, she is brilliant, and her teachers are as much stunned by her brilliance as I am. Yet, she yearns to be ordinary, which is extremely hard for her to be with her extraordinary intellectual powers. She blames me each time I applaud her accomplishments. Maybe, I am over-compensating for Sophie's parental errors. Maybe, I am failing in motherhood Sudoku.

Part VI:
Tangled Relationships

27.

University Years and Gregory

MY UNIVERSITY YEARS WERE HARD for me. The very first time I showed up at school was for a night course. I was wearing a business suit, a silk blouse and high heels. I immediately realized that my classmates were at least ten years younger than I was, and almost all were wearing jeans and sneakers. I did not own a pair of jeans, and I had always despised the informality of sneakers. Besides, I was still married at the very beginning of my university adventure, and I was an immigrant woman with a noticeable accent. I did not fit in. So, the first night, I locked myself in the university bathroom, and only came out of it a few minutes after the classes started. Once the classes started, I snuck into the room, and sat in the furthest corner possible. I felt invisible. I wanted to be invisible. Immediately after the class, I went home. I was trying to squeeze an intellectual existence into a very domesticated life. The fit was not easy. Randall did not approve the change in our home, and neither did Negrisse. Negrisse told me that the cupcakes made by her friends' mothers were much nicer than the cupcakes I made for her class. After I combed her hair and sent her back to school, I cried hysterically.

During a social gathering in our home for his colleagues, Randall told me, in front of our guests, not to make too much of my university attendance since it was just a "hobby." He had no sense of my thirst for a career. Soon afterward, I chose my journey of independence over my unsatisfactory marriage. However, my already divided universe became even more problematic after the separation. I had no money for a babysitter, and I barely had enough money for food. Hoping to appease Randall's feelings of rejection, I had forfeited all my rights to support payments, so I received not a single penny for myself or for our daughter. However, Randall did not appreciate my generosity, and expected me to crawl back to him when things got rough. Things did get very tough, but I did not crawl back. So, my ex became my very worst enemy.

Since I was not able to afford babysitters, I could only enrol in night courses for a few years. I would wait for Negrisse to come back from school, serve us a relatively simple meal like soup and crackers, and then, off we would go. At first, she sat in some of my courses with me. This was before women demanded their rights in education and other work-related environments, so Negrisse's presence during my course hours stuck out like a sore thumb. She was extremely well behaved, and never made a noise. And, although she had her own papers and crayons to keep her busy, she often preferred to listen to the lecture. This was before the 1970s, and the women's movement was still to make a dent at the universities that were male-dominated bastions. So, I was probably considered a nuisance, although no one said so to my face. I kept an A average to fend off the disdain of my male professors.

After a while, one of the only two female professors in my department took me under her wings. She herself had completed her education as a single mother; she knew the difficulties first-hand. She ended up allowing Negrisse to stay in her office, under her supervision, while I attended my various classes. When things got rough and I came close to giving up, she told me I could do it. I did. She told me things would get better, and they did. She did not tell me I might lose Negrisse's love along my thorny road to independence. If she had, I do not know what I would have done.

Flashback: Negrisse at age seven

Negrisse is seven. I am attending the university to make something of myself. It is hard. I have been out of educational institutions too long. It is hard to get into the routine of studying. I am a single mother now, and I have no money. I am afraid of ending up on welfare. I have to earn a living. Negrisse deserves better, I deserve better, so I push forward.

Another year is coming to an end, and there is not much to show for it. I have to finish school and I have to find a job. Holidays are approaching. I am just managing to put food on our plates. It is usually hamburgers or hot-dogs for Negrisse, with mashed potatoes and peas; for me, it is potatoes and peas. I say I do not care for meat, which is a little white lie.

There is no money for toys. I wanted to get the Lite-Bright kit for Negrisse, but it was fifteen dollars. Maybe, next year will be better, and I can buy the toy then. Lite-Brite is a kit that comes with different blueprints, like a Christmas tree, or a snowman. The child inserts coloured pieces, the size of small matchsticks, into designated locations. Then, you plug in the panel, and the whole figure appears, lit in colour. Although there is only a single bulb behind the panel, all the punctured holes with the coloured inserts ablaze. I am sure Negrisse will find this toy interesting, but it has to wait—maybe next year.

It was during those hard university times that I met Gregory. Like I, he was recently separated. Like I, he was a student. Like I, he had children—two girls in his case. Iris was the older one, about two years younger than Negrisse, and Daisy was the youngest, about two years younger than Iris. The girls were blonde, and very beautiful in their own right, but above all, Greg was gorgeous. My heart melted when I met him, and soon after, we became lovers. Soon after that, we found ourselves living in the same house: his. Randall insisted on selling what used to be our matrimonial house, without a single consideration of where Negrisse and I would go after it was sold. Fortunately, we moved in with Greg for a while, until I secured a graduate scholarship and moved to Toronto.

Greg was everything that Randall was not. He was warm and caring. He was loud and boisterous. He had an endearing presence. Greg was funny and his friendliness was contagious. He would even talk to people who had phoned our house by mistake, sometimes for an hour. With the exception of my father, Greg was the most generous man I had ever met. He filled up an empty room with his presence. In turn, my heart filled up with hope and joy when I was close to him. I was in love. All my senses that had gone into hibernation during my marriage were reawakened. I laughed out loud and my brown eyes regained their sparkle. Yet, I knew better than to give up my aspirations for a higher education. I knew better than to get reduced to a mother who made sandwiches in my daughter's drawings. So I pushed forward, got my As and secured a place in the graduate studies in education. I moved to Toronto, and became dizzy in a city that was so large and complex. For a while, I felt I was totally swallowed, until I learned to get around on its public transit. Soon after my move, Greg secured a scholarship, and joined me in Toronto.

I bought my very first car, a cheap forest green car that eventually received the "lemon of the year" distinction. But my car served me well, and I was absolutely proud to have it. I had no regrets. Our professors liked me, but adored Greg. Although I worked harder, and kept a much higher average than he did, he had a personal magnetism and lustre that I lacked. Our lives were simple: go to school, come back home, play some intellectual games with Negrisse, like Scrabble, then go to bed. Negrisse often won the word games, although we were the ones who were in the process of working on our Master's. We went out for long walks. We were dirt poor, but Greg invented occasions to bring excitement into our lives. We watched movies, and then dressed up in bed covers, put lampshades on our heads and replayed some of the scenes in the movies we had just seen. We went to drive-ins and to save money, we brought our own popcorn and slurpies. During the weekends, Greg's daughters Iris and Daisy joined us, and our games became crowded, less complex, but more fun. Negrisse had her own bed, but Iris and Daisy slept in makeshift beds under the dining-room table, since we had so little space. No one complained. We were happy with the arrangements, as long as we were together. Sometimes, we even found some coins under the sofa, and bought chips and dip. Our nights were private, just for the two of us. Greg was full of passion, I was full of love, and our bodies were like fine musical instruments, in perfect tune. During the nights, we lost ourselves in each other.

Flashback: Negrisse at age seven, Iris at age five, Daisy at age three

Greg and I are playing a simple word game with the three girls. We are sitting on the floor. We are in a jolly mood, making fun of each other's choices or suggestions, rolling on the floor with laughter. The game consists of a few simple rules, since Iris and Daisy are so young. Someone picks a word; all the others take turns asking questions,

and the person who picked the word answers "yes" or "no" until
someone guesses the word.

It is my turn to pick, and just to be silly, I pick the word "diarrhea."
After many "yes" or "no" probes, the girls get the inkling that the
word I picked is a form of illness, but they do not know which one.
Little Daisy asks, "But, can you get it on your face?" and I burst
out laughing. When I tell them the answer, no one laughs. Daisy
starts to cry. For some reason, they think I should not have picked
the word diarrhea, although no one can explain to me why it was
so wrong to do so.

I rush to the kitchen and bring some ice cream for the girls. Daisy
stops crying. Somehow, magically, ice cream mends all childhood hurts.

I think Negrisse was very happy during the early stages of Greg's
presence in our lives. Greg truly loved her, and she loved his ingenious
ways of keeping us busy. Besides, the two of them shared a hobby that
was all their own. They played computer games, sometimes hours at
a time. These were the very early prototypes of the computer gam-
ing industry that eventually exploded through additional advances
in technology. The games Negrisse and Greg played were not at all
visual, but much more cerebral. The characters and their actions
were described as simple word commands; there were absolutely
no pictures. The commands of the players were expressed in actual
sentences, not in computer clicks. The computers did not have too
much of a memory, and the "mouse" did not exist at the time. It was
the computer keyboard, and either a dirty amber or a disturbingly
sharp green screen that the games were played on. I did not like
these games much then, and never warmed up to them ever since.
However, I was happy to see the closeness Negrisse and Greg shared
through their hobby, since they were the only two pillars of my life.

The happier my life got, the crueller Randall became. My changing
life was constantly under his scrutiny, since we had an unbreakable
bond between us. We had Negrisse. Negrisse visited her father every
other week, and each time, came back with a new toy and some critical
comment, directed at me. In all fairness, Negrisse was not the type
of a child who carried messages back and forth. On the contrary,
she was wise beyond her young age, and refrained from peddling
information back and forth between her two families. Instead, the

cruelty in her words was reflective of what she may have heard in passing from Randall. For example, she would say that I was selfish, sacrificing her father's happiness in order to find my own. At first, these words, which I knew to be Randall's, would be uttered after each visit, and then immediately fizzle out. As time went by, the words became integrated into Negrisse's own language and thus became part of her own perceptions of me. Despite her brilliance, Negrisse never understood that women had the right to seek happiness for themselves. Negrisse unfortunately learned to associate happiness with selfishness, and held me responsible for the lack of happiness in Randall's life. During those days, I may have won a few battles, but Randall won the war by playing the part of the injured party.

28.

Punk Culture

I AM NOT SURE WHAT ATTRACTED NEGRISSE to punk culture. It could not have been the black clothes, which appeared to be the uniform of such groups. It could not have been the tall, army boots, which were exceptionally uncomfortable to wear—and smelly—during the summer months. It could not have been the rows and rows of silver-coloured chains, which dangled from boots, handbags, and clothing. It could not have been the raven-like make-up punk girls plastered all over their eyes, and finished off with cherry-red lips. It could not have been the multiple piercings around the nose, ears, tongue, and other visible or invisible body parts. It could not have simply been the music sung by young men and women who also presented themselves in black clothes, with multiple piercings and black make-up and cherry lips. It could not have been the lyrics of the songs these dark figures sang, which were about the three Ds: death, dismemberment, and generalized discontent. Maybe, it was a combination of all these things that attracted Negrisse to the culture like a magnet. Maybe, it was the bewilderment mixed with contempt that people who were not punks themselves showed toward the punks. Negrisse liked to shock people. I admit that I missed all the early signs of the transformation in my daughter, from a colourful, brilliant, slightly chubby, totally lovable little girl to the dark-clad, unhappy, sinister, but still brilliant young woman. The factors that I should have recognized as the forewarnings of this shift were the exclusively black clothes, army boots, and the loud music of discontent.

Flashback: Negrisse at age eight

We are living in an apartment building, subsidized by the university

I attend. It is for graduate students. A couple of months ago, Greg moved in with us. He is attending another university, and studying a different topic, but we are both graduate students. He seems to love Negrisse, and Negrisse seems to love him. Things are good, although money is still short. Greg and I think that there is light at the end of the tunnel, since either one or both of us are likely to get a paying job.

The three of us are taking the elevator. It is a long ride; our apartment is on the twenty-second floor. A bunch of other graduate students enter, and they push the button for a floor near our own. One of them smiles at Negrisse, and asks her name. Negrisse volunteers her name, and without skipping a beat, introduces Greg and me to the group. She says, "Greg is my mother's boyfriend. He just moved in with us. He is nine years younger than my mother." Negrisse is flexing her muscles to comment on the change in our living arrangements. Negrisse is again using language as a weapon. The elevator ride continues in an uneasy silence for all. I am not ashamed of my age, but I am hurt in front of total strangers. Negrisse is smiling one of her most benevolent smiles. She has scored.

Negrisse's transformation was not all bad. For example, it came with a heightened awareness of the environment, and a genuine care for every living being in it. Negrisse's environmental awareness preceded the yet-to-come green movement by at least a couple of decades. Negrisse read extensively, and developed a "no injury" ideology, similar to the concept of *Ahimsa* in the Jain culture. She wanted to expose and bring an end to animal cruelty, and her first target was the meat industry.

It was around those days that we discovered the presence of a mouse in our garage. The telltale signs were its droppings. So, we had to call a family meeting to decide upon an acceptable way to get rid of this uninvited creature, which was not in contradiction to Negrisse's animal protectionism. A mouse-trap was totally unacceptable to both Negrisse and I. Using poisoned food was also unacceptable, since Negrisse told us in detail about the effects of the poison on a little animal such as a mouse. But, leaving the animal undisturbed was also unacceptable, and the rationalization Greg and I used were the existence of our own cats and dogs. After all, we all knew that mice carried germs and diseases. So Negrisse took it upon herself to research the matter, and soon proposed an alternative that received unanimous approval.

The choice was a humanitarian trap, which was a small, L-shaped, plastic tunnel. The tunnel had the shorter side of the L open, and the longer side of the L closed. The trick was to place a large dab of peanut butter inside the tip of the longer side, but lay the trap flat on the short side of the L. When the mouse climbed towards the peanut butter, the L tipped over on its longer side, making backing out impossible for the mouse. Negrisse was sure that we would hear the distress of the mouse, and release it unharmed into a nearby park.

We bought the trap, which was a yellow and navy contraption, and much too expensive for its little plastic structure. We placed the gob of peanut butter on the closed tip, and laid the trap on the short side of the L, according to instructions. We were proud and bristling with our humanitarianism in the choice we made. For almost a week, nothing happened. The mouse in our garage left us its droppings, but did not get lured into the trap with the peanut butter. When we were about to give up and call another family meeting for a different strategy, it happened. It was about 3:00 am, a pitch black night, cold and snowy. Negrisse stood in the doorway of our bedroom, cold and ghostly looking in her white nightgown, and announced that she heard strange noises coming from the garage. She was absolutely sure that the mouse, which had eluded us for so long, was caught. She demanded that we take it to the park and release it.

Greg opened his eyes for a few seconds, and declared that 3:00 am was time for sleeping rather than running around in a frozen park. Greg had a general commitment to animal welfare, but obviously, he had a stronger commitment to an undisturbed sleep. So, it was I who got up, and tried to find some warm clothes to wear. Negrisse also found some warm clothes for herself, and the two of us ventured into the freezing cold of the garage. Indeed, there was a little mouse caught in the L shaped trap. We could see the tip of its ropy tail from the open side of the L. So, I picked up the trap, temporarily placed a cap on the open side, and ventured outside with my brave daughter at my side. For protection, we took Horus with us, a big, black and intimidating-looking Labrador, although he was as gentle as a stuffed toy.

Battling our way through the ice and snow, it took us more than ten minutes to reach the park. We were shivering. The long shadows of the trees and the electrical lampposts looked scary and menacing in the dark. But, we had a mission to be humane to the little mouse in the trap, so we pushed on. Horus was happy about the unexpected opportunity to walk to his favourite park at such an unusual time. Slipping and sliding, we forged on.

Soon, we reached a spot that we decided was sufficiently away from the nearest house. It would have been irresponsible to send the mouse into another house, which would surely use a method to get rid of it less humane from ours. So, I took the little trap out of its paper bag, and was amazed to feel its warmth. I carefully opened both sides of the trap, and laid it on the snowy ground. Smelling the little creature in the box, Horus started barking and running crazy circles around the trap. The poor mouse did not come out of its confining tube for a long time. It was either afraid of Horus's commotion, or its joints hurt because of its confinement. We wondered if it had been caught in there for a while before Negrisse heard the scratching and woke up. After a long wait that seemed to be hours but was probably only a few minutes, the mouse crawled out. Perhaps because of its fear, or disorientation, rather than running away and disappearing in the vast field, it charged towards us. Both Negrisse and I started shrieking, and backing away on the slippery ground. But it was Horus who got scared the most, and ran away galloping on all fours. We took Horus to protect us in the dark night, and found out that he was afraid of a little mouse! Poor Horus, he was such a gentle soul.

Flashback: Negrisse at age thirteen

My motherhood is not going well. Negrisse and I are butting heads. She has started wearing all black clothing and black boots. She wants to dye her hair black, and I resist. I say she is much too young to use hair dyes. I show her my own hair, to let her see how dyes deplete hair's natural vitality. She hates me.

Negrisse is corresponding with a bunch of people from all over Canada and the States. Each day, I find numerous envelopes in the mailbox. Her correspondence is different from all the other mail we receive. The envelopes are decorated with things like safety pins and hair braids, front and back. Often, senders use different colours of nail polish to accentuate the chaos. So, the mail Negrisse receives is luminescent, shiny, almost alive. It is difficult to see the stamp. I wonder how the post-office deals with this kind of mail, but bless their heart, they keep on delivering.

Negrisse announces that some of the people she has been corresponding with have decided to come to Toronto to visit her. It is going to be some kind of a punk reunion. She wants to hold the reunion in our house. Indeed, we have a large basement that is finished as a recreation room. The floor is carpeted and we have three sofas that open up into beds. Both Greg and I are working now. We can afford the few bottles of pop, bags of chips and cookies that she asks for. Other than that, the group is going to split on a pizza, and clean up after themselves, I am told. I think of the reasonability of these demands, and discuss the issue with Greg. He thinks there is nothing wrong in letting Negrisse have some fun. After all, what could be so bad about a bunch of girls getting together for a sleepover? Besides, I am very unhappy with the tension between my daughter and myself. Maybe allowing this visit will show Negrisse that I am not that disagreeable.

So, the arranged night arrives, and Greg and I drive to the airport to gather a bunch of black-clad girls who have been sending my daughter all those decorated envelopes. We wait for the different planes arriving from Chicago, from New York, and from L.A. The black-clad guests arrive, one by one. But none of them are girls, they are men, possibly ranging in age from twenty to twenty-five. I am dumbfounded, speechless, and enraged. How dare these men show up in my home for a pajama party with my thirteen-year-old daughter?

To be fair, later on some older girls also show up, all in black, with whitened faces and cherry-red lips. These are the Toronto contingent. In the meantime, I call Negrisse for a parental conference. I challenge her about the gender of our international guests, and why I was not informed about this before they strolled out of their respective planes. Negrisse is not apologetic. Her eyes are flashing with a thousand thunderbolts. She says, "It is YOU who claims that men and women are equal. You are a hypocrite to suggest that only *my girl friends are welcome to our house, and my boy friends are not!" I am still furious, but she does have a point. She is challenging the difference between my equality ideals, and my gendered traditionalism. I say: "But, you are only thirteen!" I think I am right, but I hear the hollowness in my argument.*

I ask Negrisse and her under-aged girl friends to sleep upstairs, after their festivities are over. I have no say over people past the voting age, so they make their own arrangements in my recreation room. It is about 3:00 am, when the black-clad group settles down. I go to bed, but do not sleep a wink. All I wanted was to mend the worn-out bridge between Negrisse and myself. All I accomplished is to reinforce in her mind that I am a tyrant and now a "hypocrite."

Shortly after our saga with the mouse, Negrisse painted her walls a dark brick colour, closed her heavy drapes once and for all, and turned first into vegetarian, then a vegan. She painted larger than life sized dragons on her walls. Some of the dragons were standing erect, with their fangs and claws showing, others were spewing fire from their mouths.

Since dragons have been long-term residents in Negrisse's drawings, this did not immediately alarm me. If I had been alarmed, I do not know what I could have done. After the fact, when the vision is 20/20, I do know that I should have done something to slow down Negrisse's transformation, to help her find alternate ways to express herself. What threw me off the most were that the signs I associated with the undesirable aspects of the youth culture, were missing in Negrisse's case. For example, Negrisse continued to attend her school, and continued to receive As and A-pluses. Negrisse did not smoke or drink or use dangerous drugs. As a matter of fact, she did not even consume carbonated drinks, and often settled for filtered water. Negrisse had a lot of boys around her, often boys who were much older than her, but she did not have a specific boyfriend for a long time. When she did, she stayed in what appeared to be a respectful, caring relationship, at least for a while. So, for the longest time, I interpreted her black clothes, her veganism, her depressive music and fierce dragons as a slightly turbulent stage within the angst of growing up.

Flashback: Negrisse at age fourteen, Iris at age twelve and Daisy at age ten

I *am taking a graduate level psychology course as an elective. I love the course, because we get to do self-awareness exercises every week. One of the exercises we do in class is called the "animal exercise." Basically, what it involves is for people who know one another well, to sit in a circle, and think very carefully about what animal would best represent each of the participants around the circle. Then each person takes a turn, telling each other person what animal they think best represents them, and why. In the second part of the exercise, the tables are turned around, and each person picks an animal to represent him/herself, and explain why. The professor who is teaching this course instructs us to be extremely careful in our selection of the animals, and to try our best to turn this experience into a growth process for all rather than calling each other names. It works, and we all learn many things about ourselves. We also learn about the discrepancies between how we see ourselves, and how others see us.*

I cannot wait to introduce the same exercise to my family. It is a good thing that Greg's daughters are staying with us for the weekend, so they can also participate. I explain the exercise, and its goals. Greg and Negrisse listen to my instructions carefully, the younger girls giggle and fidget.

We start the exercise by asking Greg's daughters to pick an animal for each of us, and explain why they chose what they chose. Both pick cats for Negrisse and I, the justification being that we love cats. Indeed, we do; by this time, we have four adopted cats in our house. The girls pick a dog for their father, the justification again being the fact that Greg loves dogs. He indeed loves Horus. The girls are obviously too young to really get to the core goal of the exercise, so they confine their choices to the simple and the obvious. We do not mind, since they seem to be having a very good time.

It is my turn to verbally declare my choice for Negrisse. I think very hard about my choice, and I think I find the perfect match ... at least in my mind. Negrisse started the exercise with an exaggerated rolling of her eyes, and the usual signs of her boredom, but she seems to be more involved now, so I am exceptionally happy that

I *introduced the exercise to my family. My pick for Negrisse is the Monarch butterfly. I explain my choice through the predominance of black on its wings and on its body. However, I insist, there is also a brilliance of colour on the wings, a marvellous orange, and an equally marvellous brilliance in Negrisse's use of words and language. I continue by explaining my choice in a second dimension, more accurately, a set of dimensions. I say, "the Monarch has fragile wings, which can easily crumble, even by a gentle human touch." Negrisse, I say, "looks equally dainty, and fragile." Yet, I continue, "birds know better than eat Monarchs because they have an aversive taste, and people around Negrisse know not to take her lightly, because she can use her oratory skills very well. Besides, the fragility of the Monarch is misleading since it can fly all the way from Canada to Mexico on those seemingly delicate wings." I complete my explanations by pointing to Negrisse's strength of character and amazing will power.*

Negrisse does not say a word, but listens carefully to my explanations. She appears neither pleased nor displeased, whereas I was expecting some kind of a positive acknowledgement of my careful selection. Others take their turns, and the second segment of the exercise arrives. It is now Negrisse's turn to pick an animal to represent herself. I cannot wait to hear what she will say. Even the younger girls stop fidgeting, and turn their attention to Negrisse.

Negrisse is prolonging the silence. She is either thinking a little more about her choice, or enjoying the cliff-hanging suspense. Then she shares her choice of an animal for herself. She says, "I see myself as a spider," and my jaw drops to the floor. I have difficulty to pull it back to its normal position. I have difficulty in closing my mouth. Negrisse continues, oblivious to—or dismissive of—my surprise. "I weave elaborate webs. I go to a corner and wait. I am exceptionally patient, and I can wait out anyone." She continues, "But then, there is the vibration in the silk, a fly is caught and struggling to get itself free. I walk on the web I have weaved as if it were a highway, and pounce. My venom dissolves my enemies." She looks around in triumph. My jaw does not seem to retract to its customary position. I think my eyes are also slightly out of their sockets. I am not able to wrap my mind around the choice Negrisse has just made. I have a hard time thinking of her as a venomous spider rather than the beautiful and graceful Monarch butterfly I see her as.

Many years later, a spider bites me on my right forearm. My arm swells up like a balloon, and changes its colour to an angry purplish black. The pain, the throbbing and swelling, and the change in colour are so frightful that there is the possibility that I might lose my forearm. The emergency personnel are baffled; they suspect a tropical disease. I am not responding well to the antihistamines and the antibiotics they are pumping into me. I am having difficulty in understanding my body's violent reaction to that little bite. I guess, without knowing it, I have developed a severe allergy to spiders.

I was wrong in a number of ways. First, Negrisse's involvement in punk culture turned out to be more than a passing phase. In fact, whatever the tenets of this culture were, they had a very long-lasting and decisive impact on her young adulthood. Secondly, Negrisse created an ironclad youth network around herself, which consisted of other young people who were as dedicated to punk culture as she was. In a way, the group powerfully catapulted each member to go to more and more extreme demonstrations of their commitment to "punkhood." The group became judge and jury passing judgment on demonstrations of one's loyalty to a punk life. The most feared label was "being a poser," which meant that someone was pretending to be punk through their clothing and make-up, but did not have what it really takes to be punk. There were continuous altercations, mostly in written and verbal form, between the true "punks" and those deemed to be "posers." Negrisse chose to go deeper and deeper into the culture, possibly to avoid being sidelined as a "poser." When I was her age, my friends and I used to fear being labelled "mousy." At my delayed university life, people stigmatized "geeks." It seems that, especially within youth culture, being something requires putting down something else.

To this day, I cannot say I know that much about punk culture. I can say that the group my daughter became totally immersed in was not necessarily a bad group. These young people were not dropouts; most of them did very well at school. None of them drank and/or used substances. To my knowledge, none of them engaged in vandalism or violence. In addition, most of Negrisse's friends showed some social awareness and responsibility. For example, most were vegans or vegetarians, most participated in environmental or animal rights demonstrations, and many were members of NGOs like the Amnesty International, Green Peace or PETA. They pooled their money to send to organizations that protected seals or whales or polar bears. So, in a way, I was extremely proud of and supportive of my daughter in many of her passions. I even joined some animal rights and environmental protection rallies Negrisse and her friends organized. I admired them when they found old and mange fur coats, painted them with red paint, and laid on the ground in public places. Their signs read: "Animals need their coats more than you do!"

To this day, I do not really understand the dark and sinister part of punk culture that existed simultaneously with the good part. Somehow, these young people were against any form of authority, starting with a deep-rooted mistrust of politicians, the legal and justice systems including the police, the educational system including the teachers, and the institution of the family. The target of their greatest cynicism was their parents. This was ironic, since most of Negrisse's friends had living parents, some in so-called intact families, some in alternate types of arrangements, such as Greg and myself. From what I could see, none of these young people were in impoverished and/or abusive situations, and again, from what I could tell, many of their parents were reasonably educated, hard-working people. What I do know for sure was that both Greg and I were trying our absolute best to provide a decent home for Negrisse, although both of us were swamped in the effort of completing our own education—albeit delayed. The trouble was, we did not have a direct line of communication with Randall, and we certainly lacked Randall's cooperation in any of our efforts to provide a seamless parenthood for Negrisse. The general distrust punk culture held towards all parents fuelled Negrisse's negative reaction to our supervision as opposed to Randall's *laissez-faire* parenting style. Negrisse began to bitterly complain about what she called my "suffocating love." I buried my love for her deep inside me, to refrain from doing what she called "suffocating." I was afraid of touching her, in case she interpreted my touch as a hug.

29.

Dungeons and Dragons

FREQUENTLY, I OPENED OUR HOUSE to Negrisse's punk friends. I am not using the word "punk" in a pejorative sense at all, since these young people did call themselves "punks" and saw this designation as an honourable badge. Dressed in their black outfits, jet-black hair, and army boots, they descended into my home like ravens. I thought Negrisse was better off where I could see—and feed—the group, rather than in another place I knew nothing about. The group did huddle together, usually many hours in a row, munching on chips, drinking orange juice, and towards the wee hours of the morning, pooling all their change together for pizza. I heard heated discussions peppered with exaggerated laughter, but everything stopped when I knocked on the rec-room door and delivered or retrieved something. The group played games like Dungeons and Dragons, but their games had more colourful names, more characters and extensive plots.

From bits and pieces of information Negrisse occasionally volunteered, I came to the realization that these games were the lifeline of the group. Each member spent days trying to invent interesting characters for themselves, and in turn, got totally absorbed in the characters they invented. In their phone conversations, and in some of their written correspondence, they would refer to each other with their game-character names rather than their given names. This is also how Negrisse's own name got forfeited, and she emerged as "Negrisse."

One of the male members of the group, an exceptionally tall and spindly man, was the designated game-master of the group. I will call him Juddah, pun intended, for reasons that will become clear when Negrisse's story unfolds. I think Juddah was the one who set the boundaries of each game, who assigned the characters, and who came up with the plot and the story line. At the end of each game, Juddah also provided feedback to the players, saying what they did right—assuming there was a right—and what they did wrong—assuming there was a wrong. Juddah, as the game-master, had a demi-god position in the group. With his negative comments, which I gathered were many, he could bring any one of the group members to tears. He also had the power to elevate them, on the basis of his feedback on how they played their roles. Negrisse was infatuated with Juddah. For her, he held the golden key to the dramaturgical universe that her punk group occupied. Eventually, and after a couple of reasonably meaningful relationships, she married Juddah. I was informed, but not consulted, about her marital choice, but that was much later.

Although I tried very hard to understand the logic behind the Dungeons and Dragons games played by my daughter's group, I really never understood the enormous power these games exerted on the players. Notwithstanding my incomplete comprehension, these games had strong plots that took place during designated historical periods. I cannot speak for others, but I know for sure that Negrisse did a lot of research in attaining some mastery over her character within the historical period the character was assumed to live. I had no problem with the research part, since I considered the love of reading as my daughter's major strength. In this regard, I was absolutely correct, since Negrisse eventually completed her doctorate degree in history, and settled in a teaching position at a university in New York.

What I felt uneasy about was the type of characters she was assigned—or the ones she chose to play. These characters were sinister, menacing, vengeful, controlling, and exploitative women. I may be wrong—and I hope I am wrong—but I have the feeling that the characters Negrisse played were based on *her perceptions of me*. I felt deeply hurt. I felt misunderstood and transgressed. The ironic aspect is that stereotypes may be built around a kernel of truth, but they end up grossly exaggerating that small kernel. Once the beholder of the stereotype believes in the representativeness of the image, all information that supports the stereotype will get highlighted while all the information that negates the stereotype will be dismissed. In other words, stereotypes have a self-fulfilling nature, for those who hold on to the stereotype. For example, I am the first to admit that

I am a little controlling: I like to be kept informed; I like to be on time, and I am a perfectionist. The role models in my upbringing, including Sophie, Agnes, and my beloved father, were all controlling people. So, Negrisse was right in attributing this negative characteristic to me; I know enough about myself to own my faults. However, I found it unfair for her to over-exaggerate my controlling nature as being sinister, menacing, vengeful, and exploitative. Regrettably, the characteristics she attributed to her characters—and indirectly to me— served to construct an image of me in her mind that neither one of us were able to dismantle over time. As my feelings of being hurt grew, so did her unabated umbrage.

Knowingly or unknowingly, Juddah played a role in widening the wedge between Negrisse and myself. But, that came second. Juddah's first successful move was to create a wedge between Negrisse and her first boyfriend, Zimbabwe. Zimbabwe was a tall, charming young man, with jet-black hair that reached his waist. Originally, he was one of the important members of her punk group. Despite the ominous appearance of his black clothes, black boots, and abundance of jet-black hair, Zimbabwe was a gentle, soft-spoken man, who was very affectionate towards Negrisse. Once I got over my initial reaction to Zimbabwe's foreboding stature, I actually became very fond of him. He, in turn, seemed to genuinely enjoy Greg's and my company, and started visiting us on his own time, outside of the supervision of the group. Greg and I, coupled with Negrisse and Zimbabwe, started to spend a lot of time together, playing card games, or Scrabble, or reading out loud some gothic literature that all of us enjoyed. After too long of a qualitative decline, I started to feel hopeful that the schism between my daughter might begin to mend. I hoped that Zimbabwe's abundant affections would wash away some of the cold cynicism Negrisse had spun around herself.

I think it was in the backdrop of these positive developments, and my full-hearted acceptance of Zimbabwe, that Juddah changed his game plan. Although I have a pretty good idea about why he did it, I am fuzzier on how he did what he did. I think he started by putting in motion small things to erode Zimbabwe's over-all standing in the group. For example, he gave less important roles to Zimbabwe in their constructed Dungeons and Dragons games. He also viciously criticized his shortfalls within the game. These were the highly valued aspects of group membership, so his harsh criticisms indeed weakened Zimbabwe's status position in the group. To my recollection, Zimbabwe did not fight back. Maybe, his much younger age made him vulnerable to Juddah's more seasoned manipulations. Maybe, he was so kind and trusting that he did not see through Juddah's schemes. Maybe, it was Negrisse's infatuation with Juddah that gave him the edge, the unfair advantage.

Whatever the real reasons behind the change, Zimbabwe became marginalized within the group. Once he was marginalized, Negrisse no longer wanted him as a boyfriend. Juddah incrementally filled in the void, and arose as Negrisse's new partner. This shift unnerved me greatly. Although I could not put my finger on what it was that bothered me so much, I knew something was not right. I had become very fond of Zimbabwe, and mourned the fact that he was no longer a part of Negrisse's, and indirectly, my own life. I missed his kindness, his easy-to-get-along ways, and subtle humour. I found Juddah cold, calculating, distant and judgmental. I think my scepticism about Juddah and his scepticism about me were mutual. I also felt a renewal of my questioning the ethical climate of the group. How was it that the group allowed the unfair excommunication of a previously beloved member? How was it that the group allowed such an "incestuous" partner exchange right in front of their eyes, since the group took pride in seeing themselves as a close family?

In one of our increasingly declining heart-to-heart conversations, I asked Negrisse about how she felt about what I considered to be an "incestuous" partner exchange within the group. Of course, this was not really a family; no one was bound by marriage or by blood. However, the group felt closer to one another than to their actual families, and they spent enormous amounts of time with one another. So, and at least in my own mind, there was some symbolic level of incest in shifting partners within the group, which would make every young woman and every young man fear about the stability of their relationships with one another. Negrisse's response to my inquiry was thought provoking. She said that precisely for the degree of closeness I had correctly perceived, that the group members had no other choice for partners than those within the group. In a way, although they lived in a many-million population city like Toronto, their self-imposed boundaries were defined by the group, like the

Mormons or the Hutterites. Although I understood her explanation, I cannot say that I condoned such close-proximity love exchanges. I felt awfully bad for Zimbabwe, who was unfairly excommunicated from the group.

During the second year of Negrisse's doctoral studies at an American university, Juddah was also accepted into the doctoral program, and moved in with her. Once the move was complete, and they settled into their graduate student routine, the emotional distance between Negrisse and I grew to new levels. She did not have much to say when I called, except to say she was in a rush. She never remembered to call me back. With the exception of rare visits that lasted hours rather than days, Negrisse stopped coming to Toronto. She always had an excuse for why I should not visit them. "Maybe next month" soon turned to "maybe next year." We were already on a slippery slope, and whatever brakes I tried were failing to reduce the rush to the bottom. The dissymmetry was that although Negrisse was an exceptionally important part of my life, I was not allowed to play any role in the life of Negrisse. Talk about life reflecting the sad and artificial casting of roles in Dungeons and Dragons.

At a totally unexpected time, I received an invitation from Negrisse. Well, it is a stretch to call that piece of paper an invitation, it was really an announcement. The announcement was printed on a single, letter-size, sheet of paper, in black and white. The contents cheerfully announced that Negrisse and Juddah were getting married, in a particular place, at a particular date and time, amongst a very small gathering of close friends. The announcement also included a note directed at the respective families of the bride and groom. Basically, it said that there may be a different ceremony for the families, in the future, but this particular occasion was only open to close friends.

To add insult to injury, the paper decree was followed up with a phone call from Negrisse. Swallowing my hurt and outrage, I tried to express my congratulations for her upcoming marriage. I felt that although my congratulations under the circumstances were not as genuine as I would have liked them to be, at least I had the courtesy to extend them to my daughter. Without spending much time on niceties, Negrisse moved right into the real reason behind her unusual call. She said that Juddah's parents were extremely unhappy with their son's decision to exclude them from attending his marriage ceremony. Apparently, his parents had threatened to come all the way from England to see their son tie the knot. Negrisse said that Juddah had threatened his parents back, by saying that he would call security if they showed up and crashed his wedding. Negrisse wanted to inform me about the firmness of their decision to keep all of us out. I was frozen to the phone. I was shaken. All I could mumble was, "Negrisse, if you really knew who I am, you would have known that I would never crash a wedding." I got off the phone, feeling that someone pushed me out of a plane, and I was free falling.

30.

Motherhood Has Nine Lives

I ALREADY MENTIONED the "parenthood as Sudoku" saying I invented. I have another one I would like to share: "Like cats, motherhood has nine lives." Negrisse's cold and calculated exclusion of me (and Randall and Greg) from her wedding must have been the eighth life my motherhood lost. During the days following what I considered to be a callous phone call, I had a hard time of dealing with Negrisse's overt rejection. During the nights, I struggled with nightmares. It was true that I was not fond of Juddah, but I had always been courteous to him during the dozens of times he showed up at my home. Although I generally despise of self-pity, I drowned in self-pity for a while.

Then, like a cat, I found the final strength in me, the ninth life so-to-speak, and sent my daughter a wedding card, and included a check towards whatever expenses they may have had. The amount was not large; certainly I could have carried a bigger share if circumstances were different. However, my goodwill was there, despite the blatant and deliberate brush-off.

For a while, I did not hear from Negrisse. This silence was not at all unusual, given her new marriage, and general tendency to avoid family communications. After a few months, rather than writing directly to me, she sent an email to Greg. In the note, she mentioned in passing that she and Juddah had decided to attend a punk concert in Toronto, using some of the money I sent them. Negrisse's note indicated the time and the date of the concert, and expressed her willingness to talk to us at the door, if we made the effort to drive to the concert gate. I should have been prepared for further rejection, but I was not. Negrisse often managed to stun me with her unsurpassed callousness. Rather than going indirectly through Greg, like she had done, I wrote a regular letter to Negrisse, and mailed it to her new address. I said that I would have loved to welcome her and her new husband in my home, especially given the fact that I was not invited to her marriage ceremony. However, I said, if the only time she could spare for me was a few minutes at the crowded gate of a concert hall, I would rather decline her invitation. The rest of the note expressing my heartbreak went something like this:

Call me greedy, overpowering, whatever else you call me but ... I would have loved to, cherished, and treasured sharing some of the events in my life with you, in some other way than disjointed e-mail messages or truncated, clock-punching, or few and far between calls. The latter are nice, but not conducive to sustain or nourish any relationship in and of themselves. I would have loved to share, in some meaningful way, at least those occasions which appeared to be once-in-a-life-time, like your recent marriage, since you are the only daughter I have in this world. I didn't, I couldn't, and the latter was never my choice.

As if the disappointment of these missed years is not enough, I have to deal with the judging words and looks of people, friends and foes alike, about your endless absences. It takes all the energy I have to look them in the eye and say good morning. Thank God, I manage to keep my head up, believing full-heartedly that I am not the monstrous dragon people may deduce me to be from your relentless absences.

There are also the small, trivial, fleeting, day-by-day things that constitute what I call the backbone of one's life experiences. Such silly things like, do you like my new hair colour, or did you smell the new rose in my garden, or did you like such and such article in today's paper, or do you still cut your peanut butter sandwich in four pieces or what material was your wedding dress made of? Can you capture the carefree laughs we had about trivial things in an email message? It is these trivialities, along with the substance of the events themselves, which make a living, breathing relationship of any kind. In their absence, what remains are cold, pre-judged, pre-screened, dissected words that occasionally appear on a computer screen. What also remains is the self-righteousness we attribute to ourselves (and attach blame to the other), to justify why things are the way they are.

In my black disappointment over the last weekend when apparently, we yet again shared the city I live in but not even a kind word over the phone, I listened to the whole set of Leonard Cohen albums. Let me close by a few of his lines, which sum up how I feel: "It's come to this, yes it's come to this. Wasn't it a long way down!"? In another song, he says, "love is the answer," let us hope and pray he is right, because I love you enough for the two of us.

Your mother

Negrisse never responded to my note, never apologized, or bothered to explain. Knowing her, this "I am holier than thou" stance was expected. What I did not expect was what followed. Negrisse mailed me a large box, addressed to my office rather than my home, containing numerous books, gifts, etc., that I had given or sent her in the last couple of years. There was no note. Thus, the ninth and the final life of my parenthood died when I received back the gifts I had chosen for her, some of them still in their original packages. Obviously, Negrisse was on a mission to reinvent herself. She changed her name, she changed her appearance, she changed schools, she changed her citizenship, and she even changed her religion. She once sacrificed Zimbabwe to the same end, now it was my turn. Like Aphrodite rising from the sea-foam, totally absorbed in her own beauty, it was obvious that Negrisse did not need a mother.

Part VII:
Completed Cycles, Incomplete Dreams

31.

Sophie's Demise

MY FATHER'S EARLY DEATH created a large void in Sophie's life. This was due to two reasons. For one, my father was a brilliant man, who possessed a keen sense of the workings of the world around him. Sophie lacked such insights. Moreover, my father loved and cherished his family. Sophie appreciated his commitment to our family and counted on his protective arms. Thus, his shoes, as a father and as a husband, were hard to fill. Sophie was both unwilling and unprepared for a life that did not include my father's protective wings. The second reason why Sophie was not able to fill the void my father left behind was because Agnes moved right in. Rather than supporting Sophie to gather her strength and pursue an independent life, Agnes reinforced her existing inclination for dependency, and she emerged as the honorary patriarch. Within the first few months after my father's funeral, Agnes and her husband moved into our parental home, and systemically rearranged the flow of our lives. As a military officer, my father was never a rich man, but he had managed to build us a nice home. Moreover, he left a rental property, health and medical coverage for life, and a reasonable survivor's income for Sophie. Thus, Sophie and I could not only have survived, but could have flourished, give or take a few months after the shock. But, Agnes took over all aspects of our lives, without a blink. Soon, Sophie and I had to get Agnes's approval for the most basic things, like what should be served for dinner and whether we could invite some friends over or not. Sophie's life-long tendency for shifting responsibility onto others helped to fortify Agnes's iron grip. Once the original crisis of losing my father was behind me, I increasingly resented living under the thumb of my sister who was only a handful of years older than I was. What gave her the edge was she was married, and I was not. In the Turkey of my youth, marriage bestowed personhood on previously unmarried girls.

Once Agnes had settled in, Sophie had no escape route, so she learned to live under the ever-growing power of Agnes. Agnes told her what to say, where to go, what time to come back, who to see, and what to do. With the exception of some child-like tantrums, Sophie never really challenged Agnes's power over her. The tables were turned, and Sophie who used to be a temperamental and controlling mother, became a well-taken-care-of, but frequently reprimanded and occasionally punished child. I had my concerns about this major power shift. However, by that time, I was living in Canada, and had my own struggles ahead of me in establishing my own independence. I became my own person only when I found the courage to leave Randall.

I must acknowledge that the way I just described the dethroning of Sophie after my father's death may not be totally fair to Agnes. The process was more like a chicken and an egg. I am not exactly sure whether Sophie's already existing dependence, or Agnes's already existing dominance, caused the final imbalance in power. Maybe, these complementary aspects worked in unison, and catapulted the change. Sophie did not seem unhappy about her increasing dependence on Agnes. Sometimes, I even got the sense that she was relieved that there was someone who made all the major decisions for her, like my father had done during their married life.

I did feel a qualitative difference though, and disliked the change. The change also gained speed after Agnes divorced Lynford. Soon, the nameplate on the door of my parents' home read "Agnes," and my mother's bank accounts were converted into joint accounts, giving full access to Agnes. The furniture in the house started reflecting Agnes's extravagant tastes, rather than Sophie's life-long preference for Spartan living. The recorded phone message asked the caller to leave a message for Agnes, as if Sophie did not live in her own house. When I asked Sophie whether I could visit her during a certain holiday, her unchanging reply was "ask your sister." Most of the time, Agnes said by all means, but some of the time, she said that that date was not convenient for her, and I should come at another time. Not once, did Agnes ask me whether the alternate time she suggested was convenient for me, although she knew that my schooling, paid-work and single parenthood left little time to do anything else. The bottom line was that even my ability to visit my mother was contingent upon Agnes's whims.

So, Sophie lived a long life, under what seemed to me as unbearable controls and limitations. I never lost my love for Sophie, not even the tiniest bit. But, I must say that my original respect for the energetic, creative, go-getter mother I once knew dwindled over time. I don't know if Sophie ever compared her own incremental demise to the demise of Beatrice. Maybe she did, maybe she didn't. Regardless, this was a comparison I could not help but make, over and over again in my mind.

Beatrice, after her husband's death, had found shelter in Sophie's home. She had brought in some wealth with her, but by the time I was around, her wealth was gone and she was totally at the mercy of my parents. I remember Sophie ordering Beatrice around, sometimes with less care and consideration than was culturally required. When the tables were turned and Sophie found herself in the dependent role, Agnes's interactions with Sophie were even less desirable than Sophie's interactions with Beatrice had been. Sophie certainly had food in front of her, clothes on her back, and medical care when she needed it. Thanks to my father, she also had a secure income, which was deposited in her joint account with Agnes. But, from what I could see, she experienced no warmth, no support or understanding from Agnes. If my father were alive, he would never have put up with that kind of infantilizing treatment. More correctly, if my father were alive, Agnes could not have garnered as much power as she did in his absence.

My transatlantic visits, although remaining as relatively joyous occasions, became more monitored, more on edge, and more prone to tension, at least on my part. I did not want to say something or do something to disturb the fragile balance in my mother's home, as unequal and as unfair as it seemed to me. After all, I was not there all the time, and the Western values I now hold high were not necessarily the same values that governed family relationships in the country I left behind. Although I was glad that Sophie was not going to be alone during my long absences, I also knew that deep down she was more alone than anyone I knew. She was as alone as Beatrice had been.

During the first couple of decades after my migration to Canada, Sophie was in very good health. She shopped, cleaned, sewed, repaired, knitted, and embroidered to her heart's content. She prepared breakfast every morning, and did all the dishes, throughout the day. Of course, her daily activities, and even her creative hobbies were under Agnes's supervision and guidance. Sophie also had a granddaughter she adored, and would do anything for. The granddaughter she treasured was Agnes's daughter Darion, not Negrisse. To be honest, I cannot blame Sophie for being partial to Darion. She was born into the house that was Sophie's, and lived in that house until she became a young woman. In a way, Darion's love for Sophie, and Sophie's love and sacrifice for Darion were comparable to my childhood relationship with Beatrice. Sophie never told epic stories, but sewed dresses, knitted sweaters, scarves and mittens for Darion. Most of all, Sophie served as the main target, a symbolic punching-ball for Agnes's anger and angst. By doing so, she protected Darion from becoming the scapegoat for Agnes's eternal frustrations. Whatever breathing space Darion experienced in her growing years was the result of Sophie's self-sacrifice.

Regrettably, Negrisse never experienced this kind of grandmotherly love, since Randall and I left Turkey before she celebrated her first birthday. Sophie, in turn, never had an opportunity to caress, feed, change, and create things for Negrisse, like she did for Darion. Knowing how imperative Beatrice's love was in my own childhood, I deeply regret the absence of such a central relationship in Negrisse's life. In my family, unconditional love between women seems to skip a generation, since mothers and daughters are caught in unending conflicts. It is the grandmothers who provide unconditional love.

Sophie was the happiest when Darion was young, and still around. In Darion's presence, Sophie's usual facial expression, stern, seemed to dissolve, melt away, and leave behind a more tender face I was not accustomed to. Her tone of voice, which often hinted at impatience, became a warm auditory blanket when she addressed Darion. Darion also bloomed within the circle of her grandmother's love. She played, ate, and slept with much less fuss with Sophie than with Agnes. In the end, and thanks to Sophie, Darion grew up to be a much more loving and caring woman than Agnes, myself or Negrisse.

It was in her declining years that Sophie's long-term dependence on Agnes produced its bitter fruits. By that time, although Agnes was still meeting her physical needs, she was considered a total nuisance. Sophie's declining health aside—which was problematic in itself—her mental health too went through a steep deterioration. She started to confuse names, dates, times, and not understand or totally misinterpret what was being said to her. She would forget to use her walker, which stood beside her bed, and fall. She would open the door of the house, and forget to close it after. She would turn on the stove, and burn whatever was on it. She would forget to eat or drink, or forget to take her medications. She eventually looked starved and emaciated. She regressed into her own childhood, which neither Agnes nor I knew much about. She claimed that she loved something one day, and hated it the next. She occasionally soiled her clothes. Once a dignified woman, Sophie increasingly became the butt of cruel jokes.

I pleaded with Agnes to find a decent facility that could provide the services my mother seemed to desperately need. Each time, she refused. In a way, I understood her vehement refusals since Turkey is still a very family-oriented society, where daughters are expected to take care of their aging parents. This crushing social pressure has somewhat declined in Canada and the U.S., but still exists in many Eastern societies. As a result of daughter-caregiver designations, there are not too many good choices in Turkey for the placement of elderly parents. The few options that exist seem to be either run under extremely poor conditions, or are so pricey that only the very rich can afford them. So, as the next best thing, I pleaded with Agnes to hire some help. That option was—and is—widely available in Turkey, and can be a very good and reasonable alternative to institutionalized care. Agnes's response was a resounding "no." She said she was not going to abandon my mother, clearly insinuating that I had done so. Although there was so much justification for my original escape, Agnes had the upper hand. She had our mother as a hostage. So, I retreated into silence and humiliation. I had to come to terms with the fact that Sophie needed help, but I was not able to help her in any shape or form.

In her last few years, Sophie lost so much weight that she reminded me of a squirrel. Her false teeth, which were fitted at a time when she had more flesh, chattered and churned in her mouth. She already had trouble speaking, because her intellectual capabilities were in sharp decline. But, the looseness of her false teeth prevented her from saying the few words she could still remember. So, in my weekly overseas phone calls all she could offer were monosyllabic responses. Until the end, however, she did manage to say, "I want to see you again," which tore into my heart.

The actual goal of my weekly phone calls was to allow Agnes to blow off some steam. She did. I heard details about every new nuisance Sophie had caused, or about things she failed to do. I heard about Sophie's talking in her sleep, or mistaking Agnes for Beatrice. I heard about Sophie feeding her own medication to the cat, thinking that the pills were cat food. I heard about some of the "unspeakable" things Sophie had done while eating, or in the bath, or in the bathroom. I heard about her falls, and sprains and bruises. I heard about Sophie's broken hip, and the emergency trip to the hospital.

Both Sophie and Agnes were stranded on thinning ice. The ice was cracking. Soon, they were going to plunge into freezing waters. I was stranded on my own piece of ice, 7,000 miles away. I heard about their constant struggles, their desperation, without being able to extend a hand on a day-to-day basis. Agnes was adamant about not hiring help, and the help I could provide from half a world away was miniscule. Even during my yearly or emergency-based visits, there was too much accumulated blame to sift through before I could be of some help to Sophie or to Agnes. By the time the worst of the dust settled, it was time for me to return to Toronto.

The years of Sophie's serious decline, both in health and in mind, are full of emotional contradictions for me. I was torn between my love and pity for my mother, versus my understanding of how hard the circumstances were for Agnes. Although I had many problems with the care—especially the emotional care—my mother received, I also knew that I could not, would not, have put myself in Agnes's place. The quality of Sophie's life was so low that, sometimes I wished she would just let go rather than hang on. I caught myself thinking about that, and then loathed myself. I loved Sophie. She was my only surviving parent, how could I even think that she should let go? I pictured her in her large sun hat, wearing her cheerful cotton dress, as she watched me during my swimming competitions. She was there for me, despite the blistering sun. I remembered my watermelon red skirt, with the exquisite poodle on it, and the weeks of my mother's creativity that had gone into its production. Yet, I was not available for her, now that her own sun was near setting. The tears swelled in my eyes, my heart imploded. Still, I wondered how she still clung to life under so much resentment and Agnes's harsh words.

The declining years of Sophie also brought into focus things I had mentally pushed away, for years. Greg was one of those whom I had pushed away. What was in my own future? Yes, Canada, which I had chosen as my own, was much better equipped with caring for its vulnerable, but only to a degree. For an aging woman like me who had no partner, no daughter, no family, who was going to advocate for me when I could not do so for myself? The few true friends I had made over the years were also aging fast, and they were also in situations where their own futures were ambiguous. In a way, Sophie's last few years shone a spotlight on a mirror-darkly, which I would rather have not looked at. I wished I could put a black silk cover on what I saw in this mirror, like Mavis once had done to cover the picture of her departed daughter, Angel.

In the mirror-darkly, I saw Beatrice's loneliness, and for the first time, I really understood its depth. Although she lived with Sophie, Sophie and Beatrice's emotional alienation from one another was intense. I never saw Sophie hug her mother, and I am sure that this was not Beatrice's choice. As little girls, Agnes and I filled some of the emotional void in Beatrice's life, but this is not to say that we were substitutes for any meaningful adult company she may have longed for. Beatrice had no friends of her own, since she moved from place to place, from an apartment to army barracks, as my father was required to move. Beatrice lived her last years, and died, in the company of four walls. Even I, as her beloved grandchild, was not there when she took her last breath. She was alone in her hospital bed, just like she was alone when she suffered her stroke.

I also see Mavis's loneliness, although I knew my paternal grandmother less well. Mavis had survived a refugee journey, in the care of total strangers, without her parents. Her own attempt to form a close-knit family was cut short when her husband died. I do not know if she actually loved her much older husband, since love in a marriage was not a requirement in her time. What I do know is that she loved her children. Mavis had suffered the pain of losing her youngest daughter, and the pain of not being able to attend her funeral. Although she had two other daughters and a son, who loved her, Mavis mostly lived a solitary life, accompanied only by her fruit trees and flowers. Sophie's negative feelings for her mother-in-law had always tainted my own perceptions of my paternal grandmother during my childhood. However, now that I am approximating Mavis's age at the time I knew her, I clearly see her loneliness, and I find a new respect for the silence she shouldered in such a dignified way.

Sophie's last few years were spent in an emotional abyss. She did not relate to Agnes, and most certainly, Agnes did not relate to her, even before Sophie totally lost her mental capabilities. She lived without seeing me, sometimes ten, other times twelve months in a row, as she waited for my annual visits. What was worse for her was not being able to see the most important person in her life: Darion pursued her education and then her career in the United States. Although Darion continued to show warmth and affection for Sophie, most of it was over the phone. As far as my own phone calls went, they were long, but they said little. I had so much to say, but my mother's ability to understand what I could say had substantially declined. So, we spoke to each other in short and meaningless sentences, such as "how are you?" "I'm okay, and you?" Besides, Agnes was always on the other line, listening.

The mirror-darkly also reflects Agnes's isolated existence. Although she was the author of some of her own isolation, even she was caught up in and swallowed by the rushing waters of life. Even she was overpowered by the circumstances that slipped beyond her control. Despite many of Sophie's contributions to Agnes and Darion's lives, no one can say that the pressure of her declining years had been kind. Despite the daily struggles and bitter complaints, when Sophie was gone, Agnes came face-to-face with her own isolation. Despite her kind heart and social disposition, Darion could only provide a transient support for Agnes, much like the transient support I had been able to provide for Sophie. Besides, Darion and Agnes have their own skeletons in the closet. If they spend too much time together, some of the skeletons may venture out into the daylight, without the abundance of Sophie's love to mediate between the mother and the daughter.

Last but not least, the darkly-mirror shows me an image that hurts the most. It is the image of my own daughter, my beautiful Negrisse. How is she going to go through her own life, having negated everything that gave that life its original existence? She chose to reject my love for her, time and time again. She chose to sever any relationship, however flimsy it may have been, with her grandmother and aunt. She chose to have no contact with Darion, although they are cousins, and very similar in age, and in educational and intellectual accomplishments. To my understanding, Negrisse has left a succession of partners, so she may not have someone to share her life with as she too advances in age. When the time comes and she confronts her own darkly-mirror, what is she likely to see? Despite all the bygones, and if I am in her mirror at all, I hope, I will still appear to her with open arms.

32.

Anna's Last Few Years

I JUST TURNED EIGHTY-FOUR, not that it was a huge celebration. I did not invite a soul. I bought myself a cheap scarf, green paisley on dirty white. Dull and dreary, it matches my mood. I am not able to digest rich foods these days, so I skipped the cake, and had pudding instead. I don't know how the years passed by me so quickly. I seem to have aged in the blink of an eye. I coloured my hair for a long time, to cover up the grey. Then, I gave up. What is the use? Besides, my hair thinned out, and whatever strands are left, look funny in auburn from a box. I looked like a baby orangutan, with deep wrinkles, beady eyes, and a bad hair-day. Now that I set my hair free from the bondage of colouring, it looks a little less unsettling in its natural grey. Still, I avoid mirrors. Mirrors that were once my friends have become unkind.

My teeth became stained, worn-out at what used to be their sharp, but proportional edges. I had caps put on them, which were expensive as hell, but which pushed back the time for a while. Although nice in appearance, caps are not equivalent to natural teeth: they have a tendency to break or to fall off. So, I have had to baby them. I wish I had babied my natural teeth when I had them. They may have stayed in my mouth longer. In her last few years of life, I remember Sophie's loose dentures and shudder. The things she tried to eat jumped summersaults in her mouth. Her dentures made her unable to say the few words she managed to remember. I can still talk, a mile a minute, but I have trouble finding someone to talk to. My older friends are dying off, and the younger ones are avoiding older people like me like a plague. People must think that age is a communicable disease; they are keeping their distance. I snicker behind my facial wrinkles, knowing that there is no escape from getting old. They too will find out. They too will have dentures.

The wrinkles on my face: well, they have always been hard to conceal. They are like stubborn little rivers, eroding more and more of their banks on each side. I gave up fighting with them as well. No matter what I did, they always won. Maybe, I could have had elective surgery, where they pull up the loose skin towards the hairline. For a few thousand dollars, I could have secured an artificial tightness to my face. But, I did not want to take the road Joan Rivers and Cher took. I remember that Rivers had to ask people around her whether she was laughing, since she couldn't express emotions on her face. One of her eyes drooped down to her cheekbone although her face was pulled back as tight as a drum. There were also endless jokes about Cher. One joke said that after she died, they couldn't decide whether she should go to hell or to heaven, since there was little that remained of her natural body. Unlike Cher, I do not want to create havoc in my own afterlife. So, I allow my new wrinkles to build up over my older wrinkles. The bonus is that I can still tell whether I am laughing or frowning, without asking for anyone's help. With the exception of my nose job in my late teens, I am still mostly in one piece, so they will know where to send me after I die. I hope it is a place where people hurt each other less. I hope there is less friction between mothers and daughters in the afterlife.

My mind: that is the most precious of all, the part that has made me who I am. My mind is the organ of learning new things; my mind is the reservoir of my memories. A while ago, I stopped searching for new knowledge. The knowledge I already have keeps me going, like the wind-up toys of my childhood. Memories … well, my memories are still vibrant. Although some are excruciatingly painful, I do not want to forget them, or to let them go, not for a moment. Like diamonds in a mine, and gold in coffers, my memories are my treasures. Losing them would bankrupt me as a person, losing them would reduce me to nothingness. So, I still take my ginko-biloba, when I manage to remember.

I still have most of my old memories, but my short-term memory is in decline. I have to check twice, sometimes three or four times, to see if my door is locked. I have to search for my keys, several times, before I can step out of my house. Each time, I tell myself to put the keys in the same place, so I do not lose them, but each time

I forget where that place is. I read the newspaper, and forget what the headlines are. Each of the books in my extensive library has become brand new reading adventures. I read them again, without a single remaining clue of having read them before. I do not recall the characters, the plots, the resolutions. I find this funny. I used to read a book and remember all its details, including the footnotes.

Food used to be one of my obsessions. I used to cook. I used to dine in above average restaurants. I used to be able to differentiate between different aromas and different flavours. I loved food from exotic places, and of course, I loved the rich cuisine of my Turkish ancestors. Not any more. My choices are limited to Jell-O, and a variety of puddings these days. I eat some pureed fruit, if it is made from fruit that does not give me gas or trigger hives. I developed allergies across the years, allergies I never used to have. Now, I cannot consume food additives, preservatives, or food colouring. I cannot tolerate clothes made of wool, or nylon, or rayon, or spandex. Soon, I am going to be reduced to wearing my birth-clothes. If I had my choice, I would have stayed young forever, I would have been the first to offer my neck to a vampire, especially if the vampire was Brad Pitt from the movie, *Interview with the Vampire*. But, there are no vampires where I live, and even Brad and Angie and their hoard of kids got old. Even Brad Pitt lost his youthful charm and vampiric taste for fresh blood.

I also have to mention the handful of pills I take. The doctors I visit tell me I need them. I used to question their judgment when I was ideologically opposed to putting foreign substances into my body. Before, I had the luxury of my youth to stand behind my moral convictions. Those days are long gone now. I need pills in a rainbow of colours to keep me from falling to the floor as a glutinous puddle. My bone mass is a mess. I have dizzy spells now, and I cannot get up too quickly from where I am lying down or sitting. I have turned into a slow-motion re-play of my former self. I have high blood pressure, which creates wind-tunnel sounds in my ears. I have irregular heartbeats and palpitations. So, I swallow my rainbow-coloured pills, and thank those who invented them. However, I would have been happier if the pharmaceutical companies were a little less greedy. I do not understand why a little box of pills costs as much as a good-size convection oven. I am happy that I made

Canada my home, but something in our healthcare systems is out of sync. From the distance of youth, it looked much better than what it is. Then again, in my youth, I hardly needed it.

So, I get up, have one of my unrecognizably mashed foods from the fridge, read for a while, without necessarily remembering what I have just read. I sleep in the afternoons, for longer and longer durations. I get up again, just in time to eat some more pureed food. I force myself to write for a few hours. I try to write down some of Beatrice's stories, but the names and the plots are long gone. I should have written them down while they were fresh in my mind. I should have taped Beatrice's voice, as she told me her amazing stories. Then, I remember that we had no tape-recorders then. All we had was an AM radio, with a lot of static. I read what I have written down about Negrisse. Unlike Beatrice's stories, Negrisse is crystal clear in my mind. She still bristles and gives me wicked looks. But preserving the past by writing about it is important. The fact that these pages will remain even after I am gone gives me some comfort.

I look out of my window, just to pass the time. As I aged, time started moving faster. Talk about the variation of the theory of relativity. I see hundreds of people scurrying around, especially in the mornings and late afternoons. For them, time cannot go fast enough. They want their paychecks sooner, they want to get married, have children, and buy a house. They want their promotions. So, they are carrying briefcases, others are holding on to manila envelopes as if their lives depended on them. Almost all are on their phones, iPods, or plasmas, or whatever else they are called these days. My own final technological advancement coincided with the simple cell-phones that had attached antennas, and then, I gave up on gadgets altogether. I had no urgent calls to make to anyone. What I want to say cannot be said over the phone. That is why I sit down and write all these pages ... using the good old paper and pencil method.

The younger people I see on the streets ooze some kind of self-importance. I chuckle. I used to be one of those people who did not have time to walk. I used to run from meeting to meeting. I used to think that I was contributing something socially important by career counselling future generations. Probably, the students of that foregone era are amongst those who are scurrying around with their briefcases and manila envelopes now. Probably, they are the ones whose ears are stuck to their phones. From my calculation, the students I counselled in the last parts of my career should not have reached the age of handfuls of pills yet. They must still be trying to save their jobs from the younger ones who may be better qualified for those jobs. Who knows? My past students may still be able to defend their territory for a little longer, before they too become obsolete. What really waits for them is pureed food. I was not aware of the unavoidable outcome that awaits all of us when I was a member of the rat race. I felt that I was important; that what I did was important. As it turns out, capitalism has made an easily replaceable peg from each one of us. When I retired, there were 157 applicants for my job. My retirement opened up a job for one of them, the other 156 had to rush somewhere else. The young workers march on, like an unstoppable army, and replace the old. Maybe it is a good thing. Who wants a geriatric work force?

So, I sit on my aching joints, arranging my bony arms and spindly legs this way and that. I am starting to look like Beatrice, without the clouds of smoke. I try to take each day in stride. I know my days lack lustre, but my dreams are still colourful and full of potential. In some of my dreams, I am five years old. I am snuggling Beatrice. I feel her bony presence against my skin. I can smell her cigarettes. Beatrice tells me about the heroes and heroines, always in some war, combating dark forces that are much larger than themselves. Fortunately, Beatrice's heroes and heroines always win in the end, no matter how long the epic story takes. Lovers meet again and embrace. No matter how much they may have been hurt, they always heal. No one gets old in Beatrice's stories, the maidens stay beautiful, and their lovers remain loyal. There are no daughters in Beatrice's stories who leave home and never come back. In her stories, there are only one or two old women. They are witches. At the end of the story, they are defeated, and the young and the innocent win. So, in my dreams, Beatrice still shelters me from the jagged edges of my own life.

I dream about the years in Mavis's garden. I am six years old. My bones do not ache as I climb from fruit tree to fruit tree. My mouth is stained a purplish-black from the mulberries. I see my father's languorous chickens, guarding the fallen fruit. I hear their noisy clucking, their hormone-laden posturing, their carefree coupling right in front of my eyes. There will be fresh eggs for tomorrow's breakfast, if I do not prematurely wake up. If I wake up right now, all I'll have is pureed food.

I dream about my pets, long departed. I see Bambo, Boomerang and Horus. I see them in their prime years, rather than in those awful days when I had to say goodbye. I see Horus, his coat jet-black and glistening again. His molten amber eyes are pleading for my love. There is no trace of the stroke that left him paralyzed waist down. He is running towards me, his bushy tail wagging, his velvet ears flopping side to side, up and down. He pushes me down, trying his best to be as gentle as he can, we end up rolling in the tall grass. I smell the crushed grass, I smell Horus's distinct doggy smell under the sun, like wet leather shoes. I see his honey-brown eyes, and they are so close to me, I can see my own face in them. My reflection looks young and happy. In my dream, I do not have to say how much I miss him, since he is right there with me. It is in my waking life that he is long gone.

I dream about some of the students from my counselling years. A young woman, who has barely left her teenage years behind walks into my office, and asks me politely if she can close the door. I know what will follow. I have been doing this work for over two decades now. The student is going to divulge something horrible, like a death in the family, or trouble with a boyfriend, or a grandfather who cannot keep his hands to himself. This meeting behind a closed door will not be about which career path to follow.

So, I sit, and shuffle the sheets of paper in front of me, and wait. Her name is Rami. She is from Sri Lanka. She asks me if I can call her professors and ask for an extension on all of her assignments. I mumble a few things, saying what she is asking me is not part of my job description. However, I still ask her what seems to be the problem. I still try to understand her conundrum. Rather than giving her the brush-off, I still want to direct her to the correct office, maybe to student services, maybe to writing services, maybe to the campus health-care, maybe to an abused women's shelter. She looks at me with her starless brown eyes; she is holding back a shower of tears. She says "look," and combs her long hair with her slender fingers. Her nails have been bitten to the bone. They look painful. When she pulls back her fingers, her palm is filled with a clump of hair. I cannot believe my eyes. I cannot move. I have seen students under great pressure before, but a student who is going bald right in my office is new, even for me. I wake up in a sweat. I feel just as bad as I did when Rami actually walked into my office, closed my door, and pulled out her hair, so many years ago. I force my mind, but cannot remember whether I was able to help Rami or not, in my real life. My memories are like a thick soup, it is hard to locate and retrieve a specific piece of information. Rami's long black hair—whatever was left of it— reminds me of Negrisse. I hope, Negrisse is not under intense pressure, wherever she is. I hope her hair is not falling out. I want to make the world a better place for Rami, for Negrisse, for all daughters, but I cannot. I am too old. I have enough trouble finding my slippers and putting them on. Each shuffle to the bathroom is a rush against time.

I went to the doctor today. He said "How are you dear?" He pinches my cheek. He is treating me like a child these days, and I no longer have the energy to scold him for doing so. Old age ground down the prickly edges of my feminism, just like it ground down the edges of my natural teeth. Instead, I act coy, and say. "I am fine." We both know this is a white lie. He asks, "How is the ticker?" as if he were inquiring about my kitty cat. This time, I do not act coy. I do not answer his question. I pout instead. He knows the state of my ticker better than I do. He has all my cardio tests in front of him. My ticker is ticking in irregular patterns. The cardiogram looks like randomly scattered volcanoes. I know he is going to prescribe additional medication since replacing the old ticker with a newer model is out of the question. I am too old to make the list of organ transplantations. I wonder which new colour will be added to the rainbow-coloured pills I already take. I wonder how much longer the pills will keep me upright.

I dream that Negrisse is eight years old. It is snowing. We are out-side, running around in the snow, throwing snowballs at each other. Negrisse is wearing her dark red snow suit, red mittens, and a purple scarf. The clash of colours bothers me, even in my dream: red does not go well with purple. Then, I remember that I knitted that scarf for her, from some left over yarn. These are the years when I am still going to school. I do not have a job, and Randall does not pay child support. Money is tight, and warmth is much more important than making fashion statements. Negrisse and I roll in the snow, wiggle our arms and legs, and make snow angels. Negrisse's cheeks are like apples, glistening and red. She is laughing. I am laughing. I look at my daughter, and I am taken aback by her beauty. I am so happy that I want this dream to continue forever. Alas, I am awake. I am in my dark and lonely bedroom. I am cold. My comforter has slipped onto the floor. My pillow is wet, so are my cheeks. I crawl out of the bed and head toward the bathroom. I need to take another pill to put me back to sleep. I need my dreams to give me strength and keep me alive.

I am about sixteen years old. It is a brilliantly sunny day. I am participating in the local swimming competitions. I have my red and black swimsuit on. In those days, swimsuits are expensive, so, I have only one good swimsuit. My body is trim and flawless, my skin is the colour of molten caramel. I am one of the contestants. I look up at the crowds who are cheering us on. Most are the parents and siblings of the contestants. Agnes is not there. She is not interested in the things that mean so much to me. So, my eyes are searching for Sophie. She always comes. My eyes distinguish her from the crowd. Although her face is hidden under a large straw hat she is wearing, I know her cotton dress with lavender flowers. I wave, and wave again, but she does not see me. She is busy talking to some other mothers. My heart fills with love towards the woman sitting under her large hat, for coming on this sizzling hot day to see me swim. I will try extra hard today, so she can be proud of me. I am the first in the water when the umpire lowers his flag. My heart starts pumping faster and faster, as my body tears the water apart. Sophie is watching me. I can feel her eyes on my back. I will make her proud! I will make her proud!

I wake up. I shuffle to the toilet. These days, even this little trip is becoming something that takes a lot out of me. Afterwards, I eat some of my pureed fruit. I think it is peaches, but it may be something else. I turned into an earthworm. I consume unrecognizable mush from one end, and discard unrecognizable mush from the other, unless I have one of my notorious constipations.

I try to read the newspaper for a while, but fall asleep again. I dream about a time when Negrisse is about sixteen years old. She is showing growing discontent with everything in her life these days. I am on the top of her list of discontentment. I am walking on eggshells, but the fissure between us is enlarging. Tonight, we have tickets to the Pink Floyd concert. It was hard to get tickets, and they were much too expensive for our budget, but we managed. Greg loves Pink Floyd, and so does Negrisse. I can take it or leave it, but I am excited about their excitement. So, we dress warmly and take small foam-cushions to sit on. We take the subway. It is an open-air concert at the Toronto Exhibition Centre. The newspapers said that the stage show is going to be awesome, and they were right. At the crescendo, the band flies a thirty-foot blow-up pig into the air. The pig is pink. There are also lasers, zipping this way and that. For its time, these effects are beyond belief. So, Negrisse is happy for the night. I am happy to see the lights in her eyes. The next day, her unhappiness resumes. Her eyes turn into dark wells. I am afraid of looking at her eyes in case I get sucked into them, and suffocate.

I am dreaming about the day Negrisse is born. I am in excruciating pain. Below my waist, my body feels like a volcano, burning with hot lava, ready to explode. The pain erases every other sensation I ever experienced in my life. No hunger, or thirst, or love or lust. Just the molten lava of pain. I dig my nails into the sides of the operating table I am lying on. Negrisse, Negrisse, please come out before I die. Hours pass by, I hang on, but there are moments I wish I were dead.

Then, like a miracle, all pain ends. Negrisse arrives. She has an inch-and-a-half long, dark hair. On one side of her head, there is a bump. The doctor spanks her bottom with his huge hands, and I hate him for doing so. It is one thing to make me suffer, but it is something else to hurt my baby girl. Negrisse cries. I am also crying, with joy. I feel *total* happiness in that miraculous day of my life. That day is full of promise. That day is Nirvana. On the white tiles of the operating room, there are no reflections of black clouds. On the white tiles of the operating room floor, there are splashes of my crimson blood. The child from my body has arrived.

I am going to see my specialist. He rarely has good news for me these days. He does not even look at me in the eye. Probably, he is embarrassed to say the things he has to say. He is a young doctor. These days, young doctors seem to know much more than older doctors do. Even the older doctors are younger than me. Things must be really cutthroat at medical schools. That is why the new doctors try to make up for their economic suffering as soon as they get out of the grind. They buy huge houses and sports cars. Most of the specialists are still men. What happened to our furious feminist efforts? The male doctors still pair up with gorgeous women, almost always many years their junior. They learn to divert their gaze from older women like me, whose lives are on the decline. So, my current specialist writes down another list of medications, two of one, four of another, morning, lunch, dinner, and on and on. I have to take some with food, some with juice, and others with milk. I am told not to drive or use heavy machinery after taking the orange ones. I laugh out loud, who is driving these days? Being old is like full-time work, with no pay, and no possibility of a promotion. When you stop working hard to live, you just die.

I stop at the drugstore and order my new pills. Most people do the ordering from their touch-phones, but I left work before the technology became advanced. I still do things in person rather than as punched-in commands on a keyboard. For a woman whose childhood coincided with the advent of AM radios, I cannot blame myself. I am a dinosaur approaching extinction. I am an aging dragon. After the drugstore, I will rush home—shuffle is more like it—and will take my new pills. Then, I will go to sleep. I am exhausted. It will not be long before the doctors will only make electronic visits. In my childhood, our family doctor actually made house calls, in person.

I am again deep into my dreams. Negrisse is about twelve years old. Her hair is not coloured yet, so she must be living in my home. She is smiling. She has a package in her hand, wrapped in newspaper. Negrisse is becoming extremely protective of the environment. To do our share, and to please her, Greg and I are also using newspapers as wrapping paper. Negrisse has a card in her hand, addressed to "Mom." The card does not have an envelope, so I can immediately see what it says. It says: "Happy Mother's Day Mom, You are the Best!" Bunches of red hearts have been drawn all around the words. Rather than a regular coloured pencil or a crayon, Negrisse has used nail polish to draw the hearts. The card is cheerful, the hearts psychedelic. I hug Negrisse, being careful not to hug her too closely. She will become irritated with demonstrations of too much feeling. I refrain from kissing her. Negrisse no longer allows motherly kisses. Nevertheless, my heart fills with joy. I say I am the happiest mother in the world. I mean it. I really, really mean it!

I wake up. I am groggy. It is the pills. What has awakened me seems to be a knock on my apartment door. How long did I sleep? What time is it? What day? Who could it be? I am not expecting anyone. No one comes to my door these days anyway. Younger people do not want to face the ravages of aging, at least, not face-to-face. Older people have their own deterioration to contend with. So, I am mostly alone.

Clumsily, I fish for my slippers. The damn things grow legs and run under the bed as soon as I take them off. So, it takes a few minutes to find them, and slip them on. I notice that my slippers are discoloured and worn out. I need to replace them one of these days, when I find the energy to engage in such a monumental task like shopping. The knock on the door is getting louder and more impatient by the minute. I shuffle harder, saying, "I am coming, I am coming."

I open the door and my jaw drops. My knees buckle. I am shaking all over. I cannot believe my eyes. I pinch myself to make sure I am not dreaming. I think I am awake, but I am not sure.

Acknowledgements

I thank Dr. Andrea O'Reilly and Demeter Press for enthusiastically embracing *Mothers, Daughters and Untamed Dragons*. I extend my sincere thanks to the editorial team at Demeter Press for their careful editing and useful suggestions for the final version of this book. I am delighted with the cover design created by Dora Chan, which perfectly captures the essence of the book.

Dr. Aysan Sev'er (Ph.D.) is Professor Emeritus of Sociology at the University of Toronto. She is the recipient of numerous national and international awards for her work on violence against women. She has numerous academic, and some non-academic books. Her most current academic research focuses on extreme forms of violence against women in India and in south-eastern Turkey. Her focus is on honour-killings and dowry murders. She is the founding editor of the *Women's Health & Urban Life Journal*. Her book entitled *Fleeing the House of Horrors* (2002) received the Canadian Women's Studies Book Award in 2004. Her edited book entitled *Skeletons in Family Closets* (with J. Trost) was published in 2011.